plea————
VESSELS

pleasure
VESSELS

◆

THE WINNERS OF THE 1995
IAN ST JAMES AWARDS

ARP
Angela Royal Publishing

Published by ANGELA ROYAL PUBLISHING LTD
PO Box 138, Tunbridge Wells, Kent TN3 0ZT

First published 1997

A CIP catalogue for this book is available from the British Library
ISBN 1-899860-60-6

Typeset by Nick Awde/Desert♥Hearts
Cover design by Nick Awde & Emanuela Losi
Cover photography by Randy Lincks
Printed in Great Britain by BPC Wheatons Ltd, Exeter

For further information on the Ian St James Awards and *The New Writer*
magazine, write to the New Writers' Club at PO Box 60, Cranbrook,
Kent TN17 2ZR, or telephone 01580 212626.

CONTENTS

THE 1995 IAN ST JAMES AWARDS

Judges

KATE ATKINSON
Author

JANE BRADISH-ELLAMES
Literary Agent

GORDON KERR
Bookseller

DENISE NEUHAUS
Author

IAN ST JAMES
Author

FOREWORD

"THE SHORT STORY," WROTE HENRY JAMES, IS FOR THE writer "a constant seduction and an exalted delight". The story, as James himself was very well aware, is a genre in its own right – not the little sister of the more grown-up novel. There are great stories just as there are great novels – Chekhov's *Lady with Lapdog*, Hemingway's *A Clean Well-Lighted Place*, James' *The Turn of the Screw*, Kafka's *Metamorphosis* – all exemplify everything we need to know about writing and more – voice, structure, style, character, invention.

However, although the story is not a lesser form of text than the novel, its very brevity makes it a wonderful place for the would-be writer to practise their art, a place to refine skills, experiment, study, play, to learn to criticise our own work and to discipline ourselves and – most importantly and somehow most mysterious of all these things – to find our own voice.

Writing is an art form like any other and just as the painter or the sculptor has to learn about his materials, about structure and form and technique, so must the writer. Writing isn't the raw stuff of feeling transposed to the page (the old 'everyone has a novel in them' adage). Writing is the raw stuff of feeling mediated by imagination and composition. The text is an artefact, an object in the same way that a Mozart opera or a Vermeer painting is – not the messy chaos of everyday reality but a world re-shaped and ordered into meaning by art.

So we've written a story, and we think it's good enough to go out into the world – but what do we do with it? The thing about writing is that it needs, well – reading. And the thing about writers is that they need approval (or, at any rate, most of them do). We need someone to say "this is good". The would-be writer often feels disheartened – who wants their manuscripts, their novels, their stories? Publishers may say they read unsolicited work but it can feel as if we're sending our writing out into the great void. This is where the story composition is like a warm light in the darkness – a focus for our energy and our desires – they actually want our stories. Best of all, the Ian St James Awards wants our stories – and if our work does have merit then that merit will be rewarded. What more can a writer ask for?

To return to Henry James: "The merit of the tale," he writes, "is ... that it has struggled successfully with its danger. It is an excursion into chaos while remaining... but an anecdote." This volume contains many such dangerous little excursions into chaos and, I hope, the promise of many more to come.

KATE ATKINSON
Ian St James Award winner 1993

STRANGE WEATHER
Maria Caruso

Maria Caruso currently lives in Portland, Oregon, where she is at work on a historical novel set in China during the T'ang Dynasty. She attended the University of California-Irvine, where she earned a Master's degree in Fine Arts in 1990. She teaches Literature and Writing at Marylhurst College.

THIS IS THE FIRST THING I NOTICED: A CHANGE IN THE sound of the wind at night as it blew the leaves of the cherry tree outside my bedroom window.

The tree's branches had always brushed against the glass, a sleepy, sweeping sound, sometimes stirring me out of sleep. It was a sound I thought of as lonely but never frightening.

But one night the wind became husky and rough, as if something wild were beating the tree, something out of balance, hissing among the branches. It was the kind of wind, though more extreme, that is the precursor to a thunderstorm in Michigan. But no thunderstorm arrived, no rain at all. I sat up in bed, watching the cherry leaves quiver, and wondered what was coming.

The next day it started – an awful stillness, and heat. The sun came closer, hovering. I could not stop going out to look at it, thinking it was too strange to last – that soon the sky would darken and a breeze stir itself and rain hush down. I could not keep cool in that weather. My face and shoulders took on a permanent red flush and in the mirror my eyes looked bright blue in contrast, the colour of something a girl would buy in a dime store.

At my high school the boys stopped waiting until they were out of sight of the schoolyard before bursting into dusty, vicious fights. And when I walked by the neighboring farms I saw the farmers spit and raise their fists like cartoon characters, angry at the sky. Everyone I knew began to look vaguely the same when the weather set; thirsty, blinking and surprised.

I was not so poetic a young woman that I thought myself responsible for the drought, or perhaps it's truer to say if I had those thoughts they were quickly followed by the knowledge that I was clearly not that powerful. I was fifteen years old and I knew my boundaries even as I pretended greater authority than I possessed. I was half one thing and half another that summer. I knew how to take a stitch in human skin but I believed if my bedroom door was not left open exactly three inches I would die before morning.

Like a portrait of a passionate woman, painted with her back to a little window through which the viewer can see a bolt of lightning striking the ground, the drought was my backdrop. The irritating heat matched my disposition, magnified it – I felt surrounded by anger and dread. You can ask anyone who has ever been in a drought if it isn't true – there is no better word to describe it than sullen. The rain refuses to fall. And under this refusal, this sullenness, is its reason.

Alone on the farm with Steven, day after day, I scarcely had to scheme to get him to do what I wanted. He felt so sorry for me. We lived on junk food and saw every movie playing at the Lido. We rode in his rusty pick-up truck, rattling as far as Saugatuck to watch the sailboats drag themselves through the waves, or to Port Huron for the horse auctions – prize geldings drooping, their flanks shiny with brushed sweat. Anything I wanted to do.

On days when he could not leave the farm but had to stay and work with our hired man on something that went wrong, again and again that summer, with the irrigation system, I paced the house. My body was the only thing in motion, and that made me feel both powerful and exhausted. The curtains hung at the windows as if they were carved from stone. The front porch was scattered with insect shells, crisp as if they had been baked. I stepped on them to hear their sharp crack. Steven saw me as he passed by.

"Go inside Cassie," he said, "you'll just make yourself hotter out here."

I ignored him, rocking on the porch swing for two minutes and then walking out to check the mailbox for the second time that day, though I knew no one who would think of writing to me. I went back into the house. In the kitchen I opened every drawer, fingering the contents. My mother's sewing scissors, in the shape of a heron with rounded legs; a box of rusted screws of my father's, a rose corsage, dried to the color of rotting crab apples. I was not looking for anything but I was angry I could not find it, and I slammed the drawers shut, one after the next. After I slammed the last one I put my hands to my head, pulling at the roots of my hair. I looked up to see Steven, leaning against the doorframe and watching me.

"You're just like your mother was," he said.

I barely knew him.

We were still in the stages with each other where he would ask me what kind of music I liked and did I want jam or maple syrup on my pancakes. I saw him hiding, and her as well, their pleasure in each other, maybe because they thought it might embarrass me. But I saw everything. Their horrible, immense happiness when they saw each other after she came home from the store or in from the garden, the way they went up to bed together. I could feel their footsteps on the stairs, trying not to race.

I had not even known him long enough to have the necessary argument with him where I was supposed to scream that he was not my father and he was supposed to say of course he wasn't, he would never try to take my father's place. We had not settled into even that much peace.

My father had been dead a long time. He remained for me mainly in photographs and certain objects; coveralls hanging on nails inside the barn, a hunting hat with fur earflaps on the shelf in the coat closet. I did not expect anything from my father, anymore. That he appeared, smiling, in a picture with me on his shoulders seemed sufficient, seemed father enough. It was my mother from whom I expected everything. It was my mother who cheated me.

After her funeral Steven and I drove to a spot by the river. At first we didn't get out the car. The river, through the trees, was just a thin slip of movement. My face was swollen and sore. Steven reached over and held me, for the first time ever besides quick hugs. He held me as if we were no longer strangers.

"It will be all right," he kept saying. My breasts were tight against his chest and I was unable to think, unable to imagine what he meant.

When I asked him what would be all right he said everything. He did not look into my eyes but he said everything.

Then he got out of the car and walked towards the river. I followed him, ducking behind trees so he wouldn't see me. He kept looking back in the direction of the car, again and again, and I believed I was watching a man who wished to lose something.

Ever since I was old enough to balance in it I loved to sit out in our tyre swing and watch the cars shoot by, the people inside turning their heads to look at our farm. "That's the LaFave farm," I imagined them saying to their children – and I thought somehow the name was written on the land itself. We lived west of the highway, and as evening came I saw them squint through their rolled-up windows to see the hay barn and the silo and the house, the rows of corn streaking by like the long striped skirt of a running girl.

In town everyone called it LaFave's farm, and they meant by this not that it was the farm belonging to my family but the farm belonging to my father. His death did little if anything to dissuade a sense of his ownership, and I occasionally heard someone in the grocery store ask my mother how the LaFave farm was doing, as if she were part of the hired help. The land too seemed to know it was his – when he was alive plants sprouted and thrived under his authority. He would not have let it be otherwise. And I was like the plants, knowing always what he expected of me. I would not have dared to make a mistake, and my childhood fantasies were rife with instances of disappointing him. I used to have a recurring dream in which the three of us woke one morning to find the fields of winter wheat stretching to the horizon around us gnawed to stubble, an act which I knew I had done during the night, crawling between the rows, moving my sharp teeth to one plant after the next, watching the sky for signs of morning, hurrying, hurrying.

Steven was at best described as a reluctant farmer. Neighbours came to give him advice and I watched from my bedroom window while he toed the dirt with an unlaced boot, looking out at the dry corn rows and letting their talk blow over him. For a while they came often, shaking their heads and pointing at sections of the crop as if they were unruly children. But I knew he never meant to be a farmer; he married my mother for her lively grace, and ten years younger than she was, he took on the land at her insistence. It was not his to begin with, and I think he remembered how it belonged to the man who loved her first.

When the neighbouring farmers stopped coming by altogether Steven began to solicit my opinion on every aspect of his farming, telling me always exactly what he planned to do, naming for me the pieces of equipment he would use as if afraid of making a mistake.

Finally he worked only a tenth of our land, in narrow strips surrounding the house. He let the hired man go. If I sat very low to the ground in the front yard I could pretend everything was as it always had been.

It became very quiet, in the middle of the drought. I was afraid I would dream of rain. It was the worst thing I could imagine – dreaming of the sounds of water and then waking to the unchanged heat, waiting for it to hit me full force – this was my real life.

The dryness began to seep into our bodies. Steven's face reddened from the sun except for the tiny white lines around his eyes where he constantly squinted when he was outside. My hands were so dry I could barely stand to turn the pages of a book. I tried to help him some days, but the heat was overwhelming. Mostly I just stayed in the house, watching the fan in the kitchen turn.

One day I summoned the energy to make oatmeal cookies. I supposed it was so hot whatever the oven might add to it wouldn't matter. When I heard Steven's footsteps on the porch I ran to meet him with a plate of the cookies and he smiled when he saw me.

"These are for you," I said.

He pulled off his shirt and used it to wipe the sweat from his face and arms. "Did you bake them on the kitchen floor?" he asked.

"The floor was too hot, I put them into the oven to shade them." I felt shy, and afraid I might have left something out of them, the sugar or something important, but he ate a couple at one crack and reached for more.

"Is there anything to drink?" he said.

I went into the kitchen and when I came back out I saw he had moved onto the porch swing and was forcing it slowly back, holding it there with the tips of his boots. When I handed him the Coke he said, "Cassie, we need to talk about what we're going to do."

I sat down on the floor of the porch with my knees pulled up, watching him. He took a long swallow from the bottle, his throat working. A fly buzzed near him and I leaned forward to brush it away. He drank down the bottle and wiped his mouth with the back of his hand.

"I think we should sell the farm," he said. He looked out at the scorched land, sienna and gold; beautiful, but not the colours it should be. The cottonwoods that lined the highway were parched. In the distance the corn moved from a rare breeze. Neither the sound nor the breeze reached the house so it looked like the plants moved from agony, or restlessness. Earlier in the day I stripped some leaves from a corn stalk and examined them. Steven watched me for a moment and then asked if I knew what I was doing, if I was looking for something. But I was just looking at the colours of the thing, creamy white where it should have been green, streaked through with red like all its blood was coming to the surface, like some transparency was beginning.

I tried to look out where Steven was looking, not just the same direction but the exact rock or post or piece of horizon. My hands began to shake.

I though about once when I was stung by a bee. It was at Easter, and my father hid my Easter eggs under the chickens in the coop. I had always been afraid of going there, the chickens were so nervous and confused, and once a big hen flew right into my face and knocked me over, leaving long scratch marks on my neck. My father said he was hiding the eggs there so I would get over my fear – that if I wanted the eggs enough I would.

There were always a lot of bees around the chicken coop – I think because there was an old honeysuckle vine back there. I had been stung on the bottom of my foot more than once from stepping on one. So while my father watched me I went out to the coop, walking carefully through the grass in my white Easter dress. I pushed open the door with one hand, then the other. The bitter yellow-jacket sting to the palm of my hand took my breath away. But I knew my father was watching so I kept walking. Inside the coop it was as dark as night. The hens shuffled softly in their places and the air was thick with dust. My hand hurt so much I was surprised it did not glow in the dark. I could not believe so much pain could be invisible. I reached under a hen: nothing. Another: again, nothing. Under the third hen I felt an egg – but the trick was to emerge with an Easter egg, not just the ordinary sort. I held the egg in front of me, trying to see it. It was warm in my palm and I let the bee sting rest against it. I emerged from the dark of the coop, almost not daring to look at it. My father came towards me and I saw the egg was the blue-green of the sea, the colour of the thinnest part of a wave, before it breaks. Someone had written my name on it, in pink, with hearts above and below. I handed the egg to my father and he told me I was a good girl. When I showed him the bee sting he took my hand and kissed it. When I could I pulled away from him and went to where my mother was sitting on the far side of the house in a straight-backed chair. I laid my head in her lap and she stroked my hair.

"We could go down south," said Steven, "where my family is. Georgia."

"Oh, Georgia," I said. Georgia meant as little to me as a foreign country. I felt as if I had been invited to a circus or some other exotic, mountebank-driven event.

"It's nice. It's got good weather," Steven said. He looked at the sky.

"I think we'll just stay here." I said, politely but with some finality, as if I were settling something and there were no further need to talk about it.

"It's good you're telling me how you feel," he said, and it sounded like the first part of something else he was going to say but he didn't say anything more.

He fried pork chops for supper. While he fixed them he told me about his sister Clary, who owned a gas station and lived with a woman named Janet. He said Clary was the sweetest thing on God's green earth, and then he amended himself by saying he didn't believe in God. He looked at me sideways to see how I was taking the news, and I told him when I was little I thought God lived in the birdfeeder in the backyard because there was a little cross on top of it. Then he started to sing *Amazing Grace* very, very off key. He plowed through the song as if it were a sun-baked piece of earth, and he the tip of a rusty old blade. Then the pork chops were done, not tender and melting like she used to make them but rubbery and black at the edges. He put them on blue plates, with store-bought bread and sliced tomatoes, still warm from the garden. He peppered everything on the plates, including the bread. He smiled and we began to eat and while we did I told him about when I made my first communion how I expected to die of happiness like Saint Agnes did and I was terrified to go up there. I tried to make it as funny as I could, waving my knife around to emphasize, and he laughed in all the right spots. Good pork chops, I said.

I never did learn to like going in the chicken coop, but I did it every day, late in the morning. I gathered the eggs from the limp chickens, trapped beneath their thick feathers. Every egg a plain colour – brownish, white or cream.

I dusted my mother's bone china and her bookcases full of Russian and English novels and cleaned the bevelled glass of the front windows but only from the inside. I spent my afternoons weaving long scenarios for myself about how I would get the farm back if Steven sold it.

A man stopped by one afternoon, walking slowly up the drive with his hat in his hand. He called out to me when he saw me watching him from the porch. He asked if Mr LaFave was looking for anyone to help out. His dark hair fell over one eye, drawing my gaze to the other and I said, without meaning to, that no one could help him now. Made braver by my uncharacteristic flippancy, and braver still by my loneliness, I coaxed him to drink some lemonade on the porch with me. He said he wouldn't mind and I listened to the creak of the swing while he waited for me to make it, hurrying to mix the sugar in, stinging a cut on my hand with the lemon juice.

I brought it to him, embarrassed before he even tasted it, and it was, as I knew it would be, too sour when I drank it there with him – though I tasted it twice when I mixed it in the kitchen and it had been all right then. He stayed on the porch swing and I sat on the steps, looking up at him. I ran my fingers through my hair, feeling his eyes on me.

"You're Cassandra, right?" he said.

"How do you know me?"

"My family used to live around here, a long time ago. I just remember you, for some reason. I remember the house."

"This house isn't so special."

"No. But you live here – that makes it different. I remember your mom, too. Black hair. How's she doing?"

"Fine," I said, "she's not here now."

"You used to wear your hair in pigtails, down low under your ears. My little sisters always wanted their mama to fix their hair the same way."

I blushed and drank my lemonade. I held still when he came and sat next to me on the steps, keeping my eyes down. Everything was motionless and hot. He touched my hair. He told me I was so pretty. He asked me what it was like, to be alone in the house. I felt myself leaning towards him, listening to his voice, which was burred and low.

"What's a little thing like you doing here by yourself?" he said.

"Everyone has gone," I said.

"You sure?"

"Well, I have a cat," I said – thinking it might make him laugh.

"That all?" he asked, not laughing, his voice serious and close to my ear.

"That's all," I whispered.

He put his hand into the top of my dress, touching my chest like that was all he wanted and then he slid his hand lower. I felt I was giving something to him; that he would think I was sweet if I let him. I wished I had just had a bath. I wished my skin smelled of orange talcum and verbena. But he put his face against me as if I were the nicest thing he'd ever smelled. It felt better than anything. Like he was stirring up the cool inside of me. He put his mouth to my nipples, outside my dress, wetting the fabric. I wanted something I could not put a name to. Can I kiss your mouth? he said. Kiss me, I said.

He was kissing me, his mouth slippery and hot, his tongue reaching into me when Steven came around the corner of the house.

"Cassie," was all he said, and he said it like one word could be a question.

17

The man stood up, looking at the ground, wiping his mouth with the back of his hand and I was embarrassed for Steven to see the man wiping me off of his mouth.

"You better go," said Steven.

"All right," said the man.

I covered the front of my dress with one arm, holding my shoulder.

The man jumped the railing on the porch, stumbled slightly, and walked down the drive toward the road. He did not look back. When he was gone Steven turned and went into the house and I followed him. He sat down in the front room and worked the laces on his boots loose.

"He's a farmer," I said.

Steven didn't say anything and I said, "He'd know how to farm this land."

Steven kicked his boot away and said, "Then maybe he can have it when we're gone."

"I'm not leaving. You go if you want to."

"You haven't got a choice, Cassie, what are you going to do? Stay here by yourself?"

"I am here by myself," I said. I think I expected him to get angry.

He rubbed his forehead with his hand. "Don't you think I know that? Of course you are. But I can't do it. This place was your mom's – everything here was hers."

"Don't you want to be reminded of her?" I said.

When he answered me he spoke so slowly I leaned toward him, waiting for his words.

"Not just now, I don't. Can you understand? Please try."

"I don't even know who you are. I wish my mother never married you."

After I spoke we looked away from each other, but it was a small room – there wasn't too much to look at. We both looked towards the window and as we did the draperies lifted, the air so hot it wasn't like a breeze at all, just a shifting.

When he got up and went into the kitchen I thought it through. If only my mother had never married him. I'd have the farm to myself. Everything would grow for me, like it had for my father. I could do whatever I wanted, all the time. My mother would come back, somehow, to keep me company. I followed Steven into the kitchen and told him I would not leave. I said it like I meant it. My father always said to me: say it like you mean it, Cassandra, or no one will believe you. My father said so many things to me like he meant them. Like there was no room for my dissension. I will not leave, I said. Well that's just great, said Steven.

"I am not a drinking man," said Steven.

He was not talking to me. I was up in my room, my ear to the heating vent on the floor next to my bed. I could hear the voices downstairs clearly. He was talking to a woman. She giggled.

"You're drunk," she said to him.

"May well be," said Steven, "but I am not a drinking man."

"Maybe that's why you're drunk," the woman said, and giggled again.

He must have gone to the window then, and pulled back the curtain, because he said, "Everything you see before you is mine. As far as the horizon are my own lands."

He sounded like a king in a cartoon but the woman said, "gosh," in a hushed tone. They were quiet for a minute and then I heard the woman say, "Why don't you take this thing off?"

I shut the vent, as softly as I could, and got into bed. My mother made my quilt, white with every shade of blue in scattered squares.

I must have fallen asleep then because I woke to Steven talking to me. I am sorry about everything, he said. I didn't open my eyes. I shifted as if I were still asleep, turning away from him. He put his hand on the quilt, touching my shoulder through its layers.

"I'm sorry about everything," he said again, more softly, "I have tried to do this, but I don't know how to be anything to you."

A couple of days after that Steven woke me very early in the morning. It was still dark. I sweated under a thin sheet, angry with him for bringing me into the heat when I had been ignorant of it only a moment before. I wanted to pull the sheet down to my waist to let the warmth escape from under it but I couldn't with him standing there.

"There are some things I need to do, Cassie," he said. He spoke slowly, clearly, as if my ears might still be asleep. The keys to the truck shook in his hand.

"Can I come with you?"

He did not answer right away. He put his hand through his hair. "No," he said.

I did not argue with him. When he left the room I couldn't fall back asleep. My legs were wet where they had lain against each other and my hair clung to my face. I listened to the sounds of him leaving the house, getting in the truck, starting the motor. I went to my window because I wanted to see him drive away, the tail lights of the pick-up glowing and then fluttering and then disappearing.

I went downstairs and began to clean the house. I pulled out the ammonia, the brushes, the bottles of cleanser. I learned from my mother it is possible to calm yourself by scrubbing. When my parents fought they often drove off, to have their fight away from me in the car. They always came home to a shining house and when I was a little older my mother would joke with me they fought so they could come home to a clean house. The night I got the call from Steven at the hospital, telling me my mother had collapsed in a restaurant, I turned the house inside out to clean it. Lemon ammonia, the grit of cleanser, the sound of a mop wrung out in the sink, these things stave off fear. Of course, they are not the final arbiters, they stave off nothing forever.

He had not taken the clothes from his closet. I checked and for a moment felt better, until I saw my mother's dresses hanging there too.

I plotted, during the afternoon, of how exactly to get him in as much trouble as possible. I took a long cold bath and put on a blue cotton dress he once said looked pretty on me. I imagined the voices of the neighbours, shocked and concerned at what had happened to me. Abandoned. I made dinner, thinking that might bring him. I sat in the kitchen while I ate it and tried to think of nothing, watching a sweat rise on my clean arms, feeling my dark hair collecting the heat and holding it at the crown of my head.

I went outside and could feel myself pale under the strong light. Everything was bright, bright. Steven kept the birdbath filled and birds sat in the water, occasionally ducking their heads under and lifting their wings in quick succession. I walked to the stone bath, the water like a bowl of light. The birds quietly flew off and I dipped my hand in, the water soft around my fingertips. A car drove by, coming slowly out of the distance like a thing that would never arrive, finally passing with the squeak and crunch of gravel, rising dust that hung in the light like a veil after it passed. Its passengers did not look up at the farm, at me. I thought he was not coming. He was the same age I am now. If I were him, would I have come?

I imagine his day's driving took him out of that strange weather altogether; that he gained, at his furthest point away from me, a day of ordinary summer, with a breeze, maybe with clouds. He never said to me directly, then or later, that he tried to leave. And sometimes I thought I was wrong for believing it.

When his truck pulled into the drive, in the late evening, I felt a surge inside me. I thought for certain I had hoped too hard for his return – I wanted it too much and therefore he would not come. That he came knocked down a piece of the philosophy I lived by, all my childhood. He sat in the truck and I clattered across the porch and down the steps and across the yard to him. I put out my hand and reached through the window of the truck to touch his shoulder. But he was dreamy, far away.

I would like to ask him, still, to show me how far he got. I would like to ask him to take me to the spot where he turned around to come back. I would like to stand there, for a moment, to see what he was looking at when he decided to retrace his path, back to the farm. I imagine a road cool and lush, shaded with pine trees.

The branches of the cherry tree brushed against my window, a soft, yearning sound. The rain was like everything I'd lost, falling from the sky. It melted against my windows and sluiced down in waves, over and over. I had awakened from a dream that my mother had uprooted everything in the vegetable garden, that she wanted me to help her. I watched the rain for a few moments and then I pulled a nightgown over my head and went to wake Steven.

When I stood at the threshold of his room I hesitated. His room was a solitary, separate place, ghostly blue. I could hear him breathing, steadily, low. He was lying on his stomach and I touched his skin with my fingertips.

"It's raining," I said.

He turned toward me, lifting himself on an elbow, and then looked out the window. The rain pinged off the eaves.

"It is," he said.

I said his name, thinking he wasn't understanding.

"O.K.," he said, " It's raining. It's raining. What do you want me to do? It's over with. The corn couldn't suck up water from a flood."

"Please."

"Please what? It's too late, Cassie." He sat all the way up.

"It's only too late because you want it to be," I said.

"I didn't ask for any of this. Listen to me. It wasn't supposed to happen this way. And I can't fix it. I only get to decide what happens some of the time. A very small percentage of the time."

I turned away from him and started to cry. He got out of bed and stood next to me. He touched my back. I could feel his fingers shaking through the cotton of my nightgown.

I said, "And me, I wasn't supposed to happen like this either, was I?"

"You? Don't ever say that," he said and his hands circled my arms.

"Everything about you happens just how it should," he said.

"My mother isn't coming back, " I said.

"She'll always be with you, Cassie. She'll always be with me."

"Oh big deal. Big deal," I said. He held me then, and I cried a long time.

It was not until the summer before I was to finish my last year at college that Steven and I returned to Michigan, to see the farm and what became of it.

We parked out on the road at evening, shy of steering up the tree-lined drive. From a distance the farm looked perfect. We walked up underneath the trees, and as we drew close I began to see the great disrepair, paint peeling off in sheets, cracked windows, a missing front step. The porch swing was suspended from only one end, with a length of knotted rope.

I did not look at Steven. A woman came out onto the porch and shielded her eyes with one hand, squinting out at us. As Steven went towards her I turned away, heading towards a birch copse between the yard and the fields. I hid myself in the trees and looked out at the farm, breathing deeply. For a moment I let myself imagine nothing had ever happened to me – that I still lived here – days passing, waking at night to the low sounds of my parent's voices.

My eyes settled on Steven and the woman in the doorway. They laughed about something, and Steven waved in my direction, though I don't think he could see exactly where I was. I came out from my hiding place, walking through the yard slowly, trying to look as if I were not particularly interested in anything. I traced the circling of ivy on the old stone bird bath. There were leaves under the water and I fished them out. Everything was not as I had left it. The hay barn looked smaller, and the distance between it and the house not as far as it used to be.

Steven introduced me to the woman and I smiled.

"She says it's been raining like crazy this summer," Steven said.

"So how long did you live here?" the woman asked him.

"Well, really," Steven said, "I only lived here for a while."

"But I thought you said..."

"It belonged to my wife," Steven started to say. "It was her first husband's..."

"No, it was Steven's farm," I said. "It was ours."

I turned and walked to the tyre swing, threaded my body through it so that I was facing the road. Steven was still talking with the woman and I could hear snatches of their conversation. Beautiful, I heard Steven say, beautiful, beautiful. I spun on the tyre swing and saw the decaying buildings, rusty old cars on cinderblocks where the kitchen garden used to be, but also the trees, in rich full leaf, the crops thick and sturdy like specimen examples in encyclopedia pictures.

After a few more minutes Steven came down the steps of the porch and we walked back to the truck together. Before getting in I turned to raise my hand to the woman on the porch, but she had already gone. We drove away, and he reached over and touched my hand. The cottonwoods swayed above us, the leaves making their sweet rush of summery noise.

LES ABANDONNEES
Nancy Lindisfarne

Nancy Lindisfarne was born in St. Louis but has lived in London since 1964 where she now teaches social anthropology. All her previous writing has been of the academic variety, including 'Dislocating Masculinity' and a book on Afghan nomads, 'Bartered Brides'. Her adventure into fiction began via a writing course with Alison Fell; 'Les Abandonnées' is her first ever short story. She has since completed a collection of short stories, 'Dancing in Damascus', which was published in an Arabic translation in 1996.

SHE WAS GOOD AT FACES, AS QUICK AS A COURTROOM portraitist. And she looked carefully as she walked through the train, locating men, loading them with families, some joy and a lot of worries. Then, to her great surprise, when she entered the last carriage she spotted a man who might just be him.

She slowed as she approached, thinking carefully of what might come next. Settling herself into the seat opposite him, she arranged her coat, and then, after a moment's pause, pulled out a copy of the TLS before putting her briefcase down on the seat beside her. She looked around her the way all seasoned rail travellers do when establishing their territory. So far, so good, no one else at the front. Well, let's see. This could be fun.

She opened the TLS and tried to read about 'Verbal violence and the law', but her concentration was nil. She felt eager, childlike, as if she were eyeing a beautifully wrapped present. The train was due out in a few minutes. She looked at him in quick flicks, while willing her impatience to behave.

She'd only seen a few photos, early ones – family snapshots which must have been taken nearly twenty years ago. It was unusual to have inherited a dossier so poor in visuals.

But he had the right configuration: large nose, small man; dapper and certainly once very fit. And about the right age – sixty-five he should be. He wasn't as bald as she would have guessed, but he had the kind of fine hair that is on the way out. And yes, otherwise hairy: she could see the hint of a tangle at his collar where he'd loosened his tie.

He was reading the kind of book she would have expected. She'd guessed he might be one of those men who read *The Silence of the Lambs* or airport trash when they think they are invisible, but who are oh-so-clever and precious at dinner parties. Whatever happened next, the TLS would give her a bit of an edge. Of course, it was a long shot. There was no way she could be sure it was him, but that didn't matter.

As the train went through Vauxhall, she looked up with intent, meaning to be seen. Lord, what a case. Either a great pretender, or completely into his book, unaware. Okay, you bugger, let's just see how well you can protect yourself, she thought.

Tilting her head a bit to the side, she leaned over. "Excuse me," she said.

He looked up slowly, forced to respond, expecting the kind of small intrusion that rail travellers often inflict on each other.

"You aren't David Morgan, are you?" Her smile, the warmth in her voice, made it clear that she'd be pleased if he were.

"Why, yes. I am." Of course he was startled, but very quick. He modulated his surprise with impressive grace.

"Oh, I'm so glad I dared to ask. I hope you don't mind, but I just thought it might be you."

He gave her one of those pulp-fiction looks. She knew she'd pass muster. She was a good twenty years younger than he was and attractive enough. Her jacket, blue silk blouse and the briefcase next to her also let him know she was solvent, respectable. Good, she thought, he's interested. Could be an easy mark.

"I'm sorry,"he said, "but do I know you?"

"Forgive me. I don't guess you'll remember, but we were neighbours when you were teaching at Highmeadows." He hadn't expected that, but she could see his shoulders relax. No doubt flattered that he'd made a lasting impression. Hooked you, she thought.

"But that was over fifteen years ago. You must have a good

26

memory." Now he's fishing. "I'm not very good at putting names and faces together." He sounded a bit worried about why he might be memorable.

This bit is easy. Still fancies himself with women. She could see the tautness in his body. "Yes, time flies, doesn't it? Tempus fugit and all that." Then she laughed, "Oh, how pretentious of me. I forgot, you're a classicist, aren't you?"

She paused, "I can imagine what it's like when you're a teacher. Just one of you and so many parents to remember. I heard that after Highmeadows you went to teach in the Gulf. Have I remembered right?"

"I did go to the Emirates." He's dropped his guard. "Quite a different kettle of fish, but pleasant enough."

"And well paid, I'd imagine," she added.

"Certainly that," He laughed. "I enjoyed being there. Less confining in some ways. Best of both worlds, I guess." He had adopted that confident style of the self-deprecating man of the world.

The train rumbled through Wimbledon. Okay, get on with it, she thought.

"Now that I think about it, I would never have guessed I'd run into you on a train. I remember you as the kind of man who likes driving. And takes a lot of pride in a good car." This too was unexpected, but accurate enough.

He grinned, but his smile was a bit tight. "You're right. Actually, this is the first time I've been on a train for years. But it made sense today. Lunch with someone who works at the Shell Centre. Spot on for Waterloo, of course." He'd retrieved the bonhomie of the lunch. It dissipated his caution.

She shifted a little to the right to sit directly in front of him as if across a table. He caught her flirt and gave her one of those deepening smiles that men use when they are dining with anticipation.

They embarked on a warm-up duet about the state of public transport and Britain's roads. She waited, then said, "You drove an Alvis once, didn't you?" His command wavered though almost imperceptibly. It was his hands, reflexing round the book, which were the give-away.

"An Alvis. Yes. I did once." He said it slowly. He was alert again.

She laughed delightedly. "Oh, I did remember correctly. In fact, what I remember is you talking about it with such enthusiasm." Momentarily, he recovered that enthusiasm. His eyes crinkled and his long lashes met in a smile. Nice effect, she thought. She could see that he was relieved: a remembered conversation was okay, money squandered during his first marriage was not.

"So, you were a Highmeadows parent?," he asked, scrambling back up to a safer place.

"No," she said. "We just kept fetching up at the same drinks parties. You remember what Surrey was – is – like. Gin and tonic belt. All those crashing bores. Major this, Chairman of the local Conservative Party that. Do you remember Lady What's-it, the General's wife? The one who would introduce herself to new people as the village Pooh-Bah." Only when the conversation smoothed and became light and comfortable again, did she confess, "I remember you so well because you were a lot more fun than the rest of them. I thought you were very amusing."

Clearly he didn't mind the flattery, but she guessed he was desperately trying to remember whether he'd made a pass at her at some party or other.

New Malden flashed past and so did some hurtful memories. She'd done a lot of marking since Robert had walked out on her and the kids. Thank God for LA. Les Abandonnées – the name still amused her every time she thought about it. LA had offered her the best self-help therapy she could have had: tormenting the bastards who pulled the same shitty stunt on other women. She looked at the man opposite her: and you, David Morgan, are one of those bastards.

She'd received his file only a few months ago. His, and a few others, littered her room. The six-month up-date was due soon. What a fluke – she'd just looked through it at the weekend. But she wasn't sure what she should do next. Getting up-date material would be easy, but this situation was a gift. And after sixty-five, on mortality rules, the bastards become fair game any time, any place. So, what the hell? Why not have a go?

"It must have been easy to travel from the Gulf to all kinds of wonderful places," she said in good Cocktail-Partyese. She hadn't a clue what his answer would be. The earlier markers had had a lot of trouble keeping the file going when he'd been abroad.

"Yes, we did at first," he answered. "Goa, Singapore, Cairo. But then we got tired of so much sun and started coming back to Britain for the summer."

"Oh, that's right. Of course, you've settled in Liphook, haven't you?" Oh god, that's a slip. She couldn't have known that fifteen years ago. He looked puzzled, but said nothing. Lucky, she thought. She didn't want the penny to drop too soon.

She retreated to the theme of holidays abroad and it was some time before she said, "But you're right, holidays in Britain can be lovely. We went to Wales last summer – Bala. Wonderful sailing. The children loved it." His hands tightened hard on the book again. Good. That was close, way too close for comfort.

"We also camped for a few days at Whitesands – you know, St. David's. It was great." Then she added a pleasant tease, "I even thought of you when we were there. I remembered a funny story you'd told about judging a good family holiday by the number of melon labels you'd stick on the cupboard doors of the caravan." He drew his legs in and practically squirmed himself into a more upright position.

Gotcha! The perfect exemplar of the power of intimate knowledge. This was trivial pursuit for real. But, careful; let out the line a little.

"Your family came from somewhere around Cardigan Bay, didn't they?"

"Yes," he said, "but you sound American. Are you?"

She was well used to Brits picking on her accent when they wanted to take charge of a conversation. "Oh, I've lived here a long time, longer than I've lived in the States in fact."

The train slowed to a stop at Woking, then after a few minutes, started again with a judder.

"How is your family?" She hoped the finesse would work: she couldn't be sure his second wife didn't have kids of her own from an earlier marriage.

"My family?" He tensed. "There's only my wife and myself." She sensed she was in sharp focus.

"Oh, I'm sorry. I'm just being nosey. I guess I must mean your first family. Didn't you have a son?," she paused and looked out the window as the train rushed forwards. Her question lingered between them; it was still, as if the carriage were the eye of a storm.

29

"Yes, a son." Then gruffly he added, "And a daughter".

The train stopped at Guildford and a voice boomed, "Platform Five for the Reading Service, calling at Wanbrough, Ash..." It didn't seem to occur to him to get off and wait for another train.

As they roared through the tunnels south of Guildford, she said, "Oh, sure. I remember now. You had a son up at Oxford. Jesus College, wasn't it? The Welshmen's college." The thunder of the train reverberated round them as she continued, "It's all coming back now. Ieuan Thomas and Angharad Elizabeth – such lovely double names. You can see I've never forgotten them. Though I must admit I was a bit surprised that they kept using their Welsh names after you left."

His face darkened.

On the other side of the Hog's Back, the evening sun shone across the water meadows along the River Wey. It was too pretty for her next question. But so be it.

"Have you kept up with them?" She waited a long while before she added, "I heard that Margaret and the children had a terrible time at first. I guess they couldn't believe you'd walked out and left them. And left all your debts as well. They still carry terrific scars."

He recoiled as if he'd been struck. But he recovered fast. He put the book down on the seat beside him and looked round quickly. Tough, Boyo, she thought. Hard to bunk off when you're on a train.

She'd never taken anyone out before. But she'd heard the other women talk about the feeling. It was a blood sport, that's for sure, but gratifyingly moral.

"I was so sorry to hear about the accident." She watched him stiffen. His considerable unease was clearly turning to pure horror. "What a tragedy. Such a clever young man, with everything before him."

"My God. You know about Ieuan too?"

"Oh, yes. I gather that when they finally found out how to get in touch with you – to tell you about his death and when the funeral was to be held – you said you had something else on that day.

"What a filthy thing to say. But I know they were relieved not to have to deal with you at a time like that. After all, they hadn't so much as set eyes on you since the day you'd left, had they? And of course for Margaret, Ieuan's death happened just when James had become so very ill."

30

His eyes narrowed; it was a violent, ugly look.

"James?" she said, knowing he didn't know. "James is Margaret's partner. And yes, he recovered. She's very happy with him. The love of her life is what she says."

The train had just left Milford. She realized she'd better not get off at Witley. The station was too small and isolated. There wouldn't be a taxi and he might just follow her.

Then she saw that his anger had collapsed. He put his hands to his face. His voice rose, "Christ. Who are you?"

She looked out towards Hindhead and Gibbet Hill. A minute or two and they'd be at Haslemere. She glanced quickly at her briefcase so she wouldn't fumble it as she got off.

Pitiless, she looked straight at him. Then, with a hint of mockery in her voice, she said, "I guess who I am rather depends on how religious you are. For some people, I'm a recording angel. But, you're not religious, are you? So, why don't you think of me as your conscience. I'm just harder to deny when you meet me in the flesh. And, believe me, you'll meet me again. But, I should warn you, I won't look the same next time, so you won't recognize me then either.

"Have a nice evening. See you again soon," she said as she stepped onto the platform at Haslemere and, as the train pulled away, she grinned pure malice at his distraught face. Then suddenly she felt giddy and a bit frightened. She'd been well-blooded. It was exhilarating.

CREATIVE ACTS
Tim Connery

Tim Connery was born in 1964. He comes from a London-Irish background. He has had a variety of jobs, including working for the British Library where the idea for 'Creative Acts' was hatched. Tim was a winner of the London Arts Board London Short Story Competition 1995, and has recently sold a story to a film company and is currently developing that story into a screenplay. He is married, has a son and lives in south London.

IF MARTIN HAD TO SAY WHEN IT ALL STARTED, HE would have said the germ of the idea was fertilized on the night he met Paul for a drink in the Phoenix and Firkin on Denmark Hill.

It was a pleasantly warm night in June (London had yet to assume its summer guise of an airless oven) and the pub was already heaving when Martin arrived at seven thirty. Packed though the place was, Martin had no trouble spotting Paul: his friend was standing at the bar in a white linen suit with a huge white Fedora on his head, oblivious to the hostile stares he was receiving from the south London misfits around him.

"Our man in Havana, I presume," said Martin.

Paul turned to greet him, and Martin noticed with some alarm that he was wearing a cravat.

"MacSweeney, you old roister-doister, you!" Paul bellowed, and everyone looked away as they realised that he was just another lunatic. "What can I get you? A Pimms and lemonade? A banana daiquiri? Quango juice?" Most of this was directed at the people who had earlier been watching him.

"Paul, don't push your luck. I'm attached to my teeth, and, judging by the amount you've spent on them, so are you to yours.

I'll have a pint of Dogbolter."

Martin watched in horror as Paul raised a silver-tipped ebony cane and rapped it on the bar.

"Service!" Paul roared. "A pint of your finest brown washing-up water for my friend!"

Much to Martin's surprise, the girl behind the bar didn't smash Paul in the face with the nearest bottle; instead she smiled sweetly and pulled a pint of the syrupy, yeasty unpleasantness that Martin liked to ruin his health with.

"Here you are, Mr Kenny," she said politely to Paul.

"She's a fan," explained Paul when they finally found space away from the bar.

"Don't you think you're overdoing this famous man of letters bit? I mean, the hat, the suit, the cane..." Martin could not keep the contempt out of his voice.

Paul shrugged.

"My agent says I should do it. Says authors these days have to be bigger than their books. You've got to be more than a famous name, you"ve got to behave like a celebrity. So many of them behave like rock stars that I thought, just to stand out, I should adopt this persona." Paul leant forward conspiratorially. "I don't mind telling you, though, when I'm walking around the streets dressed like this I can't stop shitting myself. Still," he continued, perking up, "it does seem to help shift books. And that's what writing is all about these days."

"Unfortunately."

"Realistically, Martin, not unfortunately. Anyway, how goes it with you?"

"Oh, about the same," sighed Martin wearily, swirling his malevolent drink. "Same job, same girlfriend. Same life."

"I meant writing-wise."

Paul always meant writing-wise. When they had been at university together they had often talked about writing, but in those days the subject didn't damage Martin's psyche as it did now. In those heady days when there was hope -when there was a future – Martin was going to be the novelist and Paul was going to be the poet, but things had turned out the other way round: Martin drifted towards poetry and Paul towards what he called "the English Comic Novel". Paul had been published to huge commercial and minor critical acclaim, and Martin not at all. Strangely enough, since then Paul had taken an abnormal interest in Martin's writing career (or lack of it), and when the conversation got around to it, as it inevitably did, Martin felt as if scabs were being picked off a deep, unhealable wound.

"I've done something," said Martin warily, "that you might not agree with."

"Oh yeah?"

"I've paid to have some of my poems published."

Martin did not believe that jaws actually dropped until he looked up from his beer and saw his friend's face. Paul gaped at him, and then, slowly, rearranged his features to form a countenance of total disgust.

"Paid?" Paul spat the word out, as if he had something foul in his mouth.

"It seemed the only way I was ever going to see them in print," was Martin's plaintive reply. He looked down, unable to meet Paul's eyes.

"Paid?" Paul spat the word out again.

"I thought," Martin went on quickly, guilt prompting him to justify his actions, "that if I presented my work in an attractive way publishers would sit up and take notice."

"Paid?" said Paul, still in shock. "You have been to a... a... vanity publisher?"

Martin felt his cheeks reddening.

"Blimey, Paul, take it easy. It's not as if I've raped Mother Theresa or anything."

"Isn't it?!" shrieked Paul. Aware that the lobotomised slabs around him were staring again, he lowered his voice. "Well, no, I suppose it isn't like raping Mother Theresa. That I could understand. You are only human, after all. But vanity publishing..." He was too shocked to finish his sentence; the train of thought was obviously too hideous to follow. Martin, head bowed like a carpeted schoolboy, got up to buy more drinks.

By the time Martin had returned, Paul had regained some of his composure.

"I'm sorry, Martin. You surprised me, that's all. Someone with your talent shouldn't have to pay to have his poems published. If you would just let me –"

"No!" said Martin fiercely, and that was that. The great unsaid between the two of them was that Paul was never, ever, to offer Martin help with being published. Paul paused before changing tack.

"Did you send any off to publishers then?"

"Yes," said Martin with great sadness. "I sent thirty volumes out to thirty different publishers."

"And?"

"I received thirty one rejection slips back."

"A writer's life is made of rejection slips," sighed Paul. "Although in my case I never received even one. Did I ever tell you that?"

"Yeah, but only ninety five thousand times," said Martin, contrition leaving him as alcohol entered. "Tell me again. I need help with sleeping."

Paul laughed, and the evening progressed pretty much as usual after that: they got blind drunk and most of it passed in a blur of noise and colour. One thing did stick in Martin's mind, though; at one point Paul leant across to him and slurred,

"No man but a blockhead ever wrote for aught but money."

"Eh?" said Martin, confused. "What have Ian Dury and Chaz Jankel got to do with writing?"

"Who?" Paul looked baffled, and made an effort to pull his own thoughts together. "I said no man but a blockhead ever wrote for anything other than money. That was Sam Johnson, I think. Or was it Ben Jonson?"

"I don't care who said it. They were wrong!" Martin lurched unsteadily to his feet and with an emphatic gesture knocked his drink over. "I shall prove them wrong! I shall write purely for art's sake!"

"You'll sit down purely for fuck's sake, Martin. You should go home to that lovely, lovely girlfriend of yours. You are well pissed. I shall call you a cab."

"Don't call me a cab. I am a cab. I don't need you to call me one." Martin hated the joke, but his inebriated mind couldn't let it pass.

"The pub emptied itself of its drunks like a slit belly spilling its guts," said Paul as they got caught up in the slow-flowing stream of people leaving.

"That was crap," said Martin. "How come you get published?"

"Because I make money, not art. Farewell, poet! Back to your garret!"

It was very late when Martin came staggering in, treading kebab into the carpet and scaring the cat with his maniacally affectionate greetings. Clare was upstairs in bed, reading.

"Did you have a nice time with Paul?" she asked the swaying wraith in the doorway.

"If you can call poisoning myself nice, then, yes, I did."

"I hope you are not too drunk," she said with a certain look in her eye.

Martin grinned. "I'm never too drunk," he said in his sexiest voice.

"Good," said Clare, pulling aside the covers, "because this is the year I have decided that we will have a baby." She smiled sweetly, not realising that her words had immediately rendered Martin impotent.

Two weeks later, Martin found himself at work. His job was an easy one: he worked in the preservation department at the British Library in the British Museum where, if any book or incunabulum was found to be in need of binding or repair, he recorded the details and sent the item out to be treated, and then ticked the item off when it came back in. It was easy. And boring. And dull. It ate away his soul and destroyed his mind. It ruined his day, blighted his week, aged him and turned him against humanity. But he didn't expect anything else of it; it was, after all, work.

Massimo, the weird library assistant, brought him in a trolley of books to be assessed. Massimo pushed and shoved the trolley like it was some beast of burden that he hated and wanted to kill. Martin looked at in the same way.

"Martin. How're ya?" said Massimo.

Martin dolefully kept his eyes on the trolley. Yet more work.

"I feel like I'm being buried alive," Martin said. "It is a slow process, one that began thirty five years ago when I was born. Every day since then a handful of soil has been poured over me at such a rate that I will be completely covered by about the age of seventy. As it is I'm nearly half buried. I'm half dead. I'm just waiting here in my grave for the rest to be filled in. The inevitability of it doesn't upset me, it's the fact that I never clambered out of the grave when I had the chance. I blew my chances. I wasted my life."

"Sorry," said Massimo, pulling the earphones of his personal stereo out of his ears. "I missed that. What'd ya say?"

"I'm okay," sighed Martin. "What have you got for me?"

"The usual rubbish."

Martin reached out and wearily picked up a handful of books from the trolley. Ever since Clare had decided to have a baby (and Martin's impotence had faded with the initial shock) he found that he needed to conserve all energy for nocturnal activity. His daytime movements were thus somewhat fatigued.

The books were, indeed, the usual rubbish.

"Look at this," said Martin. "*A History of Pike Fishing* in three volumes. Three volumes, I ask you. Who the hell published that?"

"Well, it wasn't me," said Massimo, stroppily. He kicked some of the books he had just brought in. "Where d'ya want 'em left?"

Martin dragged his eyes around around the cluttered cupboard that served him and his boss as an office. He felt like weeping when he saw the huge backlog of work staring unblinkingly back, but instead he just indicated a space near an untidy desk.

"There. By the führer's desk."

"Is he on 'oliday again?"

"Yeah."

"Always off, ain't they?" Massimo lifted a framed picture off the vacant desk. "Who's this? His dad?"

Martin laughed. Massimo was holding a photo of Philip Larkin.

"No," Martin said. "That's Philip Larkin, a poet. The führer is a big fan. Wants to go on Mastermind and answer questions on him. That's the thing with bosses. If they haven't got halitosis or some unsightly deformity that you can't help staring at, they've got some trainspotting obsession to bore you with when they condescend to have a conversation with you. Why did you think it was his dad?"

As a response Massimo pointed to the quote pasted near the bottom of the framed photograph:

THEY FUCK YOU UP YOUR MUM AND DAD

Martin nodded, understanding Massimo's point. Massimo stuck his earphones back in his ears and sauntered off.

Martin looked sulkily at the three volumes he had taken off the trolley. The first two were in desperate need of binding; the covers were almost hanging off. He checked the publishing details: 1953. They hadn't fared too well. The third volume looked okay. He opened it and found that it was filled with blank pages. No frontispiece, no title page, no contents page... Nothing. No writing on the spine, either. Just a blank book. He had seen weirder things in the British Library before. Perhaps a mistake had been made in printing the third volume, or perhaps the third volume had never been written and the publishers bound the pages for their own ends. Who knew? Who cared?

Seeing the book depressed him, because it looked similar to the thousand bound copies of his poems that he had sitting at home, and for all the good they had done him they might as well have been blank too. Every time he walked into his own home he was confronted with the physical evidence of his lack of skill as a writer. The ones in crates were bad enough, but the loose ones were worse as they had a habit of popping up anywhere to remind him of his failings; he had found them under seat cushions, in kitchen drawers, in the bedside cabinet, and, on doing some DIY plumbing, he had even found one in the toilet cistern. They were like some infestation: they were everywhere; they were breeding. He just couldn't get rid of them. If he went to the post office and posted a volume to a publisher, by the time he got home it would be lying on the mat with a rejection slip enclosed. And those rejection slips! They all said the same thing: "Thank you... Not suitable at this time in our schedule... Do not hesitate to send us your work in the future..." Don't ring us, we'll ring you. Of course, they tried to personalise them by dropping his name in at the top (one had read "Dear Marvin"), but this somehow made it worse – a more personal rejection.

Still, the volumes made nice Christmas/birthday/wedding/anniversary presents for his family and friends, although he had a fear that these too would come back: "Dear Son, Thank you... not suitable as an anniversary present... do not hesitate..." Yep, he had to face facts: his poems were not wanted. They would not make money. In fact, they had lost him money, and he would never (because he could never) tell Clare just how many thousands of pounds Pipkin Publishing had taken from him in order to clutter up his life with these simulated leather bound piles of crap.

Money. Did it all come down to that in the end? That appeared to be what writing was all about these days. Take Paul, for instance. Martin wasn't jealous of his talent as a writer (in fact, he had a feeling that Paul was trying to write serious novels but that people could only assume they were meant to be comedies, so ludicrous were their plots and scenes), but he was insanely jealous of his success. It wasn't fair. If only there was some way to beat the system, to prove to Paul and the publishers who seemed to hold so much power over writers that their methods of judging literary merit were entirely in error. In fact, he would like to do more than prove this to them, he would like to teach them a good, hard lesson. Give them a short, sharp shock. In fact...

It came to him in a flash. The whole plan just popped into his head fully formed. He was shocked and appalled by its audacity and amazed at its genius. His head spun. If I can pull this off... He left the thought hanging, not daring to examine it any further, and gently placed the third, empty, volume of *A History of Pike Fishing* on the top of a pile of books.

Clare came home from work to find Martin typing furiously.

"What are you doing home so early? Are you sick?" she asked.

"No. I've taken some leave."

"Oh, good. Let's go upstairs and –"

But Martin had no time for biological acts of creation, and he raised his fingers to his lips. Clare stopped when she saw the mad gleam in his eyes, and was startled into asking the obvious.

"Are you writing?"

Martin laughed. "I'm doing more than that. Much more."

Clare backed cautiously out of the room. She got very little sleep that night, but not for the usual reasons. The clatter of Martin's typewriter kept her awake most of the night. The following morning she slipped a note under the door of Martin's study. "Is it a great work of literature?" it read. The reply came scrawled back on the reverse: "Yes! As opposed to literature!".

Six days later, unshaven, unwashed, red-eyed, wild-haired and, thanks to a poor diet and no sunlight, replete with the joys of rediscovered acne, Martin finally stopped typing. He had slept for only a few hours a night at his desk. All he had eaten were chocolate biscuits and coffee that Clare, in awe of such dedication, had wordlessly brought him. His fingers were raw and bleeding, raw and swollen, and he felt great. He looked at the manuscript next to him and smiled. He rolled a fresh sheet of paper into the typewriter and typed:

GREY DAY
A Work of Fiction
by

and left it at that. Then he went to sleep for forty eight hours.

Pipkin Publishing was located underneath some railway arches (which, judging by the smell, obviously doubled as a public convenience) at Vauxhall, exactly the sort of place where Martin expected to find such a rip-off joint. Martin arrived dead on ten as arranged. Mr Pipkin met him at the door.

"Hello, Mr MacSweeney," said Mr Pipkin. "Come around to the offices. It is quieter there." They walked past the rolling presses (a bit antiquated, thought Martin, and then smiled, as that was just what he wanted), past some offices where grey haired and grey faced men and women toiled over mysterious papers, and into a tiny but soundproofed office.

"Have a seat," said Mr Pipkin, indicating a collapsed piece of furniture.

Martin had never seen a more lugubrious man in his life. Dressed like a factory manager from the nineteen fifties in a black bowler and brown overall, Mr Pipkin's face drooped in spectacular fashion. He looked like he was melting, like all his energy had seeped out downwards. Even his huge bristly moustache sagged at the corners in sympathy with his sliding jowls. His small, droopy eyes stared lifelessly at Martin.

"I'm Norman Pipkin," he said, and then inexplicably screeched "Mr Grimsdale!!"

The contrast of his normal demeanour with this sudden squawk alarmed Martin so much that he involuntarily shot out of his chair and looked around for Mr Grimsdale and whatever heinous crime he must be committing. He turned back, puzzled. Norman Pipkin kept his doleful eyes on Martin and, with no change in expression, again screeched "Mr Grimsdale!!"

Martin backed away, worried.

"Don't you get it? It's a joke. Norman Pipkin. Mr Grimsdale."

From somewhere Martin received an image of an old black and white movie. Norman Wisdom... Wasn't he always called Norman Pipkin in those films? And his boss was... Mr Grimsdale!

"Norman Wisdom?" said Martin with a dry mouth.

"Well done," said Mr Pipkin.

"Actually," said Martin, remembering the films with sudden clarity (and he would worry later about his ability to recall nothing but trivia), "I think you'll find the character was called Pitkin. That's P-I-T, not P-I-P." Martin was glad of the chance to be bitchy after the fright he'd just had. He hoped it would prevent Mr Pipkin from screaming again. Mr Pipkin stared inscrutably at Martin for a moment.

"Thank you for that insight," he said blandly. "Now. What can I do for you? More poems?"

"No," said Martin. This was it, he had to go through with it now. "It's a novel."

"Ah, the Great English Work. And how many copies?"

"One."

Mr Pipkin's expressionless face looked up at Martin. "I'm afraid the costs involved wouldn't justify the printing of -"

"Let me stop you there. Please." Martin had Mr Pipkin's full attention. He spoke quickly. "I will pay you the exorbitant sum that I paid you for printing one thousand copies of my poems if you print this novel," and Martin took his manuscript out of his briefcase, "once, and once only, onto the pages of this book," and he produced the blank third volume of the pike fishing book which he had taken from the British Library.

Martin had the impression that he could have handed Mr Pipkin two suitcases full of money, or two naked women, or two pieces of bark, and his expression still wouldn't have changed. As it was he just stared at the manuscript and bound volume for a few minutes. Martin worried that he might have fallen asleep.

"Can it be done?" asked Martin eventually.

"We would have to take the book apart. There would be binding costs and so on. And printing onto those individual pages would be very expensive indeed. It would cost much more than the printing of the poetry."

"But can it be done?"

"Yes. It can be done."

"Mr Grimsdale!!" shrieked Martin, and he laughed.

"Are you okay?" asked Mr Pipkin.

"Yes," said Martin, pulling himself together. "Yes. Sorry about that."

Mr Pipkin cast a bored glance over the novel.

"One thing, Mr MacSweeney. The title page of the MS. It doesn't have your name on it."

Here it comes, thought Martin, his heart leaping into his mouth. Don't lose your bottle now.

"That's because I don't want my name on it. I want it to read 'By... Philip Larkin'."

There was a long pause in which Mr Pipkin's bland face stared at Martin. Then he casually picked up a pencil and muttered "By Philip Larkin. Okay," and wrote that on the manuscript.

"I don't want you using laser printers or anything like that," said Martin, warming to his task. "Those old presses we saw on the way in, just how old are they?"

"Alas, they are much older than most, Mr MacSweeney. I publish unknown authors who do not make me much money. I can't afford to buy in new technology."

Martin could not believe his luck.

"Well, I'd like the book to be done using a typeface and printing method that would have been common in the early nineteen fifties."

"You have just described our most up-to-date system," said Mr Pipkin with a sad sigh. Martin took a deep breath and carried on quickly.

"I want the year of publication to read '1953'. And I don't want it to say it was published by you. I want the publisher's details left off."

"Anything else?" said Mr Pipkin, scribbling away.

God, does nothing bother this man? thought Martin.

"No. Nothing else."

And that was that.

Some time later, Martin received the proofs of the book. Apart from spelling Philip Larkin as 'Phillip Larking' it was mostly okay. The accompanying invoice was not okay; here was something that really would have to be hidden from Clare. Ah,

Clare. Things were not going too smoothly there. Their conversations had started going round on a monthly cycle. About once every four weeks Martin would come home only to have the following dialogue:

"I'm on," Clare would say.

"Pardon?" Martin would pretend he didn't understand.

"I'm on. I've started."

"Ah. Um," he would say, and she would look at him accusingly. What could he do? He was giving it his all.

And then the book arrived. Neatly bound in its original green leather covers, it looked great. But not quite perfect. In order to give it that handled-by-caring-library-staff look, Martin spent an energetic morning kicking it around the garden. He kept it hidden at home for a week, taking it out when he was alone and staring at it, sniffing it, stroking it. He read it from cover to cover twice, and both times it thrilled him. Finally, after a weekend of talking to it, wishing it luck and blessing it, he took it into work. He went in early on a Monday morning and left it at the bottom of a pile of books on his boss's desk. He felt bereaved as he left the office for the canteen.

"I don't know, I can't believe it's real. What do you think?" Paul whined. He was a crushed man. He sat in the Phoenix and Firkin in a floppy black felt hat and huge flowing black cape, but he no longer had the aplomb to carry it off. People barged into him on purpose or spilled their drinks on him. His feet were trodden on. He was frightened to go to the toilet in case he got beaten up. Martin had to go to the bar to get the drinks because Paul was too scared. The girl behind the bar was no longer a fan.

Martin, though, felt huge and powerful. Electricity flew out of him in sparks. He hummed with a barely-contained energy. He was a superman!

"Paul, it must be real. The pages – the paper used – have been scientifically dated. Even the binding is of the right period. And as for the content, well... The central character is a young man who grew up in Coventry before the war. He goes to St John's in Oxford. He writes poems which are obviously earlier versions of Larkin's more famous poems. 'Aubade' is in there in full! He is an onanist, a racist, into porn, he loves jazz... Face it, it is by Larkin."

"Yeah, but how come it's the plot of *Blue Monday*, my first novel, written in 1985? How could that happen? How could it follow that plot so closely? Have similar scenes? Now everyone thinks I'm a plagiarist! My agent won't answer my calls!"

He was almost crying, but that was nothing new. His eyes were always red these days and his nose always running. He was always almost crying. He was so miserable he could drink Dogbolter without shuddering. Martin laid a sympathetic hand on Paul's arm and excused himself, going into the toilets to laugh.

It had worked perfectly! His boss had immediately recognised the importance of *Grey Day – A Work of Fiction*, although there had been an alarming moment when Martin thought that he might have a heart attack, so excited was the man by the discovery. His boss had the wherewithal to pass the book up the chain of command at the British Library (although Martin now had to endure endless do-you-remember-the-day-I found-that-book conversations) where it attracted the attention of more and more experts. The 'Lost Larkin' created huge debate for a few months (a few nervous months for Martin) before being officially declared genuine. Then, after extracts from it were published in a Sunday newspaper, the similarities between it and Paul's first novel, *Blue Monday*, became apparent. It was well known (well known because Paul had only a handful of anecdotes for his interviewers) that Paul had written his novel in the Reading Room of the British Museum, where the 'Larkin novel' was gathering dust on the shelves, unclassified, uncatalogued... The obvious conclusion was drawn. Paul was now a literary leper, once lionised, now shunned. It was brilliant. And even no less an authority than Sir Kingsley Amis had said, "How like Larkin to slip a vanity edition of his own novel onto the shelves of our national library."

Back in the main bar, Paul was being hassled by a gang of young men, but they soon fled as Martin approached, sizzling with unearthly confidence. Paul looked gratefully up at him with his watery eyes.

"Martin, you believe me, don't you, when I say I never saw that fucking buggering book before, ever, in my life?"

Christ, he even sounds like Larkin now! thought Martin.

"Of course I believe you," said Martin in such a way so as to imply no, I don't believe you, but I'll say I do because you're my friend.

Paul stopped snivelling. "How goes it with Clare? Any developments on the baby front?"

"No. And do you know what? I'm glad."

"Why?" asked Paul. "Having children is great. When mine arrived I was literally bursting with pride."

"Literally?" said Martin sarcastically.

"You know what I mean. The birth of a child is a magical experience. You never forget that moment. It's as if the universe is condensed into that little ball of flesh and blood. When that comes into the world –"

"I thought you weren't present at the birth?"

"Well, er, no. I wasn't. But it was a very important business lunch."

"And you don't see your kid now, do you? Your wife had an exclusion order taken out on you when you pretended to be a homosexual to sell more books, didn't she?"

Paul's lower lip quivered and he stared at the table. "I think I'll become an alcoholic."

"I'll help you," said Martin, and he went to the bar to get more drinks.

When he returned he found Paul, somewhat relaxed by alcohol, singing along to the Pogues on the jukebox.

"I hate this lot," said Martin of the music as he plonked two pints of Dogbolter onto the table. He half expected the spilt beer to eat its way through the wood.

"Why do you hate them? They're Irish like you."

"They're Irish like me is right. Born and brought up in London. Those 'Oirish' accents don't fool me. They're making money out of their parents' heritage."

"And there's a lot of money to be made from it."

"What do you mean by that?"

Paul sipped heartily at his drink, glad to be off the topic of his supposed plagiarism. "Since the IRA ceased major military operations certain Yanks have been very disappointed. There were these Americans who were happy raising millions to support 'the struggle' in Northern Ireland. People with names like Riley and O'Malley living in New York and New Jersey with nothing else to do. Now they still want to raise millions to fight the Brits, but the cash isn't used to buy arms. Instead, they publish anti-British

propaganda by the shovelful. Blokes like yourself, all happily living
here but with Irish-sounding names, are sending off all sorts of
crappy poems to these Yanks and are laughing all the way to the
bank."

"Lucrative, is it?"

"I'll say. One bloke, Niall McGuinness in Boston, I think, is well
known for his generosity. The more anti-British the poems the
better. He's a maniac, McGuinness is. Hates the British with a
vengeance. Loves the crap sent to him, too. Seems to think that
only Ireland can produce great poetry. Always saying he's found
the new Yeats or whatever. Puts a lot of money behind his new
authors, who usually piss it up against the wall. But you're not
interested in this. You are interested only in writing for art, not
money, right?"

"Right."

"Y'know, Martin, that's the one thing that baffles me about this
Larkin forgery. And I am convinced that it is a forgery. I can't see
what the forger gets out of it. Apart from ruining my reputation."

Martin paused in his drinking, his glass near his mouth,
watching Paul carefully. For the first time since their coming into
the pub, Paul met Martin's eyes.

"I'm going to look into this Larkin novel," said Paul carefully. "I
will vindicate myself, and I'll fucking crucify whoever wrote it."

"Good idea," said Martin. He drank heavily after that, but
couldn't get drunk.

Martin and Clare separated in the darkness.

"That was nice," said Clare.

"Mm."

"Every time, now, I wonder, is that it? Is that the one?"

"Mm."

"Because time is getting on now."

"Mm."

"We should start saving more. Just in case. The money in our
savings account seems to be going down, not increasing."

"Mm." (He had a fleeting glimpse of Mr Pipkin buying rack
upon rack of brown overalls.)

"We really do need more money. I'll do more overtime at the
bank."

"Mm." (A heavily pregnant Clare scrubbing floors at NatWest.

Mr Pipkin looking on impassively as a cashier banks his huge sacks of money.)

"You never did let me read that novel. The one that you wrote in a week."

"Mm." (Paul, a green carnation in his lapel, hammering two planks of wood to make the shape of a cross. Clare scrubbing nearby. Mr Pipkin putting on a new bowler.)

"You haven't been right since you finished that, you know. You've been cold. Distant. It took something from you. You've changed. Even Paul has noticed it. He told me – Hello? Martin...? Never mind."

Martin was lost, lost in money troubles, in troubled dreams, in a troubled conscience.

As luck would have it, the airmail parcel arrived while Clare was out. Martin glanced at the return address on the back and ripped it open. He read the covering letter first.

"Dear Mrs O'Cunnaire," it began. "Many thanks for your sending me your son's poems. I am known as something of a hard man, Mrs O'Cunnaire, but I don't mind telling you I wept when I read your boy's verses. It took me a long time to read them because my eyes were so full of tears: tears of joy, tears of sorrow. I believe, quite truly, that your son's talent is easily equal to that of the great W B Yeats. What a loss it must have been to you when your son was mown down fighting for his country's freedom on that cold Ulster night in 1985; what a torment the last ten years must have been for you – it is no surprise that you could not bring yourself to look through his poems until now. But what a legacy he has left us! I believe your son was a genius, Mrs O'Cunnaire, and I will make sure that he lives on through his work. Please find enclosed a check for ten thousand pounds sterling made payable (as requested) to your stepson, Martin MacSweeney, and a copy of the *Collected Poems* as it will appear in bookshops. I promise you, I will make sure the world recognises the talent of your son, and everyone will sing the praises of Tighe O'Cunnaire!" The letter was signed 'Niall McGuinness' in a brutal, childish hand.

Tighe O'Cunnaire, a.k.a. Martin MacSweeney, trembled as he looked at the cheque. Then he laughed as he looked at the *Collected Poems*. The collection consisted of all the poems he had had published himself the year before, but after every second one he had inserted verses with titles like Ode to the Black and Tans, Do You See the RUC, Celtic Twilight, British Dawn and so on. The cover of the book was fantastic. It was a coloured pencil drawing depicting a moustached British Officer from the RAF (circa 1944) beating an Irish peasant with his cane. The peasant's donkey was braying in terror. The scene was taking place outside University College, Dublin, with a British tank parked nearby. Martin whistled in awe as he wondered at the ignorance of these people, then he literally laughed all the way to the bank.

Two months later, Martin was not laughing.

"My results are here in black and white, Martin!" Clare was close to tears. "I am fertile! There is nothing to prevent me from having a baby! You must have those tests! You must!"

Martin sat, trembling. At his feet lay The Times Literary Supplement. In it was an article by Paul Kenny, disgraced comic novelist, which argued that Grey Day, the 'Lost Larkin', must be a fake. The article was erudite, learned and well researched, causing Martin to muse when reading it on just how adversity can bring out the best in people. Amongst other things, Paul had pointed out that certain idioms and figures of speech in the book were too modern. "A phrase such as 'Let me run it by you,' although common enough for the modern reader to not pay particular attention to, is in fact a product of the computer age, and would almost certainly not have been used by a writer such as Larkin in 1953, even if it is said by an American character... Why would he have written a poem like 'Aubade' as early as 1953 but not have it published until much later in his life? It just does not make sense." Too right, Paul old chum, thought Martin. And Paul was not the only one to have doubts; many other literary giants had started noticing anachronistic flaws in the supposed third Larkin novel. Martin had done his best, but the holes were starting to show under close scrutiny.

There was another nervewracking article in the TLS. The British publication (in a sensible plain white cover) of The Collected Poems of Tighe O'Cunnaire had caused a storm. "Lost Great Irish Genius?" screamed the headline of the article. "The anti-British poems can be dismissed as juvenalia mixed with misplaced and misguided loyalties (the boy was only eighteen when he was tragically killed by an army patrol, just like his father was) but the other poems contain some of the most moving verses in contemporary poetry." Various leading literary lights were queuing up to sing Tighe O'Cunnaire's praises. Alarmingly, the article went on to say that Niall McGuinness, the American publisher who had discovered this "tragic genius", was coming to London to visit O'Cunnaire's "aged and long-suffering mother" and to sort out some of the more puzzling aspects regarding the deceased poet, such as why the army have no records of ever having shot an eighteen year old called Tighe O'Cunnaire in 1985 (or any other year).

"Will you have the tests, Martin? Please say you will!" The dam finally burst and the tears ran down Clare's face. Martin reached out and wiped them away, his fingers leaving an inky smear from the print of the TLS.

"Okay," he said. "Okay."

Martin stared glumly at the leaflet the doctor had given him. "Living with Infertility" was its catchy title. It reminded him of an American movie title, probably about sharing an apartment with a baby or dog called Infertility, and probably starring Ted Danson. For a worrying moment he thought he had actually seen this movie – wasn't Tom Selleck in it too? Or Macaulay Culkin? – but then he remembered it was only a leaflet, one he had been carrying around in his pocket for three weeks now, ever since the doctor had looked at him over the top of his glasses (doctors really do that! he thought wildly at the time) and announced:

"The results of your tests are here, Mr MacSweeney. I'll spare you the suspense. You have an extremely low sperm count."

Insult to injury, that: not just low, but extremely low. Martin was floored. He brooded. What was the point of weight training, muscles, facial hair, creeping baldness, watching football and behaving like a neanderthal in the pub if your sperm count was extremely low? What was the point of enduring all that male baggage if you weren't, well, capable of doing what male beings are supposed to do? What was the point of Martin's maleness when the body count of the central essences of his maleness was extremely low? Why, no point at all.

He couldn't produce children. Clare took it well, crying solidly for the first night and then only for hours at a time after that. Martin cried too, surprising himself. I didn't want children now, he thought, but I certainly didn't want to have zero chance of ever having children. "You've got your writing," Paul said, trying to be helpful (and he was being helpful, offering the support to Clare that she needed but that Martin could not supply himself as he did not have the reserves for it right now), but that was no consolation. What was the point of creating fictional characters in a real world? Why create when you can't procreate?

Martin put the leaflet away as his bus coughed and spluttered its way towards him. He carried the leaflet with him everywhere now, hoping that its constant presence would dull its ability to hurt, but all it did was make him feel as if he was carrying an albatross around in his jacket pocket. He sighed heavily as he got on the bus full of its usual daytime passengers of eroding geriatrics and psychopathic teenagers playing truant. Martin was travelling home early; depression has its plus side – your boss is only too keen to get rid of your long face if you say that you are feeling down. He had to stand for the entire journey between a woman whose carrier bag full of sharp heavy objects kept swaying into his legs and a man who had more dandruff than hair. He read the balding man's newspaper over his snow-topped shoulder:

LOST LARKIN NOVEL DECLARED FAKE – OFFICIAL

Well done, Paul.

After an eternity of listening to the gripes of the old and the lunatic abuse of the young, the bus creaked to Martin's stop and he got off, listlessly dragging himself home. As he fished his keys out he decided he needed something banal and undemanding to wash through his mind. He needed a mind-enema to sweep away the hideous detritus that was causing a blockage and he began to look forward to the prospect of an afternoon's daytime TV viewing. He went up the stairs to his front door.

Martin turned the key in the lock and all hell broke loose inside. Mad thumping and pounding came from the ceiling above him, the kind of thumping and pounding that human beings make when they are disturbed doing something they shouldn't be doing. At first, Martin thought he had interrupted burglars and got ready to flee, but then he heard a familiar voice cry out "Shit! It's him!" and he heard Clare squawk in panic. He rushed up the stairs to his bedroom.

He was greeted by a sight that looked like a scene from one of Paul's novels. There, hopping on one leg, trying to get the other through the tangled mass of trousers flapping about in his hands, was Paul himself. The bare foot he was supporting himself on hopped onto a hairbrush and he fell sideways, causing Martin to marvel at how hairy his friend's buttocks were. Clare, meanwhile, unsure as to what she should do, ran up and down the bed, clutching first the sheet then the duvet to her, like some demented peep show artist. Clare and Paul were trying to communicate but all that came out were panicky whoos and beeps; they sounded like the Clangers on a white-knuckle ride. Paul got up, holding one of his shoes. He stared, puzzled, as if he had never seen it before.

"It's a shoe," said Martin helpfully, and he left.

He thought he must've looked pretty cool, leaving like that, but out on the street his thoughts swam and made him dizzy. It was a surreal universe; now he really did feel like a character from a work of fiction. He had never thought that his relationship with Clare would end with the words "it's a shoe", but then again, he mused, I bet everyone would think that. He started walking away from his house (their house), trying to put some distance between it and him. That was his only plan – to get away – and it was while he was following this through that he became aware of a large black car shadowing him as he paced heavily along the rubbish-strewn pavements.

The black car was a huge chauffeur-driven limousine, and it looked entirely alien as it followed Martin along roads dotted with transit vans with graffiti etched into the dirt covering their rusty panels, Escorts with the wing mirrors sellotaped on and the sad skeletal remains of pecked-clean bicycles riveted to trees and lampposts. The limousine overtook him slowly and halted. The back door was eased open as he approached.

"Get in," barked an American voice. Martin got in, perceiving first the strong smell of leather and polish and wax and cigars and aftershave all of an expensive origin. Then his eyes took in Mr Pipkin, looking as nonplussed as ever, and next to him a well-dressed, squat, stocky man with close-cropped ginger hair and several constellations of freckles on his wide face. The car pulled away as Martin closed the door behind him.

"Niall McGuinness, I presume," said Martin.

"Martin MacSweeney, I presume," said McGuinness. "Or is it Philip Larkin? Or Tighe O'Cunnaire?"

"All three. At your service." Martin nodded to Mr Pipkin. "When did you find out?"

"Oh, I realised straight away that you were up to no good," said Mr Pipkin. "But I couldn't think why. Even when they published extracts from the Larkin novel I thought, why? What's in it for him? So I kept a close eye on things. I reread your poems, and I must say that they really are very good. I kept a look out for any unusual literary events. Then Tighe O'Cunnaire happened, they printed one of his – your – poems in the paper, I recognised it from your vanity edition and –"

"And then Mr Pipkin quite wisely contacted me," said McGuinness. "Y'know, Martin, I admire what you've done. You've made me look a complete asshole, but, hey, your poems are damn good. But tell me, why did you do it?"

"The O'Cunnaire poems? I needed the money."

"And the Larkin novel?"

"Literature shouldn't be written for money. Only for art."

"Jesus, kid, you are weird. Ain't he weird, Mr Pipkin?"

"The weirdest, Mr McGuinness."

"But, Martin, we ain't here to discuss your weirdness." McGuinness bit the end off a fresh cigar that was the size and shape of the leg of a large coffee table; the piece he spat out looked as big as a normal cigar. McGuinness lit the end with some difficulty, his arms being so short, and soon filled the car with thick blue smoke. Martin looked at him through watering eyes, while Mr Pipkin, bored, stared out of the window. Satisfied after drawing on his chimney, McGuinness turned again to Martin.

"Now, I don't want the Tighe O'Cunnaire thing exploded. Not yet, anyway. We can have a laugh at those jerks in the British establishment who've been duped by this. We can rip the shit out of them later." McGuinness now seemed totally oblivious to the fact that he, too, had been duped. His eyes shone through the smoke with scary fervour. "I know Mr Pipkin will keep quiet. He is a gentleman and we have come to a, er, gentleman's agreement."

"Very favourable indeed," said Mr Pipkin, his dour countenance giving nothing away. "But you, Mr MacSweeney..."

"What about me?"

"What about you, Martin?" asked McGuinness. "You've seen the interest Tighe O'Cunnaire generated. There's a goldmine there... Produce more of his poems. Hell, even a novel."

"What about a play? I've got this idea —"

"Yeah, yeah, great, kid. It can be an underwater animatronics spectacular on ice, for all I care. Spare me the details. Just produce more Tighe O'Cunnaire and we can make each other rich. Are you in?"

Martin paused, for almost a second. In that time an image of Clare and Paul and his home and his job flashed past; a messy, mixed-up vision of his life flowing down a drain. "I'm in."

Champagne was produced from some mysterious crevice and cracked open. The car sped along; Martin did not care where it was going just as long as it was away from his home. The three of them toasted each other.

"You know, this would make a great short story," said Martin.

"Don't, Martin. If a word of this gets out —"

"No, no. Don't panic. I'd change our names and everything."

"What would you call me?" asked Mr Pipkin.

"I'd call you Mr Pipkin. I'd make you a strange-looking shady printer in a brown overall and a bowler hat. And you... You'd be called McGuinness —"

"McGuinness! I like it!"

"And you'd be... American. A scary American publisher."

"And yourself?"

"Oh, I'd definitely change myself beyond all recognition. I'd be a writer called... Martin MacSweeney. I'd blur the boundaries between literature and life."

"How would it end? Would we come out of it well?"

"Oh, yes. We'd end up cruising the streets of London in a plush limousine, sipping champagne and laughing at everyone."

They all laughed and sipped champagne as the car cruised through the streets.

"And would you always have the last word?"

"It's my story," said Martin. He smiled as he lay back against the soft leather seat. "So, yes. Yes, I certainly would."

DOG IN THE YARD
Susannah Rickards

Susannah Rickards was born and raised in Newcastle-upon-Tyne. She now lives in London. After graduating from Oxford University with a degree in English, she co-founded Tattycoram Theatre Company and was joint writer of two shows, 'Mary Shelley...' and 'Three Sisters...'. She is a professional actress and for the past three years has also worked as a freelance fiction editor. She started writing regularly two years ago and has had poetry published in various magazines. 'Dog In The Yard' is her first published short story.

THEY ARRIVE SINGLE FILE, THEIR FATHER LEADING THE way like a scout master, his arms out in an aeroplane to cool his underarm sweat. So embarrassing. Their mother follows him, moving methodically under the weight of her rucksack. They are abroad and Tina feels sick most of the time. She is stranded for the summer without her friends, and the towns are full of churches with frescoes and you have to smile and say "Buona Sera" to strangers and be thankful all the time.

In the distance is her father, standing in the shade of the youth hostel porch. He turns to herd his flock and seeing his younger daughter lagging at the gate, waves her to join them. Her mother waits a few yards away from him rubbing her shoulders. Her sister Cheryl has taken off her back pack. Tina can see from the way she is circling her parents that she's asking for a can of coke. Tina's new trousers are stitched with nylon thread and the seams are rubbing her legs. She sets off at an elaborately slow pace. Maybe if she takes long enough there won't be a church this afternoon.

Half way along the path she stops outside a fenced-off yard where a ferocious dog is barking. She stands stock still and waits for it to shut up, but it barks. The dog is tied to a post and screened from her by a stretch of chicken wire but she still can't move past it. It lurches and stumbles towards her, caught in its tether.

She edges to the far side of the path and squashes up against a prickly pear bush, waiting for it to ease up, but it rears towards her, yowling and pawing the air. A sharp stone has worked its way under her jelly-bean sandal and is cutting into the little toe of her right foot. She won't allow herself to shake it out until she's passed the dog, so she has to devise a routine to allow her to pass. Close your eyes and open them three times. Each time look at the dog and see something different about it. Whenever she's frightened of something, her mother makes her describe it. Sometimes it works.

Eyes scrunched, Tina breathes in.

"Go." Its lolling tongue, the gums and goo. Her eyes snap shut.

"Go again." The pink flesh of its neck, rubbed raw by the rope.

A man comes past. You can tell from his forearms that he is Italian. The neatness of his cuffs, the gold watch, the dark hairs on his pretzel coloured skin.

"Buona Sera," Tina calls after him, and smiles. The man turns back, beaming at her.

"Buona Sera Biondina. Ti piace Il Capitano?"

Tina stares at him.

"Raff," says the man, his hands forming paws. "Raff raff."

Tina tugs at the neck of her T-shirt gesturing towards the dog with her head.

"He's sore," she says. "His neck."

"Ah. Inglese," the man says. "Eenglish – dogs. Dogs – eenglish." He pats his heart and laughs.

The man unlocks a metal gate that leads into the yard. The dog howls fiercely. Tina hangs back afraid, but the man's pretty hand closes over hers and he yanks her into the ring.

"Capteen," he says "Capteen."

The dog bounds towards Tina, but is brought short by its tether and skids in the dust. The man looms behind her, urging her forward, so close she can feel the bristly swish of his trousers

56

against her calves. In the distance her father calls her name. His voice grows louder. She feels the man's shadow move away and the back of her neck exposed to the sun grows hot. Either side of the chicken wire her father and the man are announcing themselves in Italian.

"Tina," Her father calls and she runs to him, putting her fingers through the mesh to touch his shirt.

"Daddy," her own voice sounds far away. She does not recognise it.

"Say hello to Signor Fagandini. You can do it in Italian."

"I did it already," Tina says, but she does it again. The man reels off a line of Italian and dog sounds. Tina's father laughs.

"Signor Fagandini says you can play with the dog if you like. But beware. He's a guard dog not a pet. This isn't England."

Mr Fagandini crouches to her level and speaks in careful English.

"His name is Captain." He stands up and roughs her hair.

"He is the boss, eh." He laughs and walks away. She hears the gate click and the men's feet on the hot gravel grow fainter. Just for a moment she is standing on her own with the dog. Then she pelts down the lane after them.

Up at the hostel Tina's parents are unpacking a picnic while Tina and Cheryl play adverts on the porch.

"You too could have hair as soft and shiny as mine," says Cheryl, swinging in practised slow motion round a pillar. Tina enters the frame.

"But my hair's so dry and brickle," she sighs.

"Just use what I use. New Viddle Sastoon!" cries Cheryl and canters off into a slab of sunlight, tossing her mane.

"Viddle Sastoon. Use Viddle Sastoon," Tina charges after her. On the lawn their parents are talking in low voices. The sun beats down, but their mother is hunched as if she's cold. Bread, goat's cheese and a floury salami are spread out on their father's blue waterproof. Tina sidles up on imaginary horseback and dismounts noisily but her parents don't look up.

"Maybe I was mistaken," her mother is saying. Her voice has the wobbly quality of a dud high note on Tina's recorder.

"Well if they're not transferable I could always take the train," says her father.

"We'd be back before you."

"Your choice."

Cheryl appears. "Please can I have a Fanta. Please."

Her father doesn't reply. He just shuffles round on his haunches till he's sitting with his back to his family. Tina hovers, testing the grass for somewhere to sit her new trousers. Their father wolfs his food down, chewing on only one side of his mouth. His bad tooth must have flared up again. Their mother doesn't eat. Cheryl and Tina poke around for something recognisable to feed on. Even the crisps have paprika on.

Tina feels like she does before a thunderstorm. As if an iron clamp is being winched around her skull just above the eyebrows. She tilts her face to the sun and lets it get so hot the skin feels tight. Nuala Godfrey in her class went to Spain and her mother let her wear a Mickey Mouse sticker on her neck for the whole fortnight. When they got back she'd peeled it off at break and there was a Mickey of pale skin, standing out against the brown. So far Tina has only ever freckled. There's a bottle of water on the lawn beside her. She splashes it into her hands and rubs the water on her face to attract a tan.

Her cheeks are beginning to burn and she tips the bottle directly up to her face, misjudges the angle, and the last of the water soaks into the lawn. Her mother hands her a slice of bread and marmalade, but when she bites into it, it tastes all wrong and she spits it out, half-chewed, onto the grass.

"I don't like it."

"Eat up and shut up," her father says.

"The marmalade tastes funny."

"It's apricot jam."

"I hate it. My mouth's gone all dry."

"Have a drink then," her mother says.

"I spilt it."

Her mother sighs. She gives Tina another beaker. Tina tastes it, then gags. Cheryl perks up and mock retches all over the lawn.

"I feel sick," Tina whinges.

"It's pear juice, Tina. For Heaven's sake."

"It's furry."

"Beugh," caws Cheryl, rolling her eyes merrily, "puke, puke."

Her father springs round. "See this?" He bares the palm of his hand. Cheryl squeals, he slaps and an imprint of his fingers reddens on her thigh. Cheryl's still for a moment then begins to bawl.

"Chrissake," says her father. Their mother reaches for Cheryl but she recoils and starts off into the bushes howling. Tina follows but Cheryl wedges herself under a bush and screams wordless, beastlike noises, till Tina gets bored and returns to the lawn. Her mother is standing up shaking the crumbs from her father's waterproof. Her face is as white as pain.

"Will you help me clear up, Tinnie? There's a good girl," she says. Tina's father is sitting perfectly still. Tina screws the lid back on the apricot jam, turning her nose away and holding her breath to blot out the smell. Her mother packs the food into a carrier bag. She picks the spat out bread and jam from the grass and bundles it into a paper wrapper.

"Mrs Fagandini says we can store things in her fridge, Arthur," she says.

"Very good," he says.

Tina's mother crouches beside her and puts her hand on Tina's scalp.

"You're very hot. You need some shade. Come with me."

"Daddy are you coming?"

"Come Tina," her mother takes her hand. The corners of her mouth are pointing down. Tina prods them with her forefinger.

"Smile," she says.

Her mother shakes her head. "Tina, Daddy and I have had a bit of a row."

"About Cheryl?"

"No."

Tina tests the ground with the ball of her foot. It's good for a cartwheel. Springy and firm.

"Are you going to get a divorce?" she asks and spins off into the cartwheel. Upright again and flushed, she gauges her parents' reaction. They can laugh or they can be cross; it wasn't a real question.

Nobody answers her.

"I don't know," her mother says finally. In the background Cheryl isn't screaming. Her father isn't shouting. There is no noise. Tina tries to fake a casual getaway, but she's making staccato dolly

59

movements like their cat Cora does when she's out stalking, pretending to be a bird. She walks away from her parents as stably as she can, but her legs are all brittle and stubby. She will walk away in a straight line and she won't stop till she's hit by a car or drowned in the sea.

She walks across the lawn, past the cypresses to where the grass thins out to hard brown ground. To her right are straggly shrubs, to her left a roll of barbed wire and a cement mixer standing empty. In front of her is the high wired fence of the enclosed yard, like a tennis court. The dog is in there. Tina doesn't care. She unlatches the metal gate and walks.

Captain rears up and bares his teeth. He's right in her line of vision. She has to walk. She swings her arms and digs her heels in like a soldier. The stone in her sandal is drawing blood. She stares ahead at the fence beyond. There is no dog, no obstacle. She will walk and walk and walk. The barks buzz in the distance with her mother's flat reply. She walks on and trips right over Captain's scrawny bulk. Her hand goes out to break her fall and lands in Captain's fur. Heat and a pulse she had not expected return her touch. She stays where she has fallen, concentrating on the comfortingly familiar sensation of grazed knees and the new odd one of touching a dog. She pats and strokes his bony back. Captain mewls and paws at her. His gungey tongue laps at her cheek. He smells dank, doggy, unloved. The tongue rasps and tickles. Tina giggles and wriggles and gets to her feet. His neck is rubbed raw from the rope. She pats.

"Sit." She presses the base of his spine. He yelps.

"Sit Captain."

The dog wrestles into a reluctant crouch.

"Good dog."

He circles his tether and thumps his tail. Tina pushes him towards the post to get some slack on the rope. Then she unties him and smoothes the hair down round his neck to disguise the sore.

"They never feed you do they? They never let you play."

She steers the dog to a trough in the corner of the yard and pushes his head into the water. He laps a little then stares at her. Tina scouts the yard, looking for a stick to throw.

When Kyle Hardie's parents got divorced, Kyle had climbed over the railway railings, waited until he saw a train coming, and then lain down on the track. A passer-by had spotted him in the nick of time, jumped over the barriers and swiped him up as the train brakes screeched, yards from his head. Lots of grown-ups had come to have sherry at Tina's house and said it was the luck of the devil it had been a local chuffer and not the Express, but there was no doubt about it, the child had wanted to die. At seven years old. His little sister Rosie was paralysed for nearly two years from the fright. She could only drink Coke and say "Worm." Tina throws stick after stick for Captain and when they're both tired she sits with her arm draped over his shoulders, till the sky turns a runny grey and she feels stiff.

When she gets back from playing with Captain her parents are sitting in the dusk on the steps of the Youth Hostel porch. They are sharing a plate of spaghetti and on a tray beside them is one large apple. Why hadn't they called down the garden for her to come and eat? Why was there only one dinner? Where was hers and Cheryl's?

"I'm hungry."

Her mother must know that. What would there be to make up for lunch?

"Have some of this." Her mother twizzles strands of spaghetti round her fork.

"I want my dinner."

"This is all there is."

"But when can I have my dinner?

"You can have this. There's nothing else."

"Why?"

Tina's father is trembling. His hands are white. He stands up abruptly and walks to the end of the colonnade. He jumps off the edge and heads for the cypress trees across the lawn. Tina watches until he is absorbed into their blue shadows and his outline cannot be distinguished from theirs.

Cheryl has taken the apple and is rolling it down the porch steps. Her mother puts a vague restraining hand on her shoulder twice, but says nothing when Cheryl bounces the apple down three steps and foots it along the path, chasing after it in the direction of

Captain's yard. Tina is alone with her mother in the dark.

"If you do it, I'll go with daddy."

Her mother says nothing. Tina takes hold of her mother's hair and winds it like a bandage round her wrist.

"If I do go, can I still see you?"

"Yes of course."

Why does her mother not cry? Why does she not say, "Daddy and I aren't getting divorced. It's people like the Hardies and the Corretts and the Pews. Daddy likes to live with us. Snuggle up here and let's get you a plate of your own."

But her mother says nothing, only sits.

"I'll go and tell daddy then."

Tina gets up. Her mother stays on the step. Cheryl is not visible. Tina walks down the colonnade. She walks towards the blue trees.

"Daddy?"

The trees have sucked up all the light. She moves among them blindly.

"Daddy?"

She hears a yelp to her left. It sounds like Captain did when she found him this morning with a sore neck.

"Captain?"

Now hands out in front, she's feeling her way like Murder, branch by branch. She puts out a hand and the tree flinches. It's daddy. His fists in his eyes like a baby. Shaking. She wraps her arms around his leg and squeezes. She can tell him now. Tell him she'll go with him. That he'll be alright. But her chest devil is scratching and pinching her. She has to let it out. She tightens her squeeze on his leg. That'll hurt him. And he won't know she means to, he'll think it's a cuddle. She squeezes. Now she can tell him what she came to tell him. Now.

"I won't go with you, you know!" Suddenly her fists are out and on his thigh. "Nor will Cheryl. We won't go. I won't go."

Her father stands where he's left, his woolly head rubbing the darkness.

Tina stumbles out to the lighted porch where she finds her mother, still sitting in her summer dress. The skin of her arms is cold.

"I told him."

"I see."

She climbs into her mother's lap. She doesn't care if Cheryl sees. She tugs at her mother's hair to bring her face closer to her own. She curls the hair round a finger and sucks on it. It tastes bitter but she keeps it there.

THE UNCLE
Maxine Rosaler

Maxine Rosaler's fiction has been published in 'The Southern Review', 'New York Press' and 'The Abiko Quarterly', and has been cited in The Best American Short Stories, 1990. In 1994, she received a New York Foundation for the Arts Fiction Fellowship. She lives in New York City and is currently working on a novel.

I SAW ISAAC'S UNCLE ONLY ONCE.

I showed up at his store on Orchard Street late one afternoon in July with the hope of catching Isaac there and when I arrived his uncle told me he was "out collecting".

I asked if it would be all right for me to wait, and after mulling it over for several seconds he nodded toward a carton in the back which was piled high with blue jeans wrapped in cellophane.

"It's all right.

Sit.

They don't bite," he said with a sudden grin.

And that was the last thing he said to me.

He sat staring out into the street as if he were waiting for something, though, from the look on his sad face it didn't seem to matter to him whether or not what he was waiting for would ever come.

He didn't speak.

He seemed to be as comfortable with silence as he was with waiting and after a while I gave up trying to strike up a conversation, although it made me extremely uneasy to be there, saying nothing, just waiting.

He sat on that broken-down chair as though it were a throne – his back perfectly straight, his arms folded across his chest, commanding the air.

Under the black web of his beard and the imposing bulk of his belly I was surprised to see how much he resembled Isaac.

He had the same narrow wrists and the same wonderfully long

fingers – sensitive fingers, meant for the delicate work of breaking hearts, not at all the sort of fingers to be spending a lifetime testing fabrics and counting money.

In almost every respect he seemed to be a modified version of Isaac – blown up here, stretched out and sagging there, but basically the same, except around the mouth which was stretched tightly across his teeth like an elastic band.

Isaac had lips like a silent screen star's.

I loved those lips.

When Isaac burrowed his way into the store an hour later he didn't even notice me.

He headed straight for his uncle, who listened patiently to his account of the day's business.

After he had finished, his uncle allowed several seconds of silence to penetrate the air and then he said slowly in his heavy European accent:

"The money.

It stays in their pockets.

It gets warm.

Next thing you know, they think it's theirs."

Isaac and I met when we were both reporters for a chain of community newspapers in Brooklyn.

The first time I saw him he was wearing a plaid shirt and a white tie.

I remember thinking how the outfit suited him, but later on that day I decided that it didn't really suit him at all.

It was his first day on the job, and Barry, the chubby editor, introduced us saying:

"Isaac will be covering the Coney Island beat.

He lives there, poor kid.

Why don't you take him down to Passetti's and show him the ropes?" At Passetti's, long before the coffee arrived, Isaac confessed to me that he didn't really live in Coney Island.

He was from there, but he didn't live there anymore.

He had only told Barry that so he could get the job.

He lived in a studio apartment in the East Village.

He was just out of college and five years younger than I and those seemed to be good enough reasons to forgo the possibility of romance, but when four weeks later I was offered a job on another paper the thought of never seeing him again left me with a funny feeling in the pit of my stomach.

Luckily he was there that Friday when I went to pick up my last paycheck, and without even thinking about it I asked him for his number. He wrote it down in the reporter's notebook that he carried in the breast pocket of his jacket, and, almost diffidently, asked me if I would give him mine.

I don't remember who called who for our first date, but I seem to remember every other detail of that evening.

It was a freakishly warm night around Thanksgiving time and there was a summerlike heaviness in the air that had absorbed all the sounds and blended everything – the horns honking, the car wheels sweeping across the pavement, the airplanes flying overhead – into one slightly muffled, faraway din.

We met at his apartment on East 7th Street.

Isaac sat chastely on the narrow studio bed with its boy's bedspread – the kind that is always brown with an ugly plaid – and he told me stories about his adventures as a cub reporter. As I sat across from him in his big creaky leather chair I kept on wanting to go over to him and put my arms around his neck and say:

Why are you so sad, baby?

Can't you see there's nothing to be sad about?

We went to an Indian restaurant on East 6th Street and when the check came I insisted on paying, pretending that I wanted to celebrate my new job, but really I just wanted to do something for him.

A warm breeze was blowing and the streets of the East Village were quieter than usual.

It was as though everything had slowed down to make way for the dramatic change in the weather.

On the sidewalks of St. Mark's Place the peddlers displayed secondhand clothes and books on mouldy shower curtains and torn pieces of coloured velvet, and in front of the Astor Place subway station a happy crowd of people gathered around a fourteen-piece band that was playing *Begin the Beguine*.

We saw a teenage boy whose shaven head was covered with a tattoo which said FUCK EVERYTHING, leading a pretty green-haired girl down 8th Street by a metal chain.

Isaac was wearing his plaid shirt and white tie and I was wearing a red dress – my favourite – and he kept on telling me how beautiful I looked.

We walked all over the Village – in circles it seemed – and finally when one of the straps of the shoes I had bought to go with the dress broke off at the ankle I said that it was late and that I'd better be getting home.

He walked me to a bus stop.

When we saw the bus coming up Third Avenue we looked at each other and didn't say anything.

The bus pulled up to the curb and after the last of the passengers had gotten on and it was my turn to board he bowed slightly and asked me if I'd like to come back to his place for a game of Parcheesi.

Soon we were back in his barren apartment and he was lifting a finger to his lips in a plea for silence and he was padding his way down the hall to turn off the overhead light and he was padding his way quietly back and draping his red shirt over the bright desk lamp whose shade he kept precariously balanced on two pencils.

He undressed me slowly in the red darkness, a look of grateful amazement shining across his face.

Three weeks passed before I saw Isaac again.

For some reason I hadn't expected him to call, but after calling him day after day and still not reaching him, I felt that I was going to go mad.

I kept on trying to tell myself that we had only spent one night together, but I couldn't stop playing over and over again in my mind every moment I had spent with him, and I couldn't stop remembering what it had felt like to be with him in his narrow little bed. I'd been calling his apartment and leaving messages for him at the paper, and finally I got the idea of calling Gary and on some pretense inquiring about Isaac.

When Gary told me Isaac had quit the paper, I felt even more confused, and I didn't even bother to try to hide my confusion from him.

"But I thought he was doing so well. He was so happy," I said.

"Yeah. It threw me for a loop too," Gary said.

I could see him shrugging through the phone.

"He was going to take over my job.

"Weintraub made me assistant publisher and I recommended Isaac for the job. I thought the kid was going to fall down on his fucking knees and kiss my fucking feet, he was so grateful.

"Then he calls me and tells me he can't take it.

"That he has to go work at his uncle's store on Orchard Street.

"He sounds like death warmed over and starts apologizing to me like he's let me down in some really big way or something.

"It was very emotional."

"Did he give you a number or something?" I asked.

"Yeah. Let me see – yeah here it is.

"He wanted me to let him know if any leads came in on the MTA story he was working on.

"He was writing this exposé, you know, and he asked me if it would be all right if he finished it, even if he wasn't working here anymore."

I had to dial the number three times before I got it right.

My first try I got the New York City police department.

The second time there was this Chinese man cursing me out in Chinese.

Finally, it was Isaac, sounding frighteningly unlike himself, singing into the phone, "R&B Clothing."

"Isaac?" I said.

It was a full three seconds before he responded.

But then there was that same unreal cheerful lilt to his voice. "Oh hi, Margie," he said.

"Isaac, I was so worried," I said.

"What's to be worried about?" he asked, still with the same unresponsive cheer.

"I didn't know what happened to you," I explained.

"At first I thought God-knows-what. The things that went through my head. Then I thought, maybe it was me. Maybe it was something with me."

"Oh no, Margie," he said with a groan.

"Isaac, would you like to see me?"

"Oh, yes, Margie," he said.

His sincerity engulfed me.

"Of course I want to see you, Margie. More than anything in the world."

We arranged to meet at a small Spanish restaurant in his neighbourhood.

It was a very quiet, friendly place, with only a few tables occupied and everyone smiled at us when we came in.

Our waiter, a grandfatherly man who walked with a slight limp, brought us two glasses of red wine, compliments of the house.

He seemed to know Isaac and seemed to be happy to see him out with a girl. Isaac dipped his pinky into his glass and gently rubbed my lips.

"It's nice like this," he whispered as he leaned over to kiss me, the sweet taste of the wine blending with the sweet smoky taste of his mouth.

When we got back to his apartment Isaac asked me if I'd like to take a bubble bath with him.

In his enthusiasm he ended up dumping half the bottle in the tub.

He soaped up his hands and let them glide slowly up and down my back, under my arms and across my chest.

"You're too good to me, Margie," he said as he kissed me on the back of the neck.

"I don't deserve this," he said.

I wanted to believe he was kidding, but I knew he wasn't.

I knew that he really felt he didn't deserve to be happy.

I could tell from the way he would always greet the simplest pleasure, the smallest kindness with an appreciation approaching wonderment.

It was as though he were a refugee from a totalitarian state where things like holding hands in public and eating breakfast in bed were not permitted, where having a girlfriend who loved you was against the law.

As it turned out I was the one who did the calling.

But I didn't let that bother me.

Isaac was always so happy to hear from me, so happy just to be with me.

He would always greet me with the same sweet surprised, Hello, Margie, how are you? when I called, and when we were together

70

he would always thank me just for being with him, and when we made love he would always undress me with the same delicate care and attention, yet I knew from the start that I was losing him, or rather, the possibility of ever having him.

He was always tired and two or three hours into the evening he would fall asleep, usually on top of me.

It felt good to be close to him and I would stay crushed under the weight of his body until it was no longer possible for me to breathe.

Sometimes he would talk in his sleep.

It was usually just one or two words and it was always about the business.

The longest sentence I ever heard him utter in his sleep was:

The Lees'll be here tomorrow.

He would wake up in the morning at 4:59, a minute before the alarm was set to go off, then he'd slip out of my arms carefully, so as not to wake me, and go about his morning rituals, marking each task with a deep sigh.

He would sigh when he brushed his teeth and he would sigh when he sat at his desk sipping a cup of black coffee, and standing at the window, smoking the first cigarette of the day, he would sigh again.

Then he would pace up and down the narrow room from the apartment's one window to the opposite wall that held his Abbott and Costello poster and back again – all the time muttering under his breath, Shit, Shit, Shit. Several times after Isaac started working at his uncle's store I told him I wanted to visit him there, but each time I suggested it, he would either change the subject or come up with some excuse.

There was a big shipment of blue jeans coming in that day.

There was a customer he had to see.

They were in the middle of doing inventory.

Once when he couldn't come up with an excuse right away he blurted out, "But how would I introduce you? Who could I say you were?"

It was morning and we were sitting in a coffee shop in the East Village eating breakfast and Isaac started shredding his napkin and rolling the pieces into little white balls. "Your girlfriend," I responded.

"That's what I am. Isn't it?"

He was squirming in his seat, swaying nervously from side to side like a blind man.

But still I pressed on.

"Isaac, isn't that what I am?

"Aren't I your girlfriend and aren't you my boyfriend?

"Aren't we boyfriend and girlfriend?"

I held my breath and waited for him to answer.

"He wouldn't understand," Isaac answered finally.

Then he started to tell me about his uncle.

How every day after Yeshiva, when the other boys were hiding their yamulkas away in their schoolbags and going to play stick ball in the streets, he would grab his candy bar and baseball bat to rush to take the D train to go to Orchard Street to stand guard over the underwear and jeans.

Isaac worked there throughout college too – every day of the week but Saturday, when he would drag three heavy cardboard notebooks home and spend the morning and most of the afternoon pouring over the thinly lined pages, running the columns of figures through the adding machine his uncle had given him for his bar mitzvah, making sure that all the numbers balanced out.

The uncle (that's how Isaac always referred to him) became an invisible presence in our lives.

Isaac would talk about him all the time and always with such passion and emotional abandon that everything outside of the world of Orchard Street – that site of the immigrant's struggles and triumphs – would seem unreal and insignificant, including me.

Sometimes he would make up songs for him and he would sing them to me.

Or he would buy little presents for him: a pair of suspenders, a hat and once, as a joke, an engraved bowling ball.

Once, out of the blue he said to me, "Do you know why I get up at five every morning to go to Orchard Street to wholesale?

"It's the uncle.

"I love him!

"I can't believe how much I love that man!"

The image of the uncle began to loom large in my life as well.

He would appear with remarkable clarity in my dreams:

We were always great friends, we laughed a lot together, told each other jokes, once we shared a pot roast sandwich and a can of celery soda on a giant field of bright blue grass.

Isaac never told me so exactly, but from the start I understood that I could not expect to see him more than once a week – on Saturday, the only day he didn't have to labour at his uncle's store.

Sometimes I wouldn't bother to call.

I would just show up at his door.

Of course, I always held out the hope – indeed I had no doubt – that all that would change once Isaac grew more accustomed to me, or, rather, the idea of me.

New Year's Eve fell on a Wednesday that year.

Still, I assumed we would spend it together, but when I suggested it to Isaac, he looked surprised, almost disoriented.

We were standing in front of the IRT subway station.

My arms were wrapped around his waist, my face was buried in his chest and I was breathing in the mint scent that had become so familiar.

I could feel his body stiffen slightly and I let go of my embrace and started to move away from him.

But then Isaac drew me close to him.

He put his hands on my shoulders and looked into my eyes. "I'd love to spend New Year's with you, Margie," he said.

"We'll paint the town."

Isaac had decorated his small apartment with balloons and streamers.

He smelled of soap and mouthwash and he had slicked his hair back with something wet and sticky that smelled like bubble gum. I had gotten all dressed up in a black velvet dress and stockings and high heels and after I came in the door Isaac just stood leaning against the wall gaping at me in silence.

I started to laugh and I went over to him and put my arms around his neck and kissed him. "You look so serious, baby," I said and I kissed him again.

He started tugging at the collar of my dress, clumsily, like a kid who didn't know the first thing about being with a girl.

I thought he was going to rip my dress and although I felt

inclined to let him rip the fucking thing off, I guided his fingers to the zipper in the back.

He smiled at me then, that sly smile of his, and lifted his eyebrows slightly and said politely, "May I?"

He unzipped me with special care and very carefully slipped the dress over my head.

"Wait right here, don't go away," he said as he went and lay the dress carefully over the back of his creaky wooden chair.

We made love standing up against the wall, right there in the hall.

Afterward Isaac found a paper silver star crumpled up in his bottom desk drawer and he pasted it on the spot.

He promised me that we would make love in every square foot of the apartment and that before the year was out the apartment would be ablaze with stars.

We spent the rest of the evening drinking champagne and dancing with the people at the New Year's Eve party on Channel 4.

We never did give any thought to going out and at around eleven we ordered Chinese takeout from the all-night place down the block.

Isaac gave me a pair of his pajamas to wear and we lay his plaid bedspread out on the floor and had a picnic, all the while raving about the fine cuisine and the marvellous decor.

Just before he drifted off to sleep, a little past midnight, Isaac whispered in my ear, "This is going to be my best year ever." And then, so softly that I thought I might be imagining it, he added, "And it's all because of you, Margie.

"It's because of you, you..."

Isaac arose before dawn the next morning, out of habit, I suppose.

I woke up with him and told him that I wanted to walk to the Lower East Side for breakfast.

We held hands and walked through the deserted streets in silence.

I had never before seen the city at dawn.

The street lights were still shining and the moon was still hanging in a sky that was dusty with light.

Only the crash of a garbage pail disrupted the incredible still and quiet. It was a very cold day and the streets were empty.

New York City looked like a ghost town.

We walked through the village, past the scattered remains of last night's celebrations.

A bunch of half-deflated balloons floated past us as we crossed Grand Street.

"My parents used to take me here when I was a little girl," I told him.

I remembered those Sunday morning car rides into the city from Long Island.

Even then this part of Manhattan seemed to me to hold a special enchantment.

But today there were no old Jewish merchants standing glumly in doorways, their arms folded across their chests.

There were no bins upon bins of dried fruits and nuts and nonpareils or endless barrels of pickles laid out on the streets like a carnival.

There were none of the endless assortment of shirts and dresses hanging from metal racks standing crookedly on cracked sidewalks. Today all the storefronts were covered up with metal gates and the streets were empty.

Isaac led me into a restaurant which had huge hunks of sponge cake and pieces of pie displayed on cardboard in a dirty glass window.

A woman wearing heavy black shoes and a blue-and-grey-flowered kerchief served us poached eggs and creamed spinach in efficient silence.

Sitting there with Isaac at this grey formica table at this ancient restaurant in this timeless part of the city, I felt like a tourist, and this made me feel uncomfortable, for I knew that Isaac was no tourist here.

When I told this to Isaac he looked at me and smiled.

"I got middle-aged and died here," he told me.

"What a thing to say, Isaac," I said.

"Just kidding," he said. After breakfast he asked me if I would like to visit his uncle's store.

It was covered, like all the stores up and down the street, with heavy metal gates.

Across the street a wooden sign written in Hebrew creaked in the wind. Isaac took a set of keys out of his pocket and one by one proceeded to unlock the heavy bolts that held the gates together.

He deftly accommodated himself to the idiosyncracies of each lock, jiggling one here, tugging at another there.

He rolled the gates open.

The crash of metal against metal interrupted the still quiet of the cold morning.

We walked into a room which was crowded with cartons of blue jeans.

Near the door was a glass counter patched over in several places with pieces of masking tape which were dirty and curling up around the edges.

Next to it, in an even greater state of disrepair, was an old armchair. One of its arms was worn down beyond the stuffing to the bare wood and under its sagging seat a piece of coiled metal popped out like the naked neck of a headless, upside down Jack-in-the box.

Off to the right a wall had been knocked down and there were pieces of plaster and brick lying in a heap on the floor.

Isaac explained that his uncle had recently bought the building next door.

He led me through the opening in the wall and told me about the plans his uncle had for expanding the business.

"We're going to get the material from Korea and do the manufacturing in China," Isaac said. He picked a rubber band off the floor and started twisting it tightly around his fingers.

"But, I thought –"

I paused, for I wanted to choose my words carefully. I had never asked Isaac why he had quit the paper to go to work for his uncle on Orchard Street, or why he never called me, or why he was always so difficult to reach.

I knew it would be pointless to do so.

But I knew this was important.

Isaac's whole future – our future – depended on it. All I could think of to say was, "But I thought all this was temporary." Isaac pulled the rubber band more tightly around his fingers.

The tips of his pinky and thumb turned a reddish purple. "Everyone else was killed," he said finally. "There's nobody else but me."

*

He started standing me up.

I didn't see it as a pattern at first.

Every time it happened it was such a shock, such a hurt.

It did no good to ask him what was wrong; his only explanation was that he was "out of control".

Cryptic phrases like that crept with increasing regularity into his conversation.

One night in the middle of July, I decided that I couldn't take it anymore.

Isaac had said he would call for me at 8 and by 8:30 I knew he wouldn't be showing up.

I kept on phoning him at regular ten-minute intervals, although I knew he wouldn't answer the phone even if he was there.

I could easily recall the sight of him sitting calmly in his chair, letting it ring over and over again.

It never seemed to bother him how many times the phone rang or the loudness of the ring or the fact that there was someone on the other end who wanted desperately to speak to him. I had just stupidly washed the rugs in my small apartment with ammonia and Clorox – a lethal combination to begin with and one that was made even more lethal by the hot humid air that crawled in over the windowsill.

There was no escaping the fumes or the tiny pieces of invisible lint that tickled my throat all night long.

I called in sick at work the next day and stayed balanced on the thought that I would go down to Orchard Street at five and tell Isaac that I couldn't see him anymore.

But when I saw him there with his uncle, looking so humble and defeated, I knew I wouldn't be able to go through with it.

The anger and frustration I'd felt that night with the fumes and the heat and the lint, and all the other nights of not hearing from him and not knowing why vanished in his presence.

All I could feel for him was this overwhelming love.

My love for Isaac weakened me.

It made me ineffectual.

Later on that evening he told me he loved me for the first and only time.

We were sitting in a red plastic booth in a bar in Chinatown not far from his uncle's store and a crowd of off-duty policemen had just come in to watch a baseball game on the television set that hung suspended in the air above half a dozen rows of chipped glasses.

I was trying to tell him, how much his disappearances upset me.

"Hit me.

"Go on.

"Hit me," he said and he reached out and rolled my fingers into a fist and bounced the fist against his chin.

"I deserve it."

Then he uncapped the fountain pen he'd taken from its place next to the reporter's notebook he still carried in the breast pocket of his jacket and smoothed his napkin out on the table.

On it he drew a rebus containing an eye with long curly lashes, a big heart and a U.

The paper napkin was too porous for the ink of a fountain pen and tiny beads of ink, like tiny black pearls, had formed wherever his hand had faltered.

I asked him if he would like to go away with me somewhere and we made plans to take a trip to Atlantic City the next weekend.

I knew that he had never gone away with a woman before and that made the prospect all the more wonderful to contemplate.

But I didn't hear from him all that following week.

By that time I had instituted a policy of holding off calling him for as long as I could bear it and I let another week pass before I phoned.

I knew something was wrong as soon as I heard his voice.

When I asked him how he was he said in a voice that was barely audible,

"Not good."

And when I asked him what was wrong he didn't say anything.

I asked him again.

"My uncle, my uncle," he began.

"My uncle, my uncle...," and then he burst into tears.

The funeral was in an area of Brooklyn Isaac used to refer to as Torah Town.

It was an unbearably hot day.

The heat seemed to rise from the sidewalk in curly white waves.

Despite the heat, the women all wore long skirts and wigs and heavy shoes and the men were dressed in black suits and black hats.

They had beards and paises which they tucked behind their ears.

The funeral parlor was crowded with people who spoke in whispers to each other.

No one was speaking to Isaac when I walked into the room.

He sat in the corner near the coffin with his mother.

She was a small, pretty woman with blond hair.

She was much younger than I had expected her to be and she smiled at me sweetly when I gave her my hand.

I didn't dare touch Isaac.

He looked dangerously untouchable, sternly fragile.

After the rabbi had recited the 23rd Psalm Isaac walked up to the podium to deliver the eulogy.

He told the story of his uncle.

How he had managed to keep himself and his sister alive during three years in a concentration camp, how he had come to this country with nothing and had built a business – R&B Clothing – the largest wholesale clothing store on the Lower East Side.

How after Isaac's father had died suddenly he had looked after his sister and her young family, making sure they had enough to eat and a roof over their heads.

He described how in some ways the uncle was like a kid – he loved watching bowling on TV, he loved his pot roast sandwiches and celery soda.

But most of all, he loved his business.

It had been like a child to him.

He had brought it into the world and raised it into something he could be proud of.

This was his legacy.

Here Isaac paused and turned to the coffin.

In a voice so resonant that I could feel my own breath vibrate he promised that he would not let R&B Clothing die.

He pledged to do his best to take over where his uncle had left off, to follow through on the plans he had made for the store before he died, to see that all his hard work had not been in vain.

*

I looked for Isaac outside the chapel but I couldn't find him for several minutes.

He was just about to get into a limousine waiting in front of the funeral home when I spotted him finally.

I ran over to him and grabbed hold of him with all my might.

His arms hung lifelessly at his side and his cheek recoiled slightly from the touch of my lips.

On my way past the parking lot a big, fatherly looking man who introduced himself as Ben Rabinsky asked me if I needed a ride to the cemetery.

As I sank into the soft blue velvet of the front seat of his Cadillac I felt a small wave of relief, like someone was going to take care of me.

"It's hot," he said to me in a heavy East European accent.

He took a handkerchief out of his shirt pocket and he wiped away the sweat that was pouring down his forehead and he took off his jacket and lay it carefully across the back seat.

Then he took off a pair of diamond cufflinks and he rolled up the sleeves of his shirt.

He pressed a pearl white button on the dashboard. "It will be cool in a second," he said to me. "The air conditioner in this car works like a dream."

A gust of lukewarm air swept across my face and a steady soft purring sound filled the car.

It wasn't until after we were on the Brooklyn Queens Expressway headed for the cemetery that I noticed the series of blue-black numbers tattooed on his forearm just above the wrist.

Whenever I'm confronted with some image of the Holocaust I always return to my original perception of it, when I was a little girl.

Max the Tailor, who had a shop on Long Beach Road in Oceanside, where I grew up, had numbers on his arm and when I asked my mother about them she told me about the cattle cars and the lampshades and the pillows and the soap, and the showers that weren't really showers.

Sometime after that Max gave me an old mannequin of his to play with.

She was covered with a torn brown canvas and she emanated a stale, musty odour.

I named her Mathilda and I dressed her in an old dress of my mother's and I tried to play with her, but I couldn't play with her.

I couldn't play with any of my other toys either, with her standing there in my room with her eyeless eyes, this armless, legless, faceless torso.

One night I woke up with a nightmare about faceless men sticking pins in my eyes and the next day when I came home from school Mathilda was gone. But I didn't forget about her for a long time afterward.

It was as though I felt somehow responsible for all her suffering. It was a guilt beyond understanding; it had a logic all its own.

Mr Rabinsky and I drove along in silence near the front of the row of cars that made up the funeral procession.

From the rear-view mirror I could see cars with their headlights on moving slowly through the summer heat.

The cars to the left of us and the cars to the right of us whizzed silently past, distant and removed from the business of Isaac's uncle's death.

I don't know what Mr Rabinsky was thinking about but it gave me some comfort to imagine that there was an intimacy to the silence between us.

I felt as though we were sharing a different piece of the same enormous grief.

Back at Isaac's mother's house in Coney Island the merchants of the Lower East Side gathered to pay their respects.

Isaac sat on the sofa talking to a man with a beard who was dressed in a long black coat.

His mother sat on a cardboard box which was imprinted with a mahogany pattern.

Her hands were folded in her lap and she spoke softly, every now and then bringing a hand to her cheek and turning her head from side to side, her eyes never leaving Isaac.

I sat down beside her and she extended her hand to me.

"Isaac didn't tell me he had such a pretty friend," she said to me with a weak smile.

"What?"

"You know him from college?"

"We were reporters together," I told her.

"On the school paper?"

"No. On the paper in Brooklyn."

"In Brooklyn?"

She sounded confused.

I realized that the job must have been a secret, just as I had been a secret.

I looked at her.

At her blond hair and her fair skin and her heavy eyes.

Her mouth was very thin and it was cast in a strained smile.

I hated her for not even thinking that her son might have a girlfriend.

Why should Isaac suffer, why should I suffer, because of what had happened to her?

"I'm very sorry," I said. "I know your brother was a remarkable man. Isaac loved him very much."

She looked at me and shook her head.

"Too much," she said.

"He loved Sol too much," she kept repeating to herself in a dreamlike voice.

"Yes, I know," I said.

I called Isaac every day for a week after the funeral.

After closing up the store he would go home to his mother's and I would call him there in the evenings.

She would answer the phone.

We began to establish a rapport based on our mutual concern for Isaac.

After asking how she was getting on, a matter of little consequence as far as she was concerned, I would ask after Isaac.

"Not good," she would respond with a sigh.

"He doesn't eat.

"He plays with his food, but he doesn't eat it.

"I make all his favourites.

"I know he doesn't want to hurt my feelings.

"He says, "Mom, I'm sorry,

"I know it's delicious but I'm not hungry.

"Maybe tomorrow. Save it for me tomorrow."

"And then he goes downstairs to Sol's room.

"It's not good."

*

When Isaac would come to the phone he would greet me with a cheerful hello and when I asked him how he was he would raise his voice to a high pitch and say,

"Fine. Just fine."

I told him I missed him.

That I wanted to be with him. "Don't you think it would make you feel better if you saw me?

"I just want to make you feel better, Isaac," I would plead with him, careful not to push too hard.

Usually he wouldn't respond at all, but if I persisted long enough sometimes he would abandon the facade and in a voice filled with despair he would tell me that he was so busy, that there was so much to do, that there was never enough time.

As it turned out his uncle had left everything to him.

Isaac found out that he had been the sole heir ever since he was twelve years old.

When he went back to stay in his apartment I would call him there, but he never answered the phone.

He was there.

I knew he was there.

I could see him sitting in his creaky leather chair, letting the phone ring.

I would try him at the store but he was always too busy to speak.

I resorted to writing notes.

At first I would just say that I missed him, that I wanted to see him.

When that didn't work I started looking for excuses to contact him.

I remembered that I had left a little gold bracelet at his apartment and I told him that I wanted to get it back.

Or there was a book I had lent him that I needed.

Once I just sent him a postcard with a big question mark written on it.

But nothing worked and eventually I gave up.

What else could I do?

Months passed and then one day I was in his neighbourhood and on my way home I passed his block.

It was slightly off my course but I decided to make the detour – as a kind of experiment, I told myself, to see how I would feel.

I hadn't dared walk anywhere near his street for months.

I would even avoid the neighbourhood entirely, and passing it now my heart felt an ache so strong that I had to take a deep breath and I said out loud to myself, "Oh, Margie. What are you doing?"

It was a bright cold day in the middle of November – just cold enough to cover the puddles that had collected at the curbs and on the sidewalks with thin layers of ice.

I was afraid to look up, so I directed myself to the task of inspecting what was in the puddles.

They were like little glass museums of the recent past which had made relics of the street's paraphernalia.

Whatever had passed their way at some moment before the ice had frozen lay displayed under their fragile window-panes.

In one puddle was trapped a wool mitten, three pennies and a broken comb.

Another held a bottle cap and a few of the last bright leaves of autumn.

At first I thought he was a mirage.

In all the time that had passed since I had last seen him the clearest image of him had never been more than a blink away from my mind's eye.

He was standing under the awning of his apartment building, leaning against the rail, smoking a cigarette, talking to the doorman.

He was wearing an olive green parka which I'd never seen before and he kept on tugging at the hat he had on – a navy blue cap.

It must have been uncomfortable or maybe he was trying to get the angle just right. My first impulse was to avoid him, and I crossed the street, but I didn't even get as far as the corner before I realized it was useless. He didn't exhibit one bit of surprise at seeing me.

I didn't make any motion to touch him and he didn't approach me either.

When I asked him how he was he said he was fine, just fine.

He was wholesaling.

"I buy low and sell high," he said.

"But how are you," I asked again.

"How am I?

"Ask why, why don't you?" he replied.

"Okay then, Isaac. Why are you?" I asked.

It was a familiar routine of his.

And with the comedian's timing he answered,

"For no good reason."

We went to a fancy new restaurant that had recently opened up in the neighbourhood.

He ordered the most expensive thing on the menu but he barely ate any of it.

When the check came he took out a thick pile of cash which was folded in half and he peeled off five twenties, one at a time, licking his fingers before each wrinkled bill. He told me that he had a new car and he offered to drive me home.

The seats were covered with cushioned leather and the dashboard was covered with cushioned leather also.

It had that new car smell, a smell that never fails to fill me with nostalgia.

When we got to my door I asked him to come up.

We made love on the couch.

He didn't undress me and he didn't seem to have any interest in me undressing myself either and when it was over he fell asleep on top of me.

In the middle of the night I managed to get his clothes off and put him into bed.

I dimmed the lights in my bedroom and watched him sleep.

He hugged the pillow tightly against his cheek.

He looked like the same sweet Isaac I had once known.

Somewhere at around two in the morning he started muttering something in his sleep.

I couldn't make it out at first, but I could tell he was mumbling the same word, over and over again.

Just as I was finally drifting off to sleep, my head on his chest and my legs locked into his, he woke me with his sleep talk.

This time what he was saying was so clear that I was sure he would wake himself up.

Dead.

He kept on saying it over and over again.

Dead.

Dead.

Dead.

It was still dark out, there wasn't even a trace of dawn in the sky when he disentangled his limbs from mine and climbed out of bed to start the day.

I got up to make him coffee and I went into the living room to bring it to him.

He had just finished lacing up his shoes, and, looking up, he seemed flustered to see me there.

"Have a cup of coffee before you go, Isaac," I said to him.

The apartment was so cold that my teeth were chattering and I walked over to him and pressed up against him and put my arms around his waist.

"It's so cold, Isaac.

"It's too cold to go out without something warm inside you."

He pulled away from me and rushed to put on his hat and coat.

"No, don't bother," he said as he unlocked the door.

He was almost shouting.

"I'll get it on the outside.

"I'll pay for it on the outside.

"I can pay."

And he was gone.

I locked the door behind him and sat down on the couch.

I noticed that there was a sock tucked under the rug and another one crumpled up on the night table.

When I reached down to pick them up I noticed that they were his.

They were his black orlon socks – the ones he'd get by the dozen from Milty the Sock Wizard on Ludlow Street.

They were ribbed and had a squiggle running down each side.

He'd gotten a dozen for each of us last spring – mine were black ribbed too, but without the squiggle.

He must have gotten them confused. Once before the uncle died I'd woken up at his apartment with a bad cold and I stayed in his bed when he went off to work that day.

I slept away most of the morning and in the afternoon I watched old movies on TV. He had done a wash the night before and the fresh laundry was piled high on his big creaky leather chair.

I picked up a bunch of it and pressed it to my face.

I folded the shirts and underwear and towels and rolled the socks into neat little balls.

When he came home later on that evening he was surprised to see me there at first.

From the weary look on his face it seemed that it must have been an especially hard day for him.

But it wasn't long before he was joking around with me, asking me what was for dinner, ordering me to go fetch his slippers.

I complained about the housework and how the kids hadn't stopped fighting all day.

He promised to get me a maid and to send the kids away to boarding school.

We joked around like that for a while but when he saw the neatly folded pile of laundry in the corner he stopped joking and a solemn look swept over his face.

He held me tightly and kissed me and told me he was very happy I was there.

Then he proceeded to juggle the socks in the air.

First two, then three, then he had four flying in the air at once.

They swirled around so fast that I couldn't distinguish one from the other.

They blended together into a blurred parabola of blue, black and white above his head.

That was the only time we had ever spent two nights together in a row and I thought of it fondly now.

FOOTBALL IN
BUSANZE CAMP
Dick Bayne

Influenced by a heady brew of E. Nesbit and Biggles from an early age, Dick Bayne always knew he wanted to be a writer; an ambition conveniently forgotten until, after graduating (in French and Italian), a teaching job at a Paris university allowed plenty of leisure time. He now leads walking trips in Italy and Sicily – seasonal work which still leaves time to write and travel. This story  *stemmed from a trip he made to Rwanda and Uganda in 1994 and he is currently working on a novel.*

MOTHER AND FATHER ARE DEAD. I DON'T MIND.

Swedi and Juma, my brothers, are dead too, and that's a pity because we used to play some good games. My sister Joanna looks after me now. I like her; except when she cries, because it makes me feel uncomfortable.

She told me they played football with Swedi's head. I was hiding in the maize, but she saw. The soldiers cut it off with their pangas and started kicking it. They made Father join in. He had to take a penalty, and when he missed they shot him. Joanna didn't know what a penalty was, but when she described it I told her.

I like football. At home there was a pitch with real goals. I used to watch when the big boys played, and made a ball out of woven grass to kick with my friends. So I was glad when I arrived here in Busanze with Joanna, because I saw a crowd kicking a ball. Now we play football every day.

At first there was only a grass ball, but then the Whitemen gave us a real one. Not the Whitemen who brought the plastic sheeting we use to make our shelters, and not the ones who showed us how to dig holes for when we squat. The ones who came and pushed pins into our arms.

I was hiding, but Joanna found me and made me join the line. She said she would give me an extra biscuit. The Whitemen bring the biscuits too. When they had put a pin into everybody they gave us the football.

My friend Nason looks after it. He's older than me and quite big, but lets everybody join in.

When we're not playing football there are the two hills for running down, and on the really steep parts you can slide if you have a piece of sheeting to sit on. There are the rows of shelters which are perfect for dodging through when someone is chasing you. The sheeting is blue, so if you go to the top of the hill you see all these humps in lines, like giant blue piles of cow-dung.

In the valley there's the stream where Joanna makes me have a bath. We splash and shout and throw water. At home splashing wasn't allowed because Mother had to fetch it all from a pump.

Joanna's more fun than Mother. She lets me go out and play almost all day. When I start to feel hungry I come back to the shelter and have some food. I have biscuits in the morning when I wake up, more if I want during the day, and we have rice or beans in the evening. There's plenty of food because the Whitemen bring it.

Our shelter is small – as it's just us two, Joanna says – with only half a blue sheet. We get wet when it rains, but so does everybody else. The squat-hole is just down the hill, so there's a bit of a smell. Home used to smell too.

I don't think about home very much. Once, when Joanna was crying, she asked me if I remember what it was like. I said no.

But I do remember sometimes. When I wake up in the morning and it's still too early to go and play. It makes me uncomfortable, like when Joanna cries, and I take my grass football and kick it up and down until Nason comes out too.

After a while we take his piece of sheeting and go to the slide. Lots of our friends are there: so many you have to push to get to the best place at the top. I take turns with Nason, and then we both try to sit on the sheeting together. I fall off and cut my elbow, so we go to the stream to wash away the blood. It's funny watching the red drops fall into the water. They make tiny stringy clouds in the pools, but where the current flows fast they just disappear.

While we are by the stream the Whitemen come in their big white car. They have a special hut, covered with enough sheeting for ten shelters, where they look at you if you don't feel well. We watch them until they leave again. The smaller children run after them shouting "Greetings", and the Whitemen laugh and try to repeat it; but if you look carefully when they get into the car and leave the children behind, they have stopped smiling.

After the big car has disappeared in the dust, Nason goes to fetch the football and we try to play a game like they used to on the pitch at home. There are too many of us, and everybody chases the ball, so it's not really much like a proper match, but we do have goals and two teams and I like it.

The sun is quite low when I start to feel hungry, and go back to the shelter. Joanna is cooking the rice.

After eating I lie down and go to sleep. When I wake the moon is very bright and I look outside. There is a soldier with a gun on his shoulder and a panga in his hand. The blade shines big and white in the moonlight.

He is standing by Nason's shelter and looks as if he is waiting. I slide forward a little, till my head is outside, so I can see better. The soldier looks over his shoulder, away from me, and raises the panga.

There is a loud noise, like when Nason pretends the cooking pot is a drum and Joanna tears strips of cloth to put "down there" when she bleeds, but both mixed together. I know it is the sound a gun makes because I heard it before, when I was in the maize and they shot Father and Mother.

The soldier hits Nason's shelter with the panga and starts shouting. Suddenly the noise is coming from all around and I know there are other soldiers with more guns firing. Lines of what look like shooting stars, only redder, go sweeping across the sky. After a loud pop, a bright white light appears above the hills and hangs there, making the night day.

Joanna tries to drag me back inside, but I wriggle away. I am watching the soldier. He hits the shelter again and it begins to fall down. Nason's father comes out. He is bigger than the soldier, but doesn't even look before running away down the hill. The rest of the family come out and run too; it looks as if the soldier is laughing.

Nason is still inside. The soldier drops the panga and takes the gun off his shoulder. He points it into what is left of the shelter and I see him make a little jump backwards. The noise the gun makes is just part of all the other noise.

Nason crawls out of the wreckage and tries to stand up. It takes him a long time because one leg isn't working, and he is trying to keep the football under his right arm. In the end he drops the ball and it bounces away. Then he is standing opposite the soldier and I can see he isn't really a soldier at all. They're the same height, but Nason looks stronger.

They look at each other for a moment, and then the boy-soldier laughs again. He pushes Nason with the gun and watches him fall slowly backwards as his leg folds up. Then he turns and begins to walk away.

I hear Nason shout through the noise. The word is "Baby". The boy-soldier turns again and the gun comes up. He points it at Nason for a long time, then swings to find another target.

The first shot misses, kicking up a spurt of sand. He does something to the side of the gun and then his whole body shakes to the drumming-ripping sound. The football disappears in a cloud of dust then skips high into the air.

The boy-soldier watches the ball fly and then fall, not bouncing but flattening to the ground like a ripe-rotten mango dropping from the tree. I want to kill him.

RUDOLPH
VALENTINO'S EYES
Revonne Roth

Revonne Roth was born in Muskogee, Oklahoma but grew up a few miles north of Tulsa. She is a member of Southwest Writers' workshop. For two consecutive years, her short stories have placed first in the SWW's annual writing contest and three of her stories have been published. At present, she resides with her husband in Albuquerque, New Mexico near the foothills of the 10,000 ft Sandia Crest.

"THE DEELIGHTS ARE HERE TONIGHT"

Is it possible you'll want to miss these gigantic, fantastic women? No! No! NO! They dance, they sing, they're HOT! One night only. Be here.

The poster by the ticket office says it all. It's Saturday night. On the graveled parking lot outside the Playmore dance hall people are wild with waiting. At eight o'clock sharp the crowd lines up to pay their admission. Inside the hall, sawdust is scattered over the rough boards of the floor. The three-piece band is on the stage.

"Are you ready, are you-all ready for a good time tonight?" "Yeah, yeah, yeah." The dancers answered. Jelly gives the downbeat on the drums. Nadine Deelight takes the first solo. She swings low and bluesy or loud and calling. That's her way. Her red painted lips are going every minute, and so are her feet. She's beautiful. Her kewpie doll face is sweet and girlish. Tonight she had a different look about her. It's in every move she makes. It's Herschel. He's coming tonight. She searches the dancehall with her baby blue eyes. Didn't he say in his letter that he's coming? Where is he?

"I'll be there come Saturday night," he wrote. "I'll be there if it's hot as hell, even if I have to walk all the way. Have the preacher ready, the licence bought. Have your clothes packed and your car gassed. Just you and me, we're leaving."

Nadine now goes into her first chorus. "Somebody loves me, I wonder who, I know who it can be."

Little Bernice, all two hundred and fifty pounds of baby fat harmonizes. The music is loud. The five people on the bandstand sound like a thirty-piece orchestra. Thump, thump, slide, slide, Nadine joins in the dancing. A roar goes up from the crowd. "Go, Go, GO!" They yell. These two colossal-sized women are something else. In their short red dresses, decorated from the sleeveless tops to the hems with a row of red fringe, every movement they make is multiplied a thousand times. Is this possible? Is it real? They send the people to near oblivion.

"I'm gonna marry Herschel tonight, Baby, you remember?" Nadine is feeling guilty. Herschel wrote, "Just you and me." Does this mean she has to leave her only child, her innocent baby to the ways of the world? Still, she wants this wedding more than anything. "I may never get another chance to have a preacher say the words over me and a man, sugar."

Bernice says, "Uh huh."

"I'm forty today, remember? Men don't have no use for an old woman like me. They want them young things now. But, Herschel, he is the sweetest man alive. I ain't never seen him yet, but he wrote he's the image of Rudolph Valentino. You know how I love Rudolph Valentino's eyes."

Bernice watches the men as they dance their partners past the bandstand. Can one of them be this Lonely Hearts pen pal who writes to her mama? This man who looks like mama's favourite movie star. Nadine dreams of Valentino carrying her off on his white stallion. This dark-eyed screen lover has slick black hair that shines, looks like patent leather. He wouldn't expect to elope in his bride's own 1928 Ford sedan. But, what horse can carry a three hundred pound woman like her mama?

Everybody's laughing as the songs ends. They want more, much more. Those two fanatics up there on the stage, those two big women dance like feathers floating on the wind. How can they? They're so BIG!

Jelly calls out to the crowd, "What next, what do you want to hear?"

"A fast one," someone calls out. "We want to dance until our feet are on fire."

Jelly gives the signal on the drums. His arms writhe like snakes as they weave in and out when he strikes the skins. He keeps his head down and eyes closed as he goes with the rhythm. Philly Rae is on the piano, a short fat man. Lets his fingers let loose on those eighty-eights like they have a mind of their own. Brother Skylark leans over his steel guitar cradled on his knees. His yellow hair waves like ripened wheat in a summer breeze. The band slides into *Runnin' Wild*.

It's everybody for himself on the dance floor. There are tentative rhythmic movements to the music. What is this new beat? Someone tries the two-step and another tries the waltz. Then they see Bernice come forward. Her Eton-cropped brown hair begins to fly as she Charleston's at double time. This is it. The crowd is misbehaving. Some elbow for a better look. Others try to imitate what they see. It's fast and loud, just what everybody wants.

Little Bernice isn't shy, not her mama's sixteen-year old baby. Nadine is so proud. These two beautiful women with kohl-rimmed eyes, Cupid-bow lips and thin-arched brows. They're the closest this crowd will ever come to see daring flappers.

People hover near the bandstand. This monstrous young woman is like a whirling dervish with her tiny feet almost a blur to watch. Who is she, this wonder of wonders who goes with the speed of a small locomotive. They wipe the perspiration watching her.

"And now, from New York, the latest hit song from that old Broadway. This sound you'll remember forever." Jelly introduces Bernice's solo.

But, in the distance, out on the highway, comes another new sound.

"Si—reens, si—reens," someone shouts. "Something big's a happening. It's the sheriff and his posse."

Into the dancehall a black-booted, blue-uniformed man with a shiny badge walks through the crowd up to the bandstand.

"We're here to protect you," he says.

From what, from who? This is serious.

"From up in McAlester, we got this call saying that old boy,

Pretty Charlie has done it again. He's walked right out of the penitentiary."

The crowd begins to shake their heads. Yes, yes, they've heard of this bankrobber ladies man. He's done it again, they nod.

Outside, the sky is as dark as a black-top road. Over the Washita Mountains east of town, lightning starts to sizzle and thunder rolls in the Oklahoma skies. This makes everybody nervous. Is this an omen of what this Pretty Charlie will do this time? He's never murdered anybody, but is he desperate?

"Now, don't be going out into that blackjack grove or down to the river, just hitch yourselves around this here dancehall and stay put until we have a good-looksee." The sheriff, a small man looks and talks like a giant.

Jelly stands, "It's getting to be time for intermission anyhow. You all get some of that good barbecue we've been smelling. Don't let the sheriff see you drinking none of that bootleg liquor."

A nervous chuckle goes around the crowd in the dimly lit hall. Some of the dancers follow the Deelights and the band out the front door. They walk around the end of the building to the barbecue shack.

"Bring me one of them cold beers you old rooster there behind the counter, I'm dry to my socks. Carry over one of them Double Colas for my baby here." Nadine sits down at one of the tables with the band and little Bernice.

The temporary café is a square built room of plywood seconds with a counter across one end. There is an open roasting pit outback. The rest of the room is set up with plank tables and benches.

"We'll all have some of that there cold beer, Mr Server." Skylark says as he settles down at a wooden table.

The dimly lit room is now filled with scared-eyed people. They want to be near the performers and away from the dark unknown outside. Two oil lanterns hang from posts on both sides of the make-shift room. Mosquitoes and night insects attack everybody with accuracy in the warm and spicy air.

"Now then, Nadine, just tell us. Why you gonna leave your sweet baby behind to marry up with this man you've never seen?" Jelly looks across the table at Nadine who chews her bottom lip. Her eyes begin to seep a tear. Jelly ducks when she raises one of her enormous arms. He knows she can swat him across the table and send him flying out the door.

"Because," she begins after smoothing her short blond hair and drinking half her bottle of beer in one gulp. "Because this man, bless his soul, is marrying me with a preacher. I want to be married with a preacher saying the words over me – more than anything I ever wanted before."

"But Mama, you've been married five times. My daddy, Homer Jones, Mr Carmichael, old man Slate and Skinny Leo." Little Bernice counts on her pudgy fingers, her eyes wide open and questioning her mama.

"Yeah, Nadine, five times!" Philly Rae nods.

Nadine takes her handkerchief from the bosom of her dress to dab her eyes.

"Don't none of you be disappointed in me. I ain't never had a preacher say the words, or even a judge, me and my man said the words ourselves."

"But Mama," Bernice says again, "what about my daddy?"

"Your daddy? You are a found child, honey, a found child." They all look at Nadine in wonder, but now her eyes widen and she's looking somewhere else.

"There he is, right here in that doorway, my Herschel, my sweetheart, Herschel. I'd know him anywheres."

She stands and stretches her neck forward for a better look. Nadine needs glasses but won't admit it.

"It's him, I tell you, it's him. It's my Herschel with them crazy, wonderful eyes. Go find the preacher, my man has come."

The man doesn't come into the room. He lowers his head and looks at her from under his eyelashes. "Sorry Miss Deelight, my name's Alvin Bunker. Could I have your autography? I don't know no Herschel, but I surely want to know you and your sweet baby there."

Nadine's arms fall back to her side and the smile disappears.

"Why you look like you said you did?" Not believing him for one second. Alvin Bunker has deep sun wrinkles down his cheeks and on his neck. Long strings of brown hair hang down from a centre part. He's a tall thin man.

"I've pleasured this evening more than I can say. My mama died six months ago and I miss women folk around my farm. She, if you don't mind me saying, was a fleshy woman too. I favour fleshy women myself." He sniffled, and took a clean white handkerchief from his back pocket.

"Hold it everybody, I said HOLD IT! Is there a Miss Nadine Deelight in there?" A man's voice comes from the darkness outside the open doorway. Everybody turns to look in that direction.

"Herschel, it's my Herschel this time. I know it is. Herschel, darlin' Herschel, in here darlin', in here." Nadine's heart flutters like a mockingbird's wings.

A man walks in wearing striped prison clothes. He carries a gun. His trousers are hitched up to his hips and his belly hangs over like a balloon full of water. It rolls this way and that when he walks.

"I'm come for you darlin'." He points the gun at Nadine. "Come on now, get them car keys and let's be on our way." He has a weak smile. "No one will shoot me with you along, sugar."

Nadine's mind changes within a flick of an eyelash.

"You ain't my darling Herschel. What have you done with him you law-breaker?" She screams and cries the words. Her body begins to shake like a springless car on a bumpy road.

An angry look comes over the convict's face. He waves his gun. "Herschel's my middle name Nadine, now get the keys, you fat sow!"

Some of the customers back away and out into the night screaming. "It's him in the barbecue. It's him in the barbecue." All Nadine sees is the round black hole on the end of the pistol barrel. She's dizzy and begins to wobble around. The last thing she sees before she faints is his eyes.

"They're blue," she whispers.

Through a long black tunnel of unconsciousness Nadine hears Bernice call her.

"Mama, Mama, open your eyes. You fell on him, and pinned him to the floor when you fainted. The police came and took him away." With help from Alvin Bunker and Bernice, Nadine sits up. Great sobs come from her throat like rolls of thunder going away after a mighty storm.

"I ain't lucky," she cries every word, "nobody is ever going to ask me to marry him with a preacher again."

From behind her, a soft voice answers. "Now, you ain't got that right Miss Deelight, you surely ain't," says Mr Bunker.

Nadine turns her head and looks into the most beautiful pair of Rudolph Valentino eyes, she has ever seen.

VESSEL
Heather Doran Barbieri

Heather Doran Barbieri is a non-fiction author, journalist, and creative writer. Her award-winning fiction has been anthologized in 'Writing for Our Lives' (Running Deer Press, 1996) and 'The Pursuit of Happiness' (Leftbank Books, 1995), among other publications. She lives in Seattle, Washington, USA, with her husband and three children.

MY SISTER LICKS HER ORCHID BLOSSOM LIPS. A TENDRIL of blue-black hair falls across her cheek. Her skin is clear and pure as a raindrop on a water-lily leaf. Her gentle dove-wing hands press against her chest. The most beautiful Hmong maiden sleeping deeply, dreaming most beautiful dreams, while I, her sister, plain as goat milk, stare into the night, a one-eyed frog who never sleeps.

I sit with my back against the mast of the *Cua Moj Lwg*, The Great Wind, a boat jammed with refugees from Laos and Vietnam. I listen to its fitful progress as it flounders through the China Sea: the bat-wing flutter of loose sails, the creak of rigging, the moans and retches and coughs of seasick refugees, the hiss of a man pissing over the bow, and my sister dreaming there, her head resting on a perfect *pandau* pillow she made with flowery stitches and cucumber seeds.

From the day she was born, so perfect. My parents proud, knowing she would be a good wife, all the men and boys competing for her attention.

And me. Frog girl. The day I was born, twenty years ago, the midwife told my mother to kill me, because demons had cursed my birth. I twisted and turned, a vile viper torturing my mother with days of pain, before I was pulled, feet-first, from her womb.

"That one," the midwife cried. "She is too small. See how clouds drift across her eye. See her demon-cleft lips. Do not let her drink from your breast. Drown her. Drown her now before she brings you great sorrow."

My mother staggered to her feet, supported by the midwife and my aunt. They took me to the river, wrapped in palm leaves. My mother held me over the current. White-tongued rapids churned beneath my bald baby skull. She swore that I grasped her thumb with my tamarind-pod hands and smiled my split-lipped frog baby smile.

"I couldn't let the water have you," she said.

My parents tried to make me feel loved and lovely. They sent me to school, because they knew that even though my body was slow moving over the earth, my mind was quick. Yet sometimes, I'd catch my mother watching me with her sad sambar deer eyes, wondering if she should have given me up.

"Someone will take her," I heard her whisper to my grandmother. "She's a good daughter, a good worker. Everyone can't be a lotus blossom like Niah."

I must care for the lotus blossom now. My family is gone. My father died of sleeping sickness, his skin so blue and cold, my mother of starvation, my brothers fighting the Pathet Lao in the jungles and mountains of my homeland. It is just the two of us now.

I watch my fifteen-year-old sister sleep, becalmed in strange seas. I compare her shapely arms and legs to my own, gnarled and misshapen as ginger roots, her singsong voice to my raspy croak. Every time she takes my hand, the poison inside me makes me want to tear her apart. I imagine I see her face in poppy petals cupped in my hands and I crush them, my fingers stained blood orange. I can conjure up her image in any object and destroy it. My veins sing with satisfaction and shame. Sometimes when I'm alone, as I am now, I gnash my sword-sharp teeth and dream that death or deformity befalls her, visions that leave me crying, clutching torn petals of her sesame oil scented skin to my chest. I scream into the demon darkness that makes me love and hate her so much. Scratch at my inner arms with a harvest knife when no one is looking. In those long furrows I sow seeds of despair that sprout and vine along my veins. As half-moons bleed on my skin, I think maybe tonight is the night I will spade myself bone-deep and float away on a sea of envy.

The man on nightwatch cries out from the crows-nest, interrupting my brooding. "Boat coming at us! Pirates. Thai pirates," he squawks, a ruffled bird, hopping down the rigging, a cigarette dangling from his beak.

The men stir in their sleep and pull out homemade knives. They are too young or too old or too sick to fight. Yet they are still proud. They crouch on skinny legs, pants tied up with belts, triple-wrapped beneath their sunken chests. Their eyesockets are deep caves, seeking the enemy.

The moon slips into its cocoon of clouds. I pull the sleeves of my blouse down over my arms and I squat by my sister. My bare sickled feet are damp from seaspray.

The frog monster hums in my gut. She knows her time comes.

"What is happening?" My sister flutters her lashes and rubs her eyes, eyes dark as the days before the world was created and time began.

"Thai pirates," I mutter as if in a trance. I strain my ears to hear the distant roar of the pirates' boat.

"What do they want?"

"Money, jewels, silver –" The roar rattling in my head, a Bengal tiger growling, closer, closer. I can smell its last meal, human flesh in its fangs.

"But we have nothing." My sister's voice quivers like a reed.

"Beauty." My splayed lips turn whip-like, lashing the word at her.

Even in the darkness, my one eye senses her fair skin whitening to a pale polished moon, still, suspended with fear.

"What should we do?" she asks.

"Try to be invisible," I whisper.

The boat shakes, rammed by the pirates' swift, motorized craft. Within moments, they have boarded. Wide skirts of light swing wildly from their torches, burning ghost-images of their violence into the night, so that if we had to rely only on our sight, we would wonder if that is really a man's chest laid open, his entrails dangling like worms.

His screams fly into our ears, down our throats, wail through our hearts. We press our hands to our ears, but his pain slips through the cracks in our fingers. He is there, right next to us. He pours out his suffering in a high-pitched keen, a hypnotic melody of grief.

My sister joins his voice with her own, a wailing sea maiden's song, her orchid lips betraying us.

I slap her, press my hand over her mouth.

A torch flashes in our direction, dims, flickers out. I hear cursing, low in the throat like a dog sharpening his teeth on a water buffalo bone. No sound but wheezing and panting and planks creaking as the boat rocks gently side to side. The pirates have no lights now. Their beacons are broken or burned out. They smell bitterfruit fear on our skin. They sniff us out, following the scent until they stand around us in a half circle, and there is no place for us to go.

"Come pretty girls," they murmur, their voices soft as python's breath.

Their hands reach out for us. One strokes his finger on my cheek, smelling of tobacco, dry as tea tree bark.

I dagger the digit with my teeth. His skin splits like the tough bloated pod of a sun-baked scarlet bean too long on the vine.

I spit blood from my mouth as he howls his outrage at the moonless sky. "Little bitch!"

Another laughs. "Lively ones bring good money. You a virgin, girl?"

Many hands grab me now. I chant to myself that I am the frog girl. With my wet skin I will slip from their grasping fingers. I will secrete deadly venom from my glands.

"Shut up!" One of them slaps me.

"Hey, don't damage the merchandise, eh?" Another cautions him good-naturedly.

They pull my arms behind my back, lash my wrists together with rope, gag my shrieking mouth with a sweat-drenched cloth that must be laced with some drug, because my one good eye grows as cloudy as the other and the sound of my sister's whimpering grows fainter, until it is one with the water slapping relentlessly against our broken ship.

In my sleep, I travel back to my village, to a time before the Pathet Lao and North Vietnamese Armies destroyed it with tanks and mortar attacks. I sit near my father's feet, watching him clang hammer against anvil in his forge. His arms gleam with sweat. He blasts the charcoal fire with a piston bellows, pumping air with his steady right hand. The steam wafting from the coals burns my lungs.

He is a smith, a *kws hlau*, who creates such wondrous silver objects that people come from distant villages, seeking his skills. He trades opium from our fields for silver bars, piastres, Burmese rupees, old Thai one-baht bullet coins – which he throws into bamboo baskets, where they wait to feed the fire.

I touch the neckring he cast for me after my birth to celebrate my having survived on earth for 30 days. The sacred jewelry, which has clasped my neck in its protective circle since my infancy, contains silver smelted three-hundred years ago. My father, like all smiths, cares not for the metal's age or its antique value, only for its weight.

I do not know what he makes on this day. Only that it will be the largest thing he has ever forged. He empties all the bamboo baskets. A trickle of piastres jingle, building to a roar.

I open my mouth to question him. But he shakes his head and will not speak to me. The bellows huff like a howler monkey. The steam fills the forge, until it grows so thick that it swallows my father in smoke. I try to cry out but my thick lips have melted together in the heat. I must watch silently as silver snake rises from the fire. A cold-blooded reptile twisting, transforming itself into the most perfectly-formed man I have ever seen.

The sea spits on my face, a wave of saltwater that scalds my dry lips.

"Wake up, frog girl."

The silver man stands over me, holding a dripping bucket in his hands. His eyes are milky opals. His pale body is as perfect as my dreams, tattooed with green and blue dragons.

I cough. My long pointed tongue hangs from my lips. I see my sister near the front of the boat, her eyes blank. Two of the pirates squat on either side of her. They slip morsels of rice and fish between her orchid blossom lips.

"Who are you? How do you know Hmong?" My voice is hoarse, a raspy frog rumble.

"I am the captain. I know many languages," the silver man shrugs. "I am a man who moves between countries."

"What will you do to my sister and me?" I squint up at him with my one good eye.

"We can't take you with us." He spits contemplatively near my feet.

"But my sister –"

"Your sister is beautiful. She will bring a high price at Ko Singh."

A cold mountain wind chills my blood. Niah would be chosen before me. Always before me.

"No. You must take me. I am the pure one–" Tears fill my one good eye.

"I bet you are." He crosses his arms in front of his chest. "But most men don't desire a girl like you."

"I can be beautiful too –" My chapped frog lips tremble from the weight of begging words.

"The slavetraders wouldn't want you. To them, frog girls have one virtue. They can swim with dolphins. They can live at the bottom of the sea."

"No –"

"Anybody want her before I throw her overboard?" He turns his back to me. The muscles ripple like dunes of a far desert I will never see.

The others don't even bother to look at me. All eyes are on my sister. She is there in body only. She leans against an orange life preserver, her head bobbing as the boat rocks, a glass float lost in the open sea. Her spirit has flown out over the waters I will be forced to swim.

"Maybe I should take you myself," the silver man muses. "We're both freakish in our way, are we not? An albino and a frog girl. Maybe we should join together, if only for a moment, and see what we shall see..."

I shrink from his hands, his fingers wide as elephant bamboo. The halyard chisels at my spine as I edge back. The soles of my feet squeak an alarm against fibreglass.

"Tell me, little frog girl." He winds a strand of my hair around his forefinger. "Did your mother love you?"

"Yes." My voice catches, betraying uncertainty.

"Did she smile on the day you were born, a gift from heaven? Or did she stand on the banks of a swift, dark stream, ready to cast you into the current?"

My body trembles.

"Why do you shake so? Do you wonder how I know these things? Perhaps I was there on the same stream, where my mother set me, the ghost, the albino baby, adrift in a little bamboo boat, and I have drifted ever since on the open sea, and everyone, even my own men, are afraid of me."

He pulls my hand toward his groin. "You've felt lost your entire life. But I know you. Come to me."

I snatch my hand away and press it to my chest. My nails pierce my flesh.

"Huh." The sound comes low, as though I have hit him in the gut. A flicker of pain flashes in his opal eyes, before he conceals it, rubbing his chin speculatively.

I know then that my rejection will only make him more cruel.

"Very well, if that's the way you want it – how are your gills today?"

"I don't have any." I say warily.

"Yes, you do." He traces lines on both sides of my neck with his ivory-handled knife. "Here and here."

"No!" My heart bongs in my chest, a drum beaten for a funeral procession.

"You haven't used them in many years," he says, his voice casting a spell on me. "You've lived on land for too long. It's time you returned."

"You're crazy!" Strands of spittle fly from my lips, glistening in the early morning light, threads spun by a dying silk worm.

"I'd come with you if I could. The sea is the soul of the world. Why do you fear it?"

He severs the rope that binds my hands and lifts me in his arms. I feel the pulse of blood in his wrists against my skin. I beat the hard drum of his chest, but my fists affect him no more than the brush of insect wings. My palms burn.

Before he casts me overboard, he puts a leather pouch around my neck.

"A knife for the sharks, some sweet insects for your tongue," He fingers my hair and flings me to the sea. "Swim well little frog girl."

My body spears the sea, and it closes its skin over me, taking me into itself, a fresh wound. I hear the bubble of its veins, feel its fish nibble my toes, taste the brine of its blood.

"Sink or swim, frog girl," it sighs, "I'll lick the salt from your body as you kick across my waves, or I'll build a coral reef from your bones. Live or die. It's all the same to me."

Below my drowning body, I see the wreckage of lost ships on the ocean floor, the bones of passengers who had never arrived home. Above, the white hull of the silver pirate's vessel.

I break through the surface, lungs aching, seaweed hair straggling over my face.

"Wait, wait for me!" I cry.

I swim toward them.

"Niah, don't leave me."

"Go away, frog girl," the silver pirate roars. "I'm doing you a favour. There is no life on this boat, don't you see?"

He signals the crew to fire up the engines. The sea boils. I realize that my sister hasn't moved from her throne. Her petals fall and dry at her feet. I see the wizened bloom she will become after years in the brothel at Ko Singh, as her figure grows smaller and smaller, until it is no more than a cucumber seed, then nothing, vanishing over the horizon.

I have been swimming for days. My limbs hang limp as stalks of maize, beaten down by a monsoon. I roll onto my back and face the sky. The ocean howls in my ears, and I think I hear my mother's voice.

"*Los tuam*, my first born, how could you dishonor us this way? You have become a *neeg lwj*, an evil person... My heart is heavy – I trusted you to watch over your sister."

Trusted you, trusted you, the words echo as I watch the *dab nraub ntug*, the spirit of the heavens, paint pictures with clouds – a white rhinoceros, a black bear, two women holding hands, a woman alone gazing at a full-blown poppy blossom. I take a red bee grub from the pouch the silver captain gave me and let it dissolve slowly on my tongue. Perhaps it will be my last meal.

I am tired. I do not think I can go on. What is the point? No ships have come by. And even if they did, how would they see me, an insignificant frog girl bobbing in the surf? I let my body slip beneath the waves. I see my dead body, drifting on the current, bloated with gas, fisher birds riding on my back, pecking at my neck. Blood beads strands of my hair. I do not care. I have lost everyone who ever mattered to me. My spirit will fly to my parents on the other side of the mountains.

As I lose consciousness, a smooth-backed fish that cuts swiftly through the sea lifts me up from the depths.

"Hold on to me, little frog girl," the dolphin's voice pings.

Oxygen blasts my lungs. Water and mucus stream from my nose. Salt and sun sting my eyes.

"Where will you take me?" I gasp.

"To the boat, the Great Wind." His words echo in the current.

"It must be the Great Stench by now. How do you know it?" I ask, careful to keep my head above the water.

"I've been watching you."

"Then you know that what I say is true – there is no one left," I murmur.

"Yes. Nothing survives, but the ship itself."

"I thought the pirates would have burned it."

"Sometimes they like to leave ghost ships to frighten others who attempt to sail these waters."

"Then why do you want to take me back there – to the *yeeb yaj kiab*, the abode of the dead? Have I died? Are you another demon sent to test my spirit?"

"So many questions... You live, little one. You will return to wait for the fishing boat that will take you to freedom, to Australia, and beyond."

"No one will come for me. I am evil. I am ugly."

"I think you are beautiful, for a human being. And you will learn to live with any evil deeds you have done. A new country waits for you."

"But my old problems will follow me."

"Only if you let them."

I press my cheek against his skin, smooth as the succulent leaf of a rubber tree. "I wish I could stay here with you."

"You are at the beginning of your life. There is much you are destined to do. When you are a grandmother, the sea will reclaim you, and I will be there to greet you with a silver coral crown and a necklace of one hundred black pearls."

"How will you find me?"

"We have been with you your whole life. My brother, the Irrawaddy, watched over you from the depths of the Mekong River as you were growing up," he reassures me. "Do not worry. You will not be lost."

Through the veil of mist that blows up from the sea, the dark wreck looms before us. Its mizzen-mast whines and clangs. Its sails flap, the black wings of carrion birds. The rigging is hung with severed heads, which I count while I wait to be rescued, over and over again, until they are a part of me, the stumps of their necks joined to my shoulders and arms, a council of rotten-fleshed elders advising me.

"Check my bag, there," says one. "I left some rice grains and oranges in it for you. Eat the maggots too. They'll give you strength."

"Don't be lonely," says another, consoling me in my tears. "We'll always be with you."

They will drive me mad if I let them. So, one evening while they doze, their pus-filled eyelids drooping, I stuff them into a hemp-fibre bag and push them into the sea. Their screams turn to gurgles when the sack splashes into the water.

"You must move on, my friends," I murmur. "Go to the Otherworld. Sleep well."

A few bubbles form on the surface, pop, then vanish beneath the crest of a wave. My eyes grow sharp in the darkness. Delirious from hunger and thirst, I drink in the glow of phosphorous, until my cloudy eye fills with green light. I signal the fishing boat that cuts through the black waters with this strange beacon, my aquamarine eye. But the effort is too much for me. I slump over the side in exhaustion and let the moon take over. Its pocked face breaks through the clouds, revealing the ghost vessel to the night. I clutch the roughened ship rail. Splinters drive beneath my fingernails. The moon burns bright, illuminating a living shroud of tattered sailcloth that holds my sister's image, her arms stretched out to me, her orchid lips whispering my name.

THE MAN OF THE HOUSE
Bead Roberts

Bead Roberts was born in the Potteries. She married a Scotsman and has spent most of her life travelling to wherever his work took him. She takes whatever jobs come along; when she wrote the story in this book she was living in Bavaria, making toys for a craft shop. She writes to avoid doing housework.

BEFORE UNCLE JOE WENT BACK TO THE STATES HE'D handed them a twenty pound note each. They weren't like any other notes he'd seen. They weren't wrinkled and a bit dirty like the ones his mum had in her purse and the Queen looked happier on them.

Uncle Joe said their notes were like that because he'd made them himself and the paint was only just dry. He'd laughed his American laugh, given them all a moustachy kiss, told their mum to "stay cool about all this" and promised to come back for Sally's wedding.

As soon as Uncle Joe's taxi was out of sight, he asked his mum about the notes. He thought that people, even if they were policemen from Seattle, weren't allowed to make their own money. His mum sniffed, blew her nose and called Uncle Joe a card. She told him the notes were from the bank and hadn't been used before. Sally cried because she didn't want to get married, not before she started school anyway. Mum said Uncle Joe had been joking about that as well.

"If you're both very good," she said. "We'll go to the shopping precinct on Saturday and you can spend your money."

He liked going to the shopping precinct with its fountains and see-through lifts and the big boys with big boots and shaved heads who shouted names at the security man making him lose his temper and his breath running after them.

He was allowed to keep his note just so long as he put it in his moneybox until Saturday. Mum kept Sally's money, but let her look in the catalogue to see how much doll's furniture she could buy for twenty pounds.

On Wednesday night he moved back into his own Uncle Joe smelling bedroom. He took the money out of his Ninja Turtle moneybox – that was the first place burglars would look. He sealed it in a gas board envelope and hid it under his pillow. Later he moved it to his best coat pocket, then to his secret shoebox, then back under his pillow.

He took it to school the next day and nobody, even James Wilson whose dad's girlfriend worked in a bank, had ever seen a newer note. He showed it for 'Show and Tell' remembering the number without looking at it. Mrs Murphy, whose husband was a policeman but not from Seattle, said she'd look into who the man on the back was, but it wasn't a good idea to bring money to school. She made him take it to the office and give it to the typing lady who put it in a safe place where she kept the teachers' headache tablets.

He took it to school again on Friday, but didn't show it to anybody. Every time he went to the lavatory he held it up and smelled it. Once he sniffed too close and cut a tiny red line in the wobbly bit at the end of his nose. When his class did gym he pinned it to his vest with his emergency safety pin while everybody else was looking at Ryan Evans' verruca.

He walked home on his own and when he got to the house with the curtains his mum said hadn't been washed this side of Easter he took his note out to look at it. He put the envelope on the wall while he counted the jewels in the Queen's crown. A puff of wind moved the envelope up in the air, then down again. He laughed and put his note on the wall catching it as the wind blew it into his hand.

The next gust blew the note and the envelope into the garden of the house with the Easter curtains. He pushed the gate, but it wouldn't open. He jumped up, put his arms over the top and lifted his right leg until his foot was on the rusty latch then heaved himself higher.

He was steadying himself when the wind caught his note again. He watched as it danced through the air. Jumping down, he ran after it, panting and crying as it disappeared across the main road and over the roof of the greengrocer they never went to because the manager was a 'rob dog' and the carrier bags were twenty pee each.

The 'rob dog' manager shouted at him, said his mother had more money than sense if she let him have twenty pound notes to play with.

"She doesn't know," he said.

"Well, that'll teach you to go pinching money," the manager said then turned away to sell a woman a cauliflower.

"I could tell you my name and address," he said. "Somebody might..." he could feel his lip beginning to tremble like it did when Nan told him how her dog Bruce got run over. "Hand it in."

The manager laughed. "Yeah and pigs might fly!" he said, and that made the cauliflower lady laugh.

He was halfway through the door when the manager came after him. "Here you are," he said handing him an apple. "I know you've had your troubles, I heard about your dad."

The apple had a bad bit in the middle.

His mum hoped he wasn't sickening for anything. She made his name out of spaghetti letters, but he couldn't stop thinking about his lost note.

His stomach ached, not the same way as when he ate the giant (with ten per cent extra) bag of salt and vinegar crisps, more like the way it did on Christmas Eve, except that this wasn't a good ache. He was crying, but not on the outside. His mum took his temperature and told him he could bring his duvet downstairs and watch the television when Sally was asleep.

Usually this was his favourite time, lying on the floor huddled in his Batman duvet watching the television and listening to the whispers of the gas fire and the click of his mum's knitting needles. His mum turned the television off when a man with a tattoo started kissing a lady's neck. Any other night he would've asked why the man was trying to undo the lady's bra – tonight he didn't care. All he could think about was the greengrocer's roof and the funny feeling in his stomach when he thought of his twenty pound note fluttering out of sight.

"Have you decided what you're going to spend your money on?" his mum asked when she came to the end of a row.

He shook his head, he couldn't talk because he knew if he did he'd start to cry and he'd be blamed. He was the man of the family now, he'd be six and three quarters in four days time.

His mum felt his head and took him up to bed. She asked if he was missing his dad then sat holding his hand and singing till her eyes went all dozey looking and she started to nod off. She made him promise to tell her if anything was worrying him.

"Even if it's something really bad, it's better to tell, I'll understand."

He shook his head. He couldn't tell her, dad said she didn't understand anything – that's why he'd done a bunk.

Sally's twenty pound note was now in her Beauty and the Beast handbag and they were all in one of the precinct cafés. He'd lied – just like his dad. He'd said his money was safe in his pocket. His stomach still hurt.

He'd shaken his head when his mum had asked what he wanted to eat.

"You could have your own tray," she said, then when he shook his head again she went with Sally to queue up for sausages, lemon meringue pie and Diet Cokes. He looked at Sally's handbag on the seat of the shiny red chair beside him, then he looked over to where his mum was holding Sally up so she could see the puddings under the glass counter.

He opened the bag.

His heart started beating fast. Without looking in the bag, keeping his eyes on the shuffling queue he rummaged amongst Sally's treasures. He looked down when he felt her purse and twisted the plastic clasp. He took the note and put it in his pocket. He was sure to wet his pants, he was sure of that. He didn't – that same twitchy stomach ache was there and now the feeling of needing a wee but having to hold it in.

He shouldn't have done it. God was punishing him, same way as Nan said God would punish dad. He'd never be able to hold his head up in public again. He tried – the muscles in his neck were still working, but for how long? His heart was bursting, he knew that for sure, he could hear it in his ears. He was going to die. His mum hadn't died, but then her heart had only been broken when dad did the adultery with that tart from the Post Office. This was different, his heart was going to burst like a balloon and kill him. He wondered about the blood that would spurt out when his banging heart exploded and moved the salt and pepper and sticky plastic tomato out of the way.

They were back. He heard his mum saying she was certain he must be sickening for something. Then, Sally was crying. His mum was angry now. He looked at them – their voices weren't in time with their lips, it was like the television when Kate Adie was reporting live from a trouble spot.

"I told you to let me keep it!" his mum was saying. She turned to him. "Didn't you notice her handbag was open?"

He didn't know what to say, his heart had calmed down, it wasn't going to burst, he wasn't going to die, but now he didn't want to live. He was a liar and a cheat just like his dad.

People were looking at them, it was all his fault. His mum had gone white, her lips had almost disappeared just like they did when she kept shouting at dad and waving the letter at him.

"Twenty pounds!" she said. "I could feed the two of you for a week on that."

He had to do something.

He felt in his pocket and ever so slowly took out Sally's note.

"Here you are Sally."

He waited.

Mum wouldn't shout at him here, she'd speak to him in her quiet voice. Dad said her quiet voice was worse than her tantrums voice, she'd been whispering when she'd called dad a shit and thrown his special letter at him. When they got home she'd go on and on in her quiet voice, tell him how disappointed in him she was, how he was supposed to be the man of the house. She'd never trust him again. What if she told him to leave like she told dad. Where would he go? What would he do for food? Whose television would he watch?

His mum's voice wasn't her angry quiet voice. He opened his eyes. Sally had stopped crying.

"Are you sure?" his mum was saying.

Sally began to sniff again.

His mum thought he was giving Sally his money.

"Yes I'm sure, she can have my money."

He felt so relieved, he wanted to laugh and shout – jump up and down on the table and eat a trillion billion sausages.

When Sally was in bed with her Barbie dressing table and designer bathtub, he crept downstairs with his duvet. His mum was sitting at the table with her Puzzler magazine. He walked over to her and put his head on her arm.

When he stopped shaking he said. "I took Sally's money."

His voice felt like it did when he had suspected tonsillitis.

"Mine got blown away, I tried to climb the gate and it went over the 'rob dog' greengrocer's roof, and I thought my heart was bursting." He was really crying now, great loud sobs. "I stole Sally's twenty pounds!" he said between gulps.

His mum had her arms around him, she smelled of cooking and cigarettes and soap.

"I know you did."

He watched a tear balance along the bottom of his mum's eye then drop onto her cheek. She wiped it away and sniffed.

"Mrs Murphy phoned, somebody handed it in to the Police Station. You're lucky, she'd told her husband about your show and tell." She walked across to the television.

"I'm sorry," he whispered to her back.

She didn't turn round. "I know you are, you can collect your money on Monday, Mrs Murphy says you know the number."

"I do, and how many jewels in the crown." His voice still wasn't back to normal. "Is it alright mum?"

She turned to him.

"You shouldn't have taken it to school, should have told me when it was lost." Her shoulders went up and then down again. "But you returned Sally's money."

He pulled his duvet around him and sat on the carpet with his back to the sofa.

"We'll say no more about it," his mum said. "Now let's see if there's anything decent on the box."

FIVE HUNDRED
QUID ISN'T A HAT

Edward Welti

Ed Welti lives in Edgware with his wife, two cats and the wreckage of several motorcycles. He came originally from Surrey, and studied for his degree in Politics at the University of Lancaster. After leaving university he spent several years "considering his options" then took up a career working with computers, which is now the way he earns his living. His ambition is to forget about computers and spend his time writing.

AS THE TUBE TRAIN DREW IN BECKER STOOD BACK against the platform wall, waiting for prey. He tried to look anonymous, hide his noticeably ugly face in the depths of his raincoat. But even his tousled greying hair and high forehead were distinctive. People passed, meaningless faces, a clutter of hairstyles, coats, shoes. Somewhere, possibly on the next train was his victim. A youth in jeans and a tattered tee-shirt swaggered by, a dirty baseball cap pulled down over his eyes. Becker studied the countenance, perhaps too directly. Within a few seconds he had dismissed the idea. The youth was too scruffy. Maybe too aggressive as well, liable to make a fuss about a worn out scrap of cloth and plastic. No, today was reserved for something special.

No other passengers came. Above, the electronic indicator board lied about the next train – "Kennington Oval 5 minutes". Becker's mind wandered back to the girl in the café. Strange how normal she had made him feel. So many questions he hadn't had time to think. When he told her about his room, about the wall, she had leant back on her seat and laughed, those eyes, which had been so sad earlier had twinkled with life. Later she said she would like to come to see the flat. Now he didn't believe her, but then he had gladly given her his address.

Opposite, across the track, was an advertisement. A man in a suit on a tropical beach; square jawed, good looking. People like him had worked at Becker's office. Quick and efficient, but with Gestapo eyes. They found out what Becker had known for a long time – that he was a waste of time, that his job could easily be swallowed by the department. Goodbye and thank-you. In personnel they had asked if he felt capable of the journey home: as if, after ten years, he couldn't find his way back to the dank little room he called home. They had booked him on a course the next week, "How to find a job,"which had been as useless as the various courses the people at the job centre sent him on subsequently. He grinned to himself. While they had taught him a myriad different ways to write a CV he had discovered his life's work. He spent his time, not searching for a job, but out on the tube trains working on his collection.

In the café he had spoken to her first. Her name was Sally. She came and sat down as he finished his tea. As she sat down he caught a waft of her perfume, and glanced at her face. She looked so sad that Becker, who hadn't held a social conversation with anybody in the past year, had suddenly asked if everything was all right. And it had gone from there. Now she was coming to his flat, had written down the address in that book and put it in her handbag. The thought made him panic. When the adrenaline surge had passed over and he started to be able to think again he continued to wonder about her. Becker knew that his appearance was rather bizarre, with his high forehead and that unsightly fleshy blob of gristle which grew by his hairline. What did a pretty willowy girl like that want with him – wasn't it a risky venture? For all she knew he could be a pervert. There must be a motive, one he could not yet fathom.

A train drew up. With a loud hiss, like the air blown from a burst tyre, the doors opened. The man inside it could have been Steed; Savile Row suit, expensive striped shirt, sedate, tasteful tie. And a bowler. He sat on a seat with his back to the door reading *The Times*. The prime position. With the nonchalance of experience Becker walked diagonally along the train to the next door, entered and sat down with his back to the man. The train set off. Becker weighed up the odds. Had to be careful with suits, suits and straight backs. Probably an avid squash player, like those bastards at the office. But the advantage of surprise belonged to Becker. The train drew in to the next station. The doors opened, Becker sat still. He could see the man, or rather his paper reflected in the glass. A question of timing. He stood up. The mechanism hissed, Becker jumped for the door and grabbed the bowler. The doors shut behind him as he sprinted down the platform. His coat flapped around his legs. Even now, in his mid thirties, he was still quick, not many could catch him.

Becker slowed down as the train gathered speed. A bare headed man gesticulated through the window as the carriage passed. By then Becker was turning into the exit passage so the man couldn't see his face. He pulled a carrier bag from his pocket. Nobody noticed him as he stood on the escalator and pushed the hat into the bag. Outside on the road he strode briskly. Usually after a successful raid he walked home. He avoided the chance of another meeting with an angry ex-hat owner at all cost. It was raining, an icy autumn drizzle, but he whistled as he walked.

The wall in his room was a cascade of hats. Trilbys, fedoras, three bowlers, a top hat (he had taken that from a market stall), baseball caps, flat caps and leather cowboy hats all arranged like a three dimensional quilt. Each hat was invisibly attached to the wall with a hanger specifically designed for it. Part of the fascination. Made from sections of wire cut from coat hangers. Then nailed into the brickwork. Becker's single bed was pushed up against the wall with the hats surrounding it, so when he woke up in the night he could see the shapes above him. On the other side of the room was a wash basin and a large oak wardrobe, big enough to hide a man inside. A musty smell, damp mixed with dirty socks, soiled the atmosphere. A few of the hats were beginning to grow mildew.

Becker put the carrier on the bed and walked over to the window. A double set of net curtains stopped people seeing inside. He looked down. In front of the house was an unkempt garden, a hedge which had turned into a thicket and an ornamental cherry by the gate. An old Cortina was always parked in front of the steps. On the far side of the road stood a man. He wore a long overcoat, black greasy hair swept back over his ears. As Becker watched a car drew up and the man got in. The roar of its engine reached a series of crescendos as it accelerated away through the gears. Nobody else was in view. Becker watched for a few minutes more, but the road remained empty.

He went back to the bed and carefully pulled the hat out of the carrier. It was silk lined with a leather band inside. Poked behind the leather band was an envelope. He pulled it out and opened it. Ten fifty pound notes neatly folded down the middle. His mouth twisted; his eyes stared wide. Then he went to the bathroom and threw up. In the mirror afterwards his hobgoblin face was pale, the bags under the eyes tinged with purple. He spat in the sink, took off the baggy jacket and threw it down. Never before had he really believed it was theft. Who would miss a hat? Poor people had cheap hats, rich people had expensive hats, nobody ever spent their life savings on a hat. With his knees weak and wobbly he made his way slowly back to the bedroom and over to the window. No sign of the greasy haired man or anybody else for that matter. The road was grey and empty, puddles and a mush of dead leaves by the kerb. Most people wouldn't have bothered about losing a hat. But that man would have gone to the police. Five hundred quid wasn't just a hat. They would have a description. He tried to remember who else had been in the carriage, if anybody had seen him. They would remember him easily if they had, you couldn't forget a visage like his.

Again he examined the money. Ten fifty pound notes. Crisp as a winter's dawn. Then a new flock of thoughts wheeled into his mind. After a year he could hit back. With this money he could take Sally out. Buy some new clothes. Start to look for a job again. A new era. He replaced the envelope into the hat, and put the hat back into the bag.

Instead of worrying he sat down on the bed and thought about Sally, how she was coming to see him, and how they could float away together.

The next morning he lifted the hat from its carrier and removed the envelope. The money was still there crisp and new. One note he separated out and put into his pocket. The rest he replaced into the envelope and hid it under the edge of the carpet at the back of the wardrobe. He put the hat on one of the shelves inside. It wouldn't be ready for display when Sally came round.

Later that morning he walked down to the shops. There was a bite in the air; a winter wind from the steppes. Old takeaway cartons blew up against the wooden fence by the waste ground. The old woman in the shop muttered a few things when he gave her the fifty. She held it up against the light, put it in the till, then she stared directly at him, suspiciously in silence. It unnerved him. He asked her what was wrong. She muttered a few indistinct words about change, he had grimaced in reply. Still muttering, she had pulled out the tray in the till and produced a couple of twenties, which she handed over to him, along with a few coins. With a more plentiful supply of groceries than he had had in months, he walked back towards the flat. It had been a mistake; he should split the money in shops where he wasn't known.

At the end of the road he turned the corner and walked into the greasy haired man. They stared at each other, the man apologised and continued on his way. Becker felt strength drain from each leg as if a plug had been pulled from the big toe. Unaware of his surroundings he stumbled back to the room and shut the door. From the window he could only see an empty street. The man must have followed him the previous day. He must be a policeman. He was in the shop now, interviewing the old lady, taking the note, checking numbers against a list.

He tried to find a rock to grab onto in the wash of fear. Sally, she would save him. But what did she want, what was her motive, she was too pretty to be really lonely. Maybe she was in the police too. She had seen him in the café and thought he looked suspicious. And he had told her, confessed his whole life away to her at a whim, simply because she seemed sad and interested. So that was it. The sick reality, without an ulterior motive no woman would want to associate with him, with his ridiculous big ears and bulging forehead.

He limped over to the bed, twisted round and hid his face in a musty pillow. Above the hats were gloved fists ready to batter the truth from him. Becker understood his fate; the conspiracy of the world. Now, when it had seemed as if he could have the hats, the girl and the money too, it had all crumbled. Evidence of his crimes was all around him. He sobbed gently. The doorbell rang. Becker tiptoed across the room and climbed into the wardrobe. He pulled the door shut behind himself.

Outside Sally pushed the button again. Her red hair blew in the wind. A few more dead leaves gathered around the wheels of the Cortina.

HOMING INSTINCT
A. S. Penne

Born and raised in Vancouver, A. S. Penne has also lived in Montpellier, Montreal, London and Sacramento. She currently lives in Vancouver and is working on a screenplay adaptation and a non-fiction manuscript. Her story 'The Possibility of Jack' was voted third in the shorter category in the 1994 Ian St James Awards and is published in the collection 'Brought To Book'.

WE DRIVE SOUTH, ARTIE AND ME, HEADED FOR THE U.S. border. Going to California to see if we can resurrect something between us. A year away, he says, will be good for us.

But Artie rarely says what he means. I think what he's trying to say is that he wants more of me: more of my attention and my time. This past year, while my sister was dying, I didn't have much to give him what with all the family stuff going on.

After Sheila's funeral, in the middle of all the crying and sad stuff, he said he wanted to go away for a year, take a woodcarving course at one of those weird new-age colleges in California. He didn't look at me when he said it, just sort of stood there waving a beer and explaining what he wanted to the sculpted carpet.

"Why don't you just pick up a piece of wood and start carving?" I asked. And when he looked at me, his eyes like so much west coast fog, what I was suddenly afraid of, besides getting lost in all that fog, was that he'd leave me here, alone in this cold place. "Why don't you just take a book out of the library, learn from that?" I rushed into the darkness.

He shook his head. "Can't learn everything from books, Shawn."

And without even thinking about it – without even considering how it would affect the rest of my life – I said it: "Can I come too?"

Then he smiled and I knew I'd said the right thing, the thing he wanted to hear. But my spine shrank a little afterwards, like a string pulling tight along the gather of bones.

The first few hundred miles are familiar: rich farmlands of the Fraser delta fading gradually into the poor homesteads of northern Washington. Around Everett, I started to sink into the seat a little, feeling the north receding. Artie drums the steering wheel to Annie Lennox and The The and every so often he stops, listening intently to some invisible hum under the hood of the big old Pontiac, the one we bought to tow the orange and silver U-Haul behind us. Then he turns to me and I can feel his eyes on the side of my head, but I stay staring out the rain-dribbled window.

"You okay?" he says.

"Yah – just kind of scared."

And I can feel his frown but he never actually says what he's thinking: "I thought you wanted to go" or, "I thought you said this would be fun. What the hell's wrong now?" I'm thinking I probably shouldn't be in this car, moving away from everything that is home, going somewhere that's billed as the American Eden. I'm way too messed-up right now to make decisions about the rest of my life and here's this guy who wants a family, kids and a wife, sitting so close I could touch him. If I wanted.

The grey scar of freeways intersects over Seattle and the Space Needle points heavenward, mid-20th century icon to the future, and we join the high-speed grind through the Industrial sprawl of the Seattle-Tacoma corridor. By the time we reach Olympia, we're both tense and cranky so Artie leaves the 1-5 and climbs to the top of a hill overlooking the Columbia. He gets out, stands pointed at south like a weathervane, and I watch him breathe easier again. After a minute I join him, nudging my shoulder into the armpit of his hockey jacket, grateful when he lifts his arm around me, all-forgiving.

"It's only a couple more hours to the Oregon coast. We can stay there tonight, camp in the dunes, walk in the fog – what do you say?"

And the familiar images of raw west coast fill my mind so I hug him tighter and smile, nodding into his chest.

The only person I'll really miss, the one I worry about leaving, is Ardis. A week before we left, I went to see her, took her a book. It was one of those expensive coffee-table books that people display but never really read, just move from table to shelf to box of garage sale stuff. I saw the book as soon as I went in the store and I stopped to admire the cover, a photograph taken in the eerie light of a storm. After that, the book seemed to follow me through the store, almost as if it were chasing me. I passed it on the way to the new fiction section, thinking I'd find Ardis a good novel, then noticed it again in front of the non-fiction displays. The huge butterfly on the cover kept pulling my eyes away from other books and when I finally gave in to its lure, I saw that the butterfly's eyes – two oversized beads of jet – looked right through me. Weird, I know, but after an hour in that store I decided there was a reason the book wouldn't leave me alone so I bought it.

Ardis' eyes lit up when I gave it to her and I watched her turn the pages slowly, drinking in the colours like treasure. She sank back against her pillows, ignored me in the chair beside her bed, and when I left, kissed her wispy head goodbye, I knew that those pages of butterflies would be well-worn by my return.

Leaving Oregon, a whole day of driving in front of us, Artie looks over his left shoulder before pulling on to the highway and says: "Why don't we get pregnant again down here? That'll give you something to concentrate on this year." I look straight ahead, focus on the grey highway and grey skies outside.

Artie reaches for my hand. "What d'ya think, eh?"

I squeeze back. "Maybe. Maybe we should think about it some more."

"It won't happen again, Shawn. The doctors said it was just a fluke."

I slide across the seat, put an arm across his chest so that I can look back through the rear window. Douglas Firs, branches swaying in the wind like giant arms in butterfly sleeves, wave goodbye from the side of the road. The panic rises as I watch the green retreat, out of touch, out of sight. I close my eyes and feel

Artie's pulse against my cheek, his hand on my arm, warm, soothing.

Ardis was Sheila's roommate in hospital. She had a tumor removed from her vocal chords, but she lost her voice along with the cancer. They gave her a computer-generated assistant – the androgynous voice you hear when the telephone company gives you a number from directory information – but we don't use it when I visit. I can't look in her eyes when that computer-person talks: it's like she's unplugged from the rest of herself somehow. And Ardis' eyes are something you don't want to miss: all prisms and rainbows, the colours of silence. She talks with them, as well as her hands, a fast and furious kind of speech that I have to concentrate to keep up with, but when I come away, I'm filled to bursting with something. And all that silence seems more real than any of the talking Artie and I do.

When I wake, turn frontwards again, we're headed into drier ranching country. I unstick myself from Artie, sweating where I lay against his neck, reach in the back for some juice.

"Let's drive straight through," Artie says, sitting forward and rounding his shoulders over the steering wheel. "Let's get this road trip over."

"Can't we stop for a walk or a rest?"

He shrugs. "Wouldn't you rather just get there? Then we can unpack and move in to our new home."

Artie's arranged a house for us to rent through some friends. He's saved for this year so we can get to know each other again without any more outside worries. He's a real planner.

A few hours more and the temperature begins to change: the skin on my arm out the window sizzles. This is what it must feel like to lie on a barbecue, I think.

"It's gonna be hot, hot, hot," Uncle Ed shakes his jowls, spatula waving over the burgers as he stands guard over the grill. Behind him, on the picnic table, there are all the salads – Aunt Charlene's potato, Mom's jellied vegetable – and cold beer. Over the porch, the accordioned banner says 'Bon Voyage' and the metallic letters rustle whenever someone walks beneath them.

"And you'll have to drink that American pisswater down there, ya know. You can't get real beer in the States, unless you buy imported stuff. But with the exchange on the dollar..." Ed stops waving and the spatula drips grease on his shorts.

Artie winks at me and I smile back, trying to be patient. He gets up, stands behind my chair and bends over, wraps his arms around my neck. His beard scratches against me and I reach up, stroke his rough cheek, wondering how he'll survive withdrawal from these regular family dinners. Soon I'll have to be everything – everyone – to him.

"What're you gonna do, Shawn?" Ed's bloodshot eyes drool at me from over his beer.

I shrug. "I'll find something," smiling at Ed and all the aunts who stop their last-minute fussing at the table, brows wrinkling in unison. I know what they're thinking: after four years of living together, we should be getting married, having kids. But Artie and I haven't sorted all that stuff out yet.

Sheila died slowly, changing from a kid who'd danced all her life and wanted to be a ballerina to a kid who only wanted to live. I used to sit with her after her chemo sessions, talking to fill the echo in the room. She lay there, stupefied, so drugged that she couldn't talk, couldn't eat, couldn't puke, probably couldn't even hear me. I'd babble on about the future, tell her how it was going to be, how we'd have kids and families of our own and we'd never have to go to another family dinner again, unless of course it was ours. Sheila hated the get-togethers almost as much as I do.

When she died, I felt like I'd been lying to her. All those pictures I'd painted for her, all those stories about how it was going to turn out and now she wasn't even going to be around for any of them.

What I miss most, driving through the arid hills of Northern California, is a fresh breeze. I'm wilting, gulping at the hot air blasting through the open window, wondering why Artie is pushing so hard to get there. Tears of sweat roll off his round forehead and he mops at them with the end of a bandanna tied around his neck. But he won't stop; he wants to get there.

I think about that for a minute, wonder if anyone ever gets there, wonder where 'there' is, and then I laugh out loud.

Artie frowns at me, as hot and tired and discouraged as I am, and then he smiles.

"What? What's with you?"

"Look at us: two ignorant Canucks slinking through the desert with no air conditioning, dehydrated brains and fried skin, determined to go south. Going away so we can migrate home again next spring. Pretty self-fulfilling prophecy, isn't it?"

"What do you mean?"

"I mean we're out of our element. Look at us: how the hell can we survive in a place that sucks every last bit of moisture out of our souls? Us, the people of the rainbelt! We're nuts to be doing this!"

"C'mon, Shawn. It's only another coupla hours now."

I put my feet against the dash and rest my neck on top of the front seat, stare at the ceiling above me. I consider the gold-beige interior and imagine myself as a nut, trapped inside a shell. I lift one sneakered foot off the dash and kick at the roof, slowly, determinedly.

Eventually Artie gives up, stops for the night.

"We'll get up before dawn tomorrow," he says. "Be there by midday."

We pitch the nylon pup tent at some bulldozed site where each spring the owner slaps up a sign – CAMPSITE – on the only tree, mostly dead, and crawl inside the orange walls, exhausted. I dream of northern rains and mountain streams, silver water bouncing off my face in slow motion beads, long drinks of smooth coldness reaching down inside me, my face in ripples of river reflected off black granite. But by morning I feel like a Californian raisin again, all wrinkled and brown, the humidity sucked out of me into the miles of emptiness stretching ahead. Behind, nothing but scrub oak and oleander marking our passage.

"Let's sing rounds," I put my arm across the back of the seat, curling Artie's wispy pony tail around my finger, cajoling his attention away from the endless road.

"Don't, Shawn," he pushes my hand away. "I just want to concentrate on the signs. Put a tape on."

And after I've played all the tapes and cut my toenails and looked at Artie once or twice to see if he's ready to talk yet – even about babies, but he still says "Not now, Shawn..." – I let my mind drift, filling up all the quietness with noisy thoughts.

I got pregnant right after we found out Sheila had leukaemia and then I had to walk around with this big secret inside of me so everyone could focus on my sister instead of the baby. When I finally told Sheila about it, because I had to fill up the emptiness in the hospital room, her eyes brimmed like fishbowls. I think I was more scared than she was then: scared of what lay ahead of us and scared that she might die, leave me all alone with this kid and no sister.

And then she said: "Will you name it after me if it's a girl?" And I knew what she was thinking so I had to make a joke of it. I told her that would be stupid because then there'd be two people answering whenever someone called out "Sheila!" Back then I was still so sure of life that I couldn't understand why she wasn't. Afterwards, after she slid into a permanent silence and I couldn't tell if she was sleeping or slipping across the line, towards coma or death, I wondered if she'd just given up, shown the cancer cells her submission and let them take over.

But the baby died before Sheila. Didn't even make it through the first trimester. The doctors saw it on the ultrasound and told me I had to have D&C because it was already dead inside of me. I cried pretty hard about that, and Artie, he cried too, two wet trickles curling down his stubbly cheeks. He never said anything – didn't want to talk about it, he said – just cried. We sat in the doctor's office, our two chairs and our grief side by side, without touching. Later, in a hospital room several floors below Sheila's, I curled on my side trying to calm all the sobs and the long shudders that ran over me like a dying heartbeat. The ironic part was that I wasn't even sure I wanted that little peanut-sized thing inside of me. After all, it had no face, no name, no eyes.

When we first see Sacramento, I churn at the haze of smog over all those strip lights. We drive by car lots and fast-food outlets, the bane of the American existence, and I remember that somewhere beyond my window, closed now, is the California I left Vancouver for.

We spend the first three days lying on the cool tiles of the living room floor in our rented house, amazed at the squealing of kids outside in the 110 degree sun. We leave the air conditioner off, afraid of utility costs in a land where rivers are sparse and hydroelectricity is sometimes imported from Canada. We tell each other that eventually we'll acclimatize, here in the home of the free where nothing is free, but I begin to wonder why I came south at all.

And then, on the fourth evening, we venture out. In the still-simmering dusk, we move nervously, like cats, padding past the tangled jungles of neighbourhood gardens – camellias the size of giant rhododendrons, palms like towering umbrellas – and jumping at the first shrill of cicadas. Our hands reach instinctively for each other and when the cool desert air sweeps in from the east, we run down the middle of the street, fingers entwined like a passion flower vine, laughing at our delicate state.

"We're icebergs in Hell!" I yell when we stop at the top of a rise. To the north of us, the panorama of rolling hills and yellow grasslands run away home.

"Yeah, but we made it!" Artie spins me round, kisses me with his tongue halfway down my throat and then I feel his other hardness against my thigh. He pulls away suddenly, tugging at my hand. "Let's go back and celebrate!"

"What's a home without family?" Artie says.

But when he says it, I fade out, remove myself like a dream, spinning away and watching him get smaller and smaller.

I try to come back: "I already have a family," I tell him. "I've got you and Mom and Dad. And Ardis." But Artie's got this thing about having a kid of his own and I'm only making him sadder. "Let's get a dog."

Artie's face pinches with anger at my suggestion. I sit beside him, take his hands, but they just lie there, lifeless. I wonder if there is something wrong with me, a woman without the urge to create life.

When Artie's classes begin, I explore my new world, pushing at unfamiliar borders until I discover the river snaking through the Sacramento Valley. Standing at its edge and watching it slink towards the coast, I remember pictures of the Pacific Ocean and the childhood summers spent there with Sheila.

Eventually I write to the family back home, tell them about the murky American River on my early morning explorations, the lanky eucalyptus and palms throwing shadows like fly rods at me. But I don't tell them how, when I lie back against the rocks in the sun, Sheila's image becomes attached to the insect-humming wildflowers and the mistletoed copses of oak. I don't tell them how, when I walk through the scream of dense greenery along the bank, I pretend I'm in Africa, on the other side of the world, scattering Sheila's memory.

And with each discard, a part of me passes over to this land, caught in its spell.

Artie, though, pines for home. "I don't know how anyone can live here," he bursts through the door after a bike ride in the carbon monoxide. He rants about the automobile fetish of Americans and I listen sympathetically, taking a jug of water from the fridge and pouring him a glass. While he drinks, I show him my sketches: 'asparagus trees', 'sword' and 'spear' cacti, plants I have christened according to their strange appearance, momentarily diverting him. But soon he returns to his lamentations about the Californian weather, Californian roads, Californians. At least his rampage over foreign territory covers up my reluctance for new family.

In November the temperatures drop and Artie stops talking about going north for Christmas, "to a civilized climate". We spend a weekend at Lake Tahoe, passing through green farmland and old mining towns, and I buy Christmas cards with scenes of the ski resort in winter. I sign the insides of the cards from both of us, though Artie shakes his head at them. "That's probably man-made snow," his finger jabs at the picture. "They don't have real snow here."

He's happiest at school, I write to Ardis. He's met new friends to commune with – a replacement for his family, I guess. And when he comes home, energized about his carving, the people there, their ideas, he is full of life. We grow well again.

I put the pen down, remembering how Ardis' hands covered her chest over her heart, a glossy tear flashing out of her eye. "Won't you be lonely?" she asked.

"No. It'll be a good time to slow down, figure things out again...?"

Her grim smile was full of fear. She held her palms out then put them back against her heart.

I knew even then, I think, what I was doing, but I couldn't admit it. Instead I said, "I'll be back soon. We'll be home again next spring."

She hugged the book – those big butterfly eyes – to her chest as I left.

Artie started in about kids again at Christmas. He even bought a gift for the child we didn't have, wrapped it in baby-shower paper and put it under the tree. Every time I walked into the living room, that lumpy package of yellow and blue and pink stared at me. Waiting.

"You know, Artie," I finally said. "I don't think we were meant to have kids. We've tried three times now and none of those kids have come into this world, so maybe we should just close the book on that part or our life." And after it was out there, floating between us like a barbed-wire fence, I felt a lot lighter.

He looked straight at me, and for a minute I saw Ardis' eyes flashing, but it was only Artie's anger heating up, his corneas changing from grey calm to black rage. His face struggled to master some kind of neutrality, but only succeeded in forming a cold, superior look. His jaw worked rapidly, as if tonguing a too-big jawbreaker, and then he turned, crashed his fist against the wall.

"You just don't want to have my kid!"

"It's not that I don't want your kid, Artie," I say. "I'm not sure I want a kid at all." Better and better; cleansed.

Not for Artie, though.

"What the fuck did we come down here for, Shawn? What were you thinking of when you said you wanted to come with me?"

"Artie..."

"Did you just come for the free ride?" he sneers. I can tell he's scared, but doesn't know how to say so. And for some reason I remember Sheila's fishbowl look when I told her I was pregnant. I guess that's when I realized that Artie would never be able to say what he's feeling; that he'd only be able to yell – or hit – when he's upset.

"You never have loved me, have you?" Artie wants to pull me back into the fight so I shake my head, sad but not denying, and he raves on. "Well you're no screaming catch either, you know!" I nod in agreement and remember the butterfly's eyes, the way they'd seen through me. I smile, thinking about how life has a funny way of working things out without us.

"Oh, it's funny, is it? Well fuck you too, Shawn. Fuck you too!" Artie slammed the door so hard the molding cracked.

I wake in the middle of the night, alone in the bed, the temperate climate of a California winter too mild for the goose-down comforter on top of me. I kick the cover onto the floor, too hot to understand that it's not the heat that niggles me awake. The ovenlike dark feels claustrophobic, suffocating.

A keening noise slips through the open window and slides across my sweat-damp skin, leaving goose-bumps. The mourning sound repeats, louder, and I shiver, temperature dropping and sleep leaving. Again the keening and I recognize the bleat of a single donkey above the stillness of the valley, unanswered by miles of quiet. I hold onto the Californian night and smile in the darkness, relaxing.

The braying increases as I lie, rolled onto my side now, face towards the window. I open my mouth, breathe in through clenched teeth – "Eeee" – out through a slack jaw – "awww," softly, trying to communicate. The digital clock slips red numbers past my eyes and sometime later the sky lightens, like a Christmas Eve over Bethlehem, all starry and blue and night. When it's bright enough to see, I stand at the bedroom window, search the distant blaze of pastures – horses, goats, and chickens in the midst of a residential blur, but can see no donkey, neck hung over a fence rail, crying.

I crawl back into bed, stretching across the coolness of empty sheets on the side that is Artie's.

Artie doesn't come home until the afternoon and when he arrives, he sits outside, passenger in a classmate's Volkswagen, talking. When I look out the window, I see him, hand on his brow, and her, hand on his cheek. I close the venetian blinds against the hot Californian sun and sigh.

I wake again that night, hot and sticky in the quiet of the sleeping world. Artie lies beside me, his chest steadily rising and falling and I watch him sadly. After a while, I slip off the bed and go to the window, drawn by the new moon and the cicadas in the empty shadows of the garden. I listen and then, from across the dark distance, beginning slowly and tentatively, I hear the loneliness of the vigilant donkey. His bray drifts towards me, lifting through the air like a night choir. I whisper back, wanting to go to his darkness, wrap my voice around his warm, bristly neck and sing to his whiskered ears.

Towards dawn, when the red numbers say 5:07, the roosters begin. Even Artie, in the lure of a heavy morning dreamscape, can't sleep through the volume. I watch as his eyes fidget beneath their lids, whip frantically before opening a crack, widening when he sees me on the floor beneath the window.

"It's a new day, Artie," I smile at him.

Later I write to Ardis:

I took Artie to see the wildflowers I'd found along the banks of the river. We sat in the middle of a big clearing to talk and a cloud of butterflies lifted around us like a flock of ducks. Artie held out his hand and a big black one with white spots at the bottom of its wings and dabs of turquoise on the tips landed on his palm, just sort of fluttering. We watched for a few minutes while it lay there, next to the warmth of his skin. And then its wings closed together, shut like an old suitcase, and it died. We were in a kind of butterfly cemetery, all these beautiful creatures coming home to die. It made me think of Sheila and how she had slipped away before I could even tell her that the baby was dead.

Artie's coming back next month, and he's bringing you something from me. I'm going to stay here for a while, but I'm sending you some pictures of my new home. The cat and goat don't have names yet – ideas are welcome – but the donkey's Tosca. They're my family now – we hope you'll come visit us one day.

I put the butterfly in a little box with tissue paper around it so its wings won't break. It's the first time I've ever touched something dead and I hope Ardis doesn't mind that I'm sending her a corpse. I hope she'll know that it's good for me to do this, to send her something from the south, from home.

WORK
Justina Hart

Justina Hart was born in Birmingham in 1968 and studied English at Oxford University. Her first collection of poems and photographs, 'The Rhythm Of Stones', was recently published by The Carnival Press and launched at the Birmingham Readers & Writers Festival. Her poems have appeared in the 'Daily Poem' section of The Independent, as well as in several literary magazines.

I HAD BEEN MANY THINGS I HAD NOT MEANT TO BE: barmaid, chambermaid, teacher, typist, insomniac, sucker, smoker, postal worker, 'A' grade student, voice-over artist and shoplifter. There were many things I had wanted to be but had not yet been: actress, photographer, painter, deep-sea diver, international something or other, saxophonist, chauffeur. There were many things I was which were almost enough, but which didn't pay the rent.

"Some people work very hard but still they don't get it right": the song lyric was running around my head. Tinker tailor soldier sailor rich man poor man beggar man thief. Cacophonies. The air is full of them, especially when you spend too long in one place. Full of old wives with malicious tongues and tales. You ought to do this, we expected you to do that, I thought you would have been this, your dead grandfather said you would definitely be that. This is right and that is wrong, and when you know you are right, the voices club together to ensure that doubt derides decision. There are many lies scratching around in Dickensian offices believing smugly in the myth of self-justification. And then there is the cocktail party smalltalk which backs up the myth with an aura of respectability: What have you been, what are you and what will you be? Flesh and blood with a mainframe underneath and a voice that comes out with fresh violence. These days I try and curb a desire to scream silence into blind ears.

I met a nutter on a plane once when I was trying to be next to nothing, who said ad nauseum: "Who are you, how do you justify yourself, what do you do?" He had a point perhaps because I could not answer, but then sensing the victory, asked me out for a drink. Sometimes I want to crawl up a mountain laden with beer and sandwiches and stare at the ground down below from inside a bandage of cloud. Better than Grub Street. I could be a slow worm, seeing by feeling without sight.

I don't want to be about, of, in or out. I just want to be and be left alone. I want the plurality of a singular life. I set out to see a straight line and walk down it, only have failed and fallen off every few yards, right off my sanctimonious perch and ended up with a hangover or concussion or both. I am always fooling myself by leading multiple lives, by doing one hundred things at once and walking up and down a moving elastic stair.

It makes me feel good sometimes to do the things I don't want to do, as though I have fooled everyone on the outside and can go on living unharmed inside. Invariably though, it doesn't work out because it's a game, and I start breaking up like meringue from the inside out and looking for strangers to pick up the pieces. If I have to be and I do have to be – I do not have a patron to patronise my being an unbeing – I would really rather do things that I want to do. I don't want to lead lives I'm not cut out to live if it means cutting myself out in order to live them. That is like being a doll cut out of newspaper which unfurls to show hundreds of identical, meaningless dolls holding hands: reflections of the same nullity. But again, it's much easier to conform and say you are an astronaut or a mechanical engineer or a street sweeper, than explain that you are looking and searching in order to find meaning or the lack of it.

One of the sweetest jobs I have done involved sitting on my own in a theatre box office, selling tickets for a kids' pantomime, mostly over the phone. I was in a booth with a computer and behind a grilled, perspex barrier like the ones in British railway stations. There was a sign on the plastic sheeting that said, SPEAK HERE. Occasionally someone came in or someone went out, but if they tried to speak there, I heard only a muffled cottonwool whisper. I had the keys to the theatre, including the Victorian safe, and spent whole days reading in my box with the door bolted for safety. There was a job satisfaction in this that I had not known before. I was trusted implicitly and sold hundreds of tickets on automatic pilot whilst barely looking up from my books.

In this substitute prison I found myself thinking of an old, Irish car park attendant I had met who fought for years in the Belgian Congo. He had known horror upon horror and what it feels like to be locked up against your will without food or water. He once had to sleep standing up in a dug out hole, which was filled with rainwater up to his neck. Yet he was now working in an underground car park patronised by rich executives, spending most of his time shut inside a tiny portacabin. When I asked him what he did all day, he said he wrote poems and stories, tearing them up each night before he locked the gates to go home. He had the sort of dedication that I had never had. His straight-down-the-lineness made me and my perennial dithering about being this and not being that seem less consequential than the life of a stone being tossed out to sea.

After the theatre job, I was offered full-time employment by a small firm in the country. I signed an initial three-month contract and felt full of remorse and self-betrayal. I imagined the prospect of a life-sentence – being incarcerated from sun up to sun down in an office, staring longingly at unobtainable patches of sky. The word 'career' had always made me want to bury my head in the sand or climb up a tree and not come down. My 'Go Guide for Enterprising Graduates' had lain safely encased in its cellophane wrapper for three years, yet now I had wittingly signed my own death certificate. Being in an office, I thought, was like believing in God: you didn't have to think; it was all wrapped up, in the bag, with a user-friendly job description tacked to the front.

Then it dawned on me that the chance to do a nine to five job could in fact be a radical opportunity in disguise. I hoped it would not lead to a perverse enjoyment of doing the opposite of what I had planned, but instead would allow me to experiment on a day-to-day basis. Rather than moping around with plenty of time but no money with which to enjoy that time, now I would have some money and a limited amount of thereby more valuable time which could be called freedom. I would try and exploit the Catch–22. I reckoned that to the prisoner an inch of freedom is more comprehensible and useful than bewildering miles of open road. To conform for a while need not mean entering the house of the dead.

The job did not start out well. My appellation was 'Associate Researcher', but it should have been 'Associate Liar'. I was conned into doing the job, and in turn was duty-bound to con the company's clientele. I took the honest road to dishonesty and told people straight out that I was duping them. I had to phone up prospective 'customers' and offer them one of a number of choice lies designed to entertain and take them away from the humdrum of their routine. "Dear Sir/Madam," I would say, "it has taken me many years to learn my craft, will you listen to this fabrication recited especially for you and chosen from amongst my company's vast, sophisticated repertoire?" They would respond in the main to my adrenal attempts: "Yes, that is a very good lie indeed, a lie I will gladly pay for. Please send the invoice to my M.D. Have a nice day." But sometimes they would say: "We are cynical bastards in our industry and far more experienced in the art of lying than you. Get off your high horse and piss off." Fortunately I had many and varied pseudonyms to leave with their acerbic secretaries when cold-calling. It was a job without satisfaction; I got paid per lie and was bad at being full-time who I was not.

My employer was a temperamental man, overly fond of American psycho-jargon and hence, glib pep talks. On the first day, he gave me a list of his Ten Commandments which I was to obey to the letter:

1. You will arrive at 9.00am sharp and not leave until 6.00pm.
2. You will win.
3. I do not listen to what you say you can do, I listen to what you do do.
4. You will not let the phone ring more than three times before answering it.
5. You will make me coffee with milk and sweeteners three times per day and tea twice (as per previous instruction).
6. You will not be told what to do; I expect you to be sufficiently intelligent to work it out.

7. You will not complain, but be polite and cheerful at all times.

8. You will not swear.

9. Although I have specified a one hour lunch break, it will be deemed bad practice to take more than ten minutes.

10. You will not kindle fire in the office (or smoke any flammable material/s).

As I glanced through it, he turned sharply, saying, "I have a small window on Thursday, come and see me if you wish to discuss any difficulties." A window? I thought that windows were for looking through, for imagining that life was perpetually greener on the other side. He walked out without awaiting my reply. Fuck you, I didn't say. I stared longingly through the window above my desk at the unobtainable sky and did not go to see my boss on Thursday.

I was determined each and every day to leave for the allotted ten minutes even if it was simply to walk down the street with my numbed face uplifted to the wind or the rain. No-one else seemed to come in or go out during office hours. I discovered Norman churches and towers with rough stone walls against which to press my forehead and imagine I was sane for a few deep, desert breaths. The churches had graveyards that were always cool and empty but beautifully kept. I walked over the graves and it felt good.

Then I discovered a secret garden, to become my favoured haunt, where I would sit on a white, slatted bench and inhale an illicit cigarette. This was a public garden which people mistakenly thought was private. It lay down an alleyway and one had to lift the latch of a heavy, iron gate beneath a hidden archway to get inside. It was my minuscule Eden, removed from the scurry and flurry, the hustle and bustle, the shouting and shifting, the chastisements. Here I felt instantly vacuous, in a giddy, abandoned way. In this garden I would always have the time and freedom to be anything that came to mind.

The garden was a garden of surreal Russian dolls. As I gently peeled off each petal, a new centre would appear until I got back to the minute enormity of me. As a kid might write in a book: this belongs to .... of x street, y county, z country, the world, the universe, infinity, amen; the garden opened up without boxes, without categorisation, to a larger and larger feeling.

At its core was a sundial which stood on a plinth, then came the grass, then the path, the border, the hedges, the trees and finally, the four walls which contained it. The vital thing about the garden was the square of its walls, which, by virtue of enclosing, promised a richer wilderness in the landscape beyond.

All I needed was to scale the walls and run out toward the hills.

I whispered to myself over and over: "Art happens. It has no limits. It knows not confinement. Art happens. It has no..."

As I had predicted, the office goaded me, pushed me ironically into a new determination. The weird pleasure I got at being stuffed inside its meaninglessness for eight hours a day came from the essential discipline of being locked inside four walls, which increased in me hourly, daily, the desire to be, to go, rather than to do and do. I dreamed that later or sooner, I would leave the treadmill in mid-flow and walk away toward the hills, leaving a message painted in thick, black strokes across the windows:

SOME PEOPLE WORK VERY HARD BUT STILL THEY DON'T GET IT RIGHT.

EXPECT JAIL
Nick Kelly

Nick Kelly gave up the study of law on the second of May 1985, the day he qualified as an Irish solicitor, and spent the next eight years based in London as lead singer and songwriter with his band, The Fat Lady Sings. Having released two critically-acclaimed albums and toured the world, Nick split the band early in 1994 and began to write fiction. He has since moved back to his native Dublin, where he is now working on his first novel.

EVERY WEEKDAY FOR THE PAST THREE MONTHS MY WIFE and I have been riding the Piccadilly Line, the section from Acton Town to Cockfosters.

These journeys have been the most exciting events of our thirty-one year marriage, more delicious than our honeymoon, more fulfilling than the day I became a partner with my firm (Whelkstall & Amersham, 1 Lincoln's Inn Fields, London ECIR 3AU, Telex: Bluechip, London), more thrilling than even the births of our two now full-grown sons, Edmund and Alexander.

Alicia, my life's companion, knows me better than I know myself. I think she had been planning for my retirement for months, years maybe, although she never so much as mentioned it to me.

For myself, to be honest, I had given it very little thought; like most professional men, I suppose I had just assumed that it would be all late lie-ins, rounds of golf, a glass of good wine with every lunch, at least two with every dinner, plenty of reading, long leisurely conversations with other similarly carefree friends and perhaps a new hobby, such as water-colour painting or researching my family tree.

How surprising then, eleven days after my grand retirement dinner at the Savoy, to find myself in tears in my favourite armchair in my study, not knowing what to do with myself and the fearfully empty hours that stretched before me.

But, apparently, not a surprise to dear Alicia at all.

"There, there, my old bulldog," she crooned to me, dabbing at my wet face with her no-nonsense matron's handkerchief. I had not even realised that she was in the house. She must have sensed that that day would be the day of my disintegration, and postponed her appointments (she is the chairwoman of the Committee of Friends of the Victoria & Albert Museum) to be ready to appear by my side.

She did not wait for me to offer an explanation. I suppose she knew that I would not have one.

Moving slightly away from my chair, she lowered her head, just letting me catch the mischievous glint in her dark eyes: "I think it's time we did a little work on our Naughties, my darling" – she smiled at my obvious shock – "now that we've got all this time on our hands."

"But what can you mean...?" I breathed.

She stooped slightly forward, and with her slim gloved hands – she was, I now noticed, dressed for going out – she lifted the hem of her neat skirt to her waist: she wore no underthings!

My vision clouded and starred as if I had bumped my head. The sudden understanding of what she was suggesting, the sudden realisation that she was perfectly and happily serious, made my stomach acid with lust.

"The Naughties" was our phrase for our one recurrent shared sexual fantasy, a fantasy that had had its first, tremulous airing some six years into our marriage (Alicia was, of course, the first to take the plunge by relating some of her imaginings one night to her weary and ever-so-slightly-bored husband in order to make him sit up and take his nose out of his bedtime book).

We would be on a train, or some other form of public transport together. We would be sitting next to one another, but we would pretend that we were strangers and would not talk to each other, or take any discernible notice of one another's actions. I would be reading a paper, so that my face would be hidden to most of the other travellers. Alicia would catch the eye of some fellow passenger sitting opposite. He would be a handsome man, not young, by appearance a successful doctor or lawyer. She would smile at him. My newspaper would be completely blocking my view of her, but I would be able to peep surreptitiously around the other edge and see his reaction to my wife. Alicia would then, very discreetly, make some rearranging movement with her skirt, allowing this handsome man to see that she was wearing no underwear. I would only know the precise moment of her revelation to him by the change in his expression. He would show a flicker of amazement, but then regain his controlled, professional composure. She would repeat the movement some minutes later, and then once or twice more if necessary, to make him understand that it was no accident. Eventually he would drop something (a coin, a book) onto the carriage floor, and using the retrieval of this as an excuse to stand up he would reseat himself beside my wife, so that she would have one of us on either side. They would then start to talk. Although they would speak quietly, Alicia would make sure that her words would be just audible to me, anonymous behind my paper, though his might not. She would then begin to say outrageous things to him, sexual things, carnal invitations and suggestions. Although his verbal responses would be muted, by peering around the edge of my paper across the carriage I would be able to see his physical reactions to her reflected in the carriage window in front of which he had been sitting until just a few minutes before.

That was it; The Naughties never went any further, nor needed to. Just the relating of the scene was enough to make us as erotically-charged as schoolyard virgins. And I suppose, in truth, I had never given it serious consideration outside of our own, lights-out love-making. It was always a private thing, a joke with just enough truth to be really amusing. There was, to misappropriate a phrase much in vogue with the younger partners at Whelkstall, a glass ceiling: a barrier beyond which The Naughties could never even contemplate going.

But now, as Alicia stood beaming before me, I realised that the glass ceiling had evaporated. There was no reason why we should not do it. We would do it. Why shouldn't we?

My bold, brave, darling Alicia!

There have been more than twenty by now. We chose the

Piccadilly Line over the other local option, the Central, principally because of its extremities: our plan would work better when, city striving towards country, the gaps between stops became longer, and we felt that we were more likely to find suitable candidates (late-middle years, professional, of good stock and breeding) travelling to Cockfosters and Southgate than to Hainault or Ongar.

They have been tremendously varied.

The first, perhaps because Alicia was new to the practice and unsure of herself, was the youngest: he cannot have been much more than forty.

He was a big, burly man, with a face that looked ready to fly into a rage at the slightest provocation. He had little guile, and his jaw dropped comically open when he first became aware of my wife's selective undress. He coughed very loudly and looked immediately away, reddening furiously. For the next minute or two he was beside himself, mortified, staring down at the carriage floor, fiddling with his big, ugly watch, waiting for my wife or one of the other passengers to laugh at him or demand an angry explanation for his unforgivable behaviour, as if he had himself removed Alicia's knickers. When he finally realised that nobody else in the carriage had noticed anything untoward, he allowed himself another furtive glance. This time, finding that my wife, so far from objecting to his interest in her, was unmistakably pleased, he allowed his eyes to linger, and, as I could clearly see, his body began to react, causing him to shift awkwardly in his seat and dig his hands deep into the pockets of his expensive (but not perfectly cut) grey pinstripe. When (as we had discussed beforehand) she looked directly into his eyes, smiled, and discreetly patted the vacant seat to her left with her gloved hand, he hesitated only for a moment (one last check to make sure his intolerable behaviour had really gone unnoticed) before clumsily crossing to sit beside her. She used the same kinds of words as she had always used to me for The Naughties. I could not hear how he replied, but his posture – viewed in the window opposite – was not masterful; he craned his head so that his ears were almost at my wife's lips, as if to ensure that she did not feel the need to raise her voice. Later on Alicia told me that he had not responded to her with any erotic talk of his own. All he had been able to bring himself to do was mutter "yes...I know...yes...," and make one final, adolescent suggestion of a rendezvous later in the week in a hotel. This (as we had arranged) was politely turned down. At Southgate (the last stop but two) Alicia said a friendly "goodbye, so nice to have met you" and, to the man's utter horror, we both stood up simultaneously, linked arms and left the train. We found a nice, ordinary café near the station where she gave me a complete run-down on The Shy Quantity Surveyor.

Number Two, much older and more suave, was The Aftershave Greek. He barely raised an eyebrow at the initial approach, as if middle-aged women flashed him on trains every day. He did talk back, but, perhaps predictably, it was in the hackneyed imagery of English soft-pornography, all barrow-boy clichés. When we left him at Arnos Grove, he hardly reacted at all, turning his attention back to his briefcase, as if he had had better things to be doing all along and had only talked to her out of courtesy.

After him came The Nearly-Millionaire, The Cummerbund Man, Doctor Smarmy, The Councillor, Little Lawman, Big Lawman. These nick-names owed more to guess-work than hard information: rarely did one of our subjects reveal much about himself outside of his fantasies.

The encounters, of their nature, were very brief. I think the longest – Little Lawman, Knightsbridge to Turnpike Lane – was only about twenty minutes. It is to my wife's great credit that she managed to glean such a rich yield of erotic information and experience in such short lengths of time. But, then again, Alicia has never been a dawdler, nor an utterer of platitudes. I truly think she has a talent, an ability to cut through to the fundamentals at astonishing speed. I had noticed small hints of this capacity before, but these last three months have been a revelation.

Some were terrified throughout their little adventure and barely spoke at all. Some were predictable in their smuttiness, like The Aftershave Greek. Some had fantasies which seemed so mundane that it was difficult to be sure whether they were completely sexually pedestrian or, on the contrary, so acutely sexually aware as to be able to find pleasures where less sensitive fantasists could see nothing of interest at all. And some were born erotic tale-tellers, relaxed, powerfully descriptive, sparing with profanity so as to preserve its full exquisitely shocking effect for when the moment was just right, full of surprising and exciting counter-suggestions, giving far more than they received from Alicia.

It may seem surprising that we have never been confronted by the same subject twice. But, in fact, the more advanced in years one becomes, the more one is a creature of routine, and by varying the time of day travelled and the carriage entered – and, of course, by keeping our eyes open – we have not had any embarrassing second meetings. (Once we did see The Cummerbund Man entering a door at the far end of our carriage, but we managed to escape before the doors shut, and I'm sure he noticed nothing).

On all but two occasions, Alicia politely terminated the encounter and we left her admirer at Southgate, Arnos Grove or an earlier station if necessary. On the days when we got a 'catch', we never travelled as far as Cockfosters. It would obviously have been unwise to disembark at the same station as the gentleman concerned, and my wife seemed instinctively able to tell how soon his destination was approaching and take appropriate action. Quite how she managed this, I am not sure. Possibly some urgency began to creep into his mumbled carnality, or he tried to shift the conversation from fantasy-relating to actually making erotic proposals (always gracefully ignored or declined). At any rate, Alicia almost invariably took the person by surprise with her farewell and we would step out of the carriage just as the automatic doors began to slide shut. We would then spend a wonderful three-quarters of an hour huddled close at a corner table in some cosy hostelry like student lovers, discussing that day's gentleman, his attributes and his shortcomings, and speculate from what we already knew of him as to what else might lie unrevealed.

Our journeys back to Acton Town – we decided from the start to confine Alicia's attention-seeking activities to the outbound trips – were full of giddy, hard-to-conceal excitement. For no sooner were we back in the sanctuary of our large bedroom than we would tear at each other's clothes and gurgle and gasp with lust, laughing and moaning as we consumed each other. I used to imagine our intimate life as about average, good enough but necessarily dulled by familiarity and the passage of years. Now, I occasionally feel that we must really have been rather a staid couple as regards these things. I find myself wondering whether any of our close married friends have been enjoying the kind of relations Alicia and I have just discovered ourselves capable of throughout their own long marriages. For she has been set ablaze by the intimate attentions of these total strangers she has encountered, as I have by the knowledge that their attentions will be unrequited and that, whatever their qualities and charms, at the end of our tube trip, it will not be they that beds my irresistible wife, but I. Together we revel in the treasure-trove of intimate data that she has gleaned from the gentlemen she has spoken to on our expeditions, their stories, their bragging, their own fantasies and insecurities. We have amassed an unrivalled database of erotic detail, which we can access at any time. We – at our age, can you credit it? – have become experts in the clandestine craft of sex.

As I say, on only two occasions has an encounter not resolved itself in the ordinary way, by Alicia suddenly abandoning her suitor, taking him by surprise as she and I made our clean getaway.

The first was six or seven weeks ago. The rather intense little man we later christened The Repentant Perv, who had initially leapt at the bait of Alicia's bare thighs, and who had regaled her with some of the most forthright stuff that she had yet heard, seemed all of a sudden to be smitten by belated guilt, and, breaking off in mid-mutter with a stricken "Excuse me, please," he jumped up from the seat and rushed off the train at Turnpike Lane in a state of extreme agitation.

The second was today.

He got on at Green Park, a busy station. It was just after ten o'clock, but in Zone One the rush hour is never really over, it just eases slightly. I noticed him straight away.

He wore a long blue overcoat, buttoned up, a mustard-coloured scarf, and black leather gloves. His black shoes gleamed. His hair was thinning and completely white. His air was relaxed. He was clearly a successful and distinguished person, possibly a barrister or a senior clergyman. He could even have passed for a member of parliament, the kind who has inherited a safe rural Tory seat from his father and effortlessly retained it over five consecutive general elections.

He was an extremely handsome man, but his presence was of a kind that even had he been grotesque one would still have paid him attention.

The seat immediately opposite Alicia was already occupied by a young mother who struggled to control the fidgety three-year-old on her knee. There were two other seats free further along the carriage. But he was content to stand, it seemed, his gloved hand enfolding the ball-ended safety grip that hung from the ceiling, his body swaying easily with the train in a manner that belied his obvious years.

Alicia had noticed him too. I did not have to see her face to understand this. I simply felt, through some surprising intuition, her gaze lock on to him.

At Leicester Square, the struggling mother and her son left the train.

There were many people crowding in through the doors, and it seemed likely that the seat would be immediately re-occupied by a lank-haired girl in a floral dress and clumping army boots, but – with startling grace – the man released his grip on the hanging handle, glided along the aisle and sat down in the place exactly opposite Alicia, just before the obviously amazed girl could reach it.

What a move!

I had never in the course of our recent adventures been so tempted to say something to Alicia, to make some kind of contact with her, just to express my excitement, just to share it with her. But naturally I did nothing of the kind, knowing that on no account must I jeopardise the encounter that seemed certain to take place.

I knew that this fellow was something special.

I fixed my eyes on his face, holding my *Telegraph* up in front of me but in such a way as to allow me a narrow unobstructed view around the right-hand edge (Alicia, as usual, was sitting to my left). I knew that by the time the train had reached Covent Garden, my wife would have made her first move.

Extraordinarily, I saw no start of surprise or shock, not even the merest flicker to signify that my wife had uncrossed her legs. He sat, perfectly comfortably, his hands clasped lightly together as if in an attitude of prayer. Yet I had distinctly heard the swish of skirt against stocking-top.

And it was not because he had been looking elsewhere and had not seen. In fact, he was looking directly at her. I could not at first decipher his expression. His brown eyes held her steadily. He did not change his body position in any way, neither craning eagerly forward nor folding shyly inward, the two most usual responses to Alicia's revelations. And, unless I was deluded, his mouth was actually twitching as if he was suppressing an attack of the giggles.

He sat like that, twinkling at her, for several minutes. I dared not look at her, of course, but she must surely have been as surprised as I by the lack of any of the standard reactions.

Notwithstanding this, she must have finally decided that it was time to make her standard hand-patting-the-seat offer, for he stood up in a leisurely fashion, and moved across to her side.

"Well, thank you, that would be very nice indeed."

He spoke quite normally, and made no effort to lower his voice. He was, to my surprise (but, then, everything about this man surprised me), an Irishman. You could not, however, have confused his tones with those of Ian Paisley or Bob Geldof: his accent suggested culture, learning, wisdom, affluence. I suppose the nearest likeness I can find for him among my admittedly limited set of images of the Celts would be that of Oscar Wilde.

He lowered himself into the seat and, as I could now see reflected in the window above the place he had just vacated, he was no less relaxed than before, his hands once more held loosely together. He seemed to have no self-consciousness whatsoever.

I heard Alicia make her standard opening remark, using the phrase which she invariably used when her prey had taken the bait and was sitting beside her. Her voice seemed a little uncertain, and she spoke more quietly than usual. She asked her admirer to tell her exactly what he had seen that had made him want to come over to sit with her.

"Oh, I could just tell that you wanted a bit of an old chat."

His voice seemed to boom around the carriage, though none of the other passengers appeared to hear. I just wasn't used to hearing Alicia's gentlemen speak out loud. (Previously, strain though I might, I had never picked up much more than muffled sibilance or grunts).

Alicia herself was clearly taken aback. She paused for some seconds. When she asked her follow-up question – but had he liked what he had seen when she had uncrossed her legs? – her voice was even lower than before, like a mother whispering to a roaring child in the vain hope that he will reduce his volume to match hers.

"Well, you're certainly a very attractive woman," he replied, with a laugh in his voice, "but, to be honest, I'm not much of a ladies' man, and I expect that someone with a little more experience in the field would be a better judge when it comes to that kind of thing."

He had not taken the hint; in fact, I think his voice was a little louder still.

My wife, for the first time in three months, was seriously rattled. I did not have to look at her to know that. Our genteel Mr Wilde seemed to have no concept of what was required of him, and little tact or discretion. People around us would surely overhear him. Perhaps, despite initial appearances, he was a drunkard or mentally unbalanced. Perhaps he would begin shouting at the top of his voice, telling the entire train that this seemingly respectable lady here beside him was a sexual deviant. Perhaps he'd leap gracefully up and pull upon the emergency lever.

The train was beginning to slow down as it approached Russell Square. I sensed that Alicia was waiting for the precise moment to stand up, grab me by the arm and rush me out of the carriage just before the doors shut. This mission would have to be aborted.

But just then, Mr Wilde spoke again, and this time his voice was much lower, barely audible to me.

"But I would enjoy talking to you. I'd enjoy that very much, my dear lady."

I looked across at his reflection. His head was now much closer to hers. His posture was just as relaxed, but somehow, magically, whereas before he had sat like a stranger sits beside another stranger, now he complemented Alicia as if they were a long-married couple. No casual witness would have doubted the propriety of his connection to her.

The train pulled up, the doors slid open. But the tug on my sleeve from Alicia that I was expecting never came.

As the doors shut again, and the train began to pick up speed, I realised that my wife had decided, in an instant, to prolong this disturbing encounter. More than that, something in Wilde's voice and manner had suddenly struck home, had turned Alicia's fear into trust.

And, as the journey continued, and as he spoke to her, Alicia seemed actually to forget where she was. She ceased to be aware of the other passengers or of the ebb and flow of the passing tube stations. She also forgot about her husband, sitting mutely to her right.

Always, during our little adventures, I had been aware that, although I played the part of a total stranger, a passive, covert witness to her behaviour, everything she said or did was for my benefit, for the benefit of us both. This secret understanding was what made her escapades so thrilling.

But, as I quickly became aware, this encounter between Wilde and her had somehow been transformed into a truly private contact, no longer one engineered by Alicia to be shared between us later. Wilde had taken her somewhere else, had spirited her away from me.

He spoke and she listened. His voice was not loud now, but somehow every word he spoke reached me, every pause, every gentle stress.

"Life takes us on strange journeys, does it not, my dear?," he began.

"I was born just sixty years ago, on a small farm in the west of Ireland. I was the second of eight children, six boys and two girls. It was a lovely part of the world. The land was not great land, but it produced a higher yield than any other farmland in that area, which was a tribute to my father, and to his father before him, and to the hard work that they put in. It fed us all, anyway, and clothed us and sent us to school.

"My older brother was very bright. He was just fifteen months my senior, but the gulf between us was much greater than fifteen months. He had an ability to retain information and to process it the like of which I have never known before or since. We were in the same class in school. When the teacher would start showing us something new in chemistry or mathematics, Fingall would always be the first to pick it up. He truly had a raging thirst for knowledge and learning.

"While the rest of us happily helped out at harvest-time, destroying as many haystacks with our playacting as we ever built, freckling our noses and reddening our bare backs in the hot sun, skinning our knees as we tripped and chased each other home at dusk along the stony narrow boreens which ran between the rock-walled fields, Fingall would be sitting palely indoors, straining his eyes at some book he would have had specially ordered from the mobile library that passed once a fortnight.

"When he was sixteen, and I had just turned fifteen, we sat the National Intermediate Certificate Examination. For the young people in our locality this would generally be our final contact with education, and most of us were not sorry to see the last of the damp pebble-dashed schoolhouse. Once the Inter was over, we would be grown-ups, workers, part of the real world.

"Fingall got nine 'A's. He got three prizes, for achieving the highest marks in the whole of Ireland in mathematics and biology, and the third highest in chemistry. Each prize – a medal – came with a letter of congratulation signed by the Minister for Education.

"A news photographer came out from Galway City, and another all the way down from Dublin, to take pictures which later appeared, with laudatory captions, in the papers concerned. For the Galway paper my parents were asked to pose with their genius son, and so they did. My parents had only ever had one photograph taken of themselves before, on their wedding day, and in the cutting – I still have it somewhere – they are like rabbits caught in headlamps. In between their two awkward, nervous faces, Fingall looks almost casual, as if he had not a bother on him, as if he was bored.

"It was not boredom on Fingall's face, however. It was resignation.

"The morning of the arrival of the Minister's letters, Fingall had requested a private chat with my father. Once in the back room, he told my father that he wanted to stay in school, to study for the National Leaving Certificate, to seek a scholarship to go to university in Dublin and to take a degree in the Sciences. He wanted to become a forensic analyst, to join the police force.

"My father, not knowing what to say in response to this flabbergasting proposal from his normally silent eldest son, sent one of my younger brothers to ask Father Lannigan to call down to the house. Father Lannigan ran the school, and had taught us Irish and Latin. He and Fingall had never got on. Fingall's brains and his unanswerable questions and his logical argumentation outraged Lannigan. He was a jealous and ignorant man, a man threatened by progress and science and all forms of intellectualism.

I think he thought Fingall was a heretic, perhaps even the Devil himself.

"When my father told Lannigan about Fingall's plans, the priest instructed him that on no account should he let my brother have his way. What about the fine farm that my father and his father before him had built up with their honest toil? This country was founded on tradition, Lannigan said, a Christian tradition and a rural tradition. Patriots had died to ensure that this land belonged to a good Irish family. The Convention that land should pass from eldest son to eldest son was sacrosanct. Without Convention, without the strength of knowing where we all stood, Ireland would quickly go to rack and ruin. It was my father's duty as a Christian and an Irishman to banish these dangerous notions from his son's head, by force if necessary.

"Force was not necessary. I suppose that nowadays a youngster might consider running away from home or a father might decide to go against the wishes and advice of his priest, but that was not the Convention in those days and in that place.

"Fingall stayed on the farm, and, after my father died, he dutifully took up his inheritance. He never read another book from the day of Lannigan's visit. He spent his life working the land, a job which he hated and for which he had no calling.

"I would gladly have stayed there and helped him, for I loved working out in the open air and could not imagine another, indoors life. But that would have run against Convention too; a farm was not built up over generations only to run the risk of being split up again among squabbling siblings. Daughters were expected to marry into other nearby farms, and younger sons to leave the area entirely, to look for work in the villages, the towns, the cities, and very often overseas.

"I came over here when I was eighteen, though it broke my heart to leave.

"Things went well for me, I was very lucky. I stumbled, somehow, into some kind of an education, I worked out how things were done over here, and I did all right.

"In forty years I only went back there twice, for two funerals: my father first, and then, barely five months later, my mother. Fingall received us all, all his younger brothers and sisters, grown now and awkward sitting in the little parlour in smart clothes bought in Galway, Coventry and Chicago. He wore my father's threadbare second suit. It was all he had to wear. He didn't argue with us or discuss things with us, or with any of the other mourners, and I knew that he never did with anyone any more. He only made small talk.

"I was back there again last week. For Fingall's own funeral. He never married. He hadn't been well for months. I bought a suit for him last Christmas, I had it made in Savile Row. Although I made light of the gift in the card I sent with it, he was not fooled, I'm sure. We both knew that I had bought him a suit so that he would at least have something decent to wear in his coffin. It was a little too big for him, in the end.

"After the funeral, and the dinner and drinks with my greying brothers and sisters and all my multi-national nieces and nephews, I was told by the solicitor Kilbride that Fingall had left me the farm.

"In the will he said that I was to have it, I 'who should have had it all along'.

"So here I am, six months from retirement, with the farm I would have happily lived on all my life.

"But I'm too old to work it, of course. And I never married either, nor had any children. If only I could have lived Fingall's life; if only he could have lived mine.

"I tell you, dear lady, Convention made a mockery of us."

He paused for a little time. I realised that, while he had been telling Alicia (and, incidentally, myself) this story, I had become completely oblivious of my surroundings. I had fallen under his spell, just as Alicia had. I had been unaware of the train's stops and starts, or of the other passengers' movements. I began to focus my eyes again. My arms were stiff from holding the paper up, still open on the Obituaries page. When I lowered it to look around I saw that we were alone in the carriage, the three of us. And I realised from the landscape passing outside the windows that we were now travelling overground and were already past Bounds Green, past Arnos Grove, past both Southgate and Oakwood. The next stop was the last, Cockfosters.

I felt suddenly afraid, and for the first time in the entire encounter (in fact, for the first time, really, in all of our adventures of the past three months put together) I half-turned in my seat, and faced towards my wife. What should we do now, when the train stopped, how should we deal with this unexpected development? I realised that she had not spoken since the story began. I needed her to make a decision, to be her resourceful, intuitive self, to get us out of this pickle.

But Alicia was unavailable to me. She, too, was turned in her seat. Her back was to me, she only had eyes for Wilde.

He spoke again, but with a slightly different tone. He was not telling a story now.

"Of course," he said softly, "if I could find a beautiful woman somewhere who could put up with me and my foibles, and who wouldn't mind living out her days with me, just the two of us together, in a little cottage in the loveliest corner of the universe..."

I heard a strange sound: Alicia sighing, just once, but not in a way I'd ever heard before.

"... Well, then, perhaps I could have my last laugh at Convention's expense."

I really thought, at that moment, that I had lost her to him.

I realised that I was the stranger, not he. The rules under which Alicia and I had boarded this tube train, under which we had lived our whole married lives together seemed suddenly to have been rescinded. I had never imagined that our special bond together could be broken, was vulnerable to attack. All my life, since the day we left the church together, I had felt that she and I shared a small bunker for two, from which we could laugh at the world and at each other, impregnable and safe. But Wilde had seen something in her, a yearning or a need, which I, her husband of thirty-one years, had not spotted. It would not have been a spectacular thing to witness, perhaps, but the combination of her concentration, her back turned to me, and that small, alien sigh, was as profound and shocking to me as if she'd turned around from the kitchen sink and plunged a knife into my stomach. I have never felt so lonely.

The brakes squealed as we slowed down into the terminus. Wilde spoke again.

"Why don't we go and have a cup of tea together..."

Alicia moved to stand up, her face turned towards his and away from mine. So this was how it would be, I thought. She would leave me for him.

"... Just the three of us?"

As we walked along the road to our regular Cockfosters teahouse, he explained that he was a policeman. His name was not Wilde, of course, it was Duignan, Chief-Inspector Michael Duignan. There had been several unusual complaints from passengers, in consequence of which a plain clothes policewoman had been assigned to travel on Piccadilly Line trains looking for a suspect answering Alicia's description. She had spotted Alicia, and, from several seats away, had witnessed the Repentant Perv incident. Waiting to see which station Alicia would alight at, this WPC had been rewarded with the sight of my wife and I linking arms and departing together.

"To be honest, in a situation like this, in the old days, I would simply have done nothing," he told us, his eyes crinkling kindly at us across the formica-top table, "what harm have you caused anybody?"

He took a sip of his tea. He was as relaxed as ever, no different to before.

"But, there's been a lot of pressure on us lately, what with all this talk of family values" – the expression was clearly distasteful to him – "from various idiotic hypocrites in high places, and it was decided that you should be arrested and charged."

He looked at Alicia, whose face was still drained of colour, as I suppose mine must have been.

"But I'm not very impressed by these people and their zeal for Convention, so I persuaded my superior to let me approach you to give you just a warning."

He was smiling at us as he spoke, now, and it was the smile of an ally, a confidant.

"I'm really of too senior a rank to be dealing with this kind of matter myself, but, because they know I'm retiring shortly after a long and distinguished service in the force, they humour me a little. They find my interest in you two quaint.

"You see, I really did want to meet you. I wanted to tell you that if you can't bring yourselves to restrict your adventures to more discreet locations you are liable to be arrested and prosecuted, which I know you would both find embarrassing. It's my duty to tell you that, and now I have.

"But I also wanted to meet you so that I could tell you" – and his lips were once again twitching as they had when he had first sat down opposite Alicia – "how much I admire your guts, the pair of you. I envy you your closeness. Well done."

He then shook our hands in turn, bid us a warm farewell and left the café.

We travelled back to Acton in silence. We would be all right, despite everything. We would be fine.

I unfolded my *Telegraph*, and for the first time that day, I made an effort to read.

"Expect jail, judges warn porn peddlers," ran the headline. From tomorrow I shall be taking a different newspaper.

CONCERNING THE EYE OF THE MASK
Kristina Amadeus

*In 1993, after thirty years of hectic
eclecticism in the USA, Kristina Una
Amadeus returned home to England with
6,000 books and an elderly wolf-dog
named Blue. She has published three
esoteric short stories in 'Sufi – A
Journal', and several exhibit catalogues
for American painters. Many years were
spent as a theatrical agent and film
production associate. Now living high on
a granite cliff on the north coast of Cornwall, she hopes to resist
the seduction of sea, sky, kestrel and ancient stone circles and stay
inside to write.*

MY MOTHER SAID THAT OF ALL OF HER CHILDREN I
lay the quietest in her womb. "My sleepy little fish," she would
whisper affectionately, and rub her belly to make me stir.

When I finally emerged, neither late nor early, sliding into the
warm air of the small back bedroom, she had already named me. I
was to be Jamila, the Beautiful.

My mother was a stubborn woman having never been known to
change her mind once it was set. A strong woman, she kept both pain
and pleasure to herself. And, if she ever cried we never knew it. When
I was placed in her arms, I'm told that she looked at me for a long
time with teeth clenched, sweat running down her neck, her large
breasts heaving from the labour. She wiped my forehead with her
long hair, and counted my fingers, toes, and verified my sex; F. She
was silent. Finally, she nodded, handed me to my father and said,

"Her name will be Jamila."

My father cried. I'm told that he tore his hair and blackened both his eyes with his own fist; that he sobbed like Pagliacci; that he stayed away from our house for more than a week; that he went to the house of that woman; that he bought spells of dried monkey gonad and silver charms dipped in blood and sealed by moonlight; that he stayed away from the small back bedroom forever (or twelve years, whichever is the most); that he was a changed man who no longer smiled just for the joy of feeling his cheeks puff and his lips open; that he never laughed again; that he gave up the guitar; that he took to gambling; that he developed psoriasis; that he lost his hair, and that he could not look at me without weeping.

I was born with no face. Where my face should have been was smooth, white translucent skin, from chin to forehead. No eye openings, no eyelids, though eyes were there, hidden beneath the skin. Instead of a nose there were two slits like gills on a minnow, fluttering with each breath as delicately as pink rosebuds in the early morning breeze.

Yet I was lucky, even then. I had ears. I could hear. My mother tells that my hearing from the very beginning was phenomenal, I could hear whispers rooms away, storms while they were still on the far side of the desert. I could hear pain, pleasure and love in the marketplace and the strained silence from the small back bedroom at night. And I could hear my father crying as he laced his shoes.

The doctors at the local hospital were kind. A collection was taken to fly in a reconstructive surgeon from a great city on the coast. He was to look at me and decide what could be done.

"We must give her light," he said. "She must be allowed to see or her eyes will atrophy and the optic nerves will die."

My parents nodded gratefully, their hands clasped together in joint supplication. They were simple people and knew how to be grateful.

"And she must eat or she will die." The doctor examined the separate jaws beneath the smooth unblemished skin. My parents nodded, yes, yes.

"I will make three holes. Two for her eyes, one for her mouth." My parents raised their clasped hands in a salute.

"It will not be a pretty sight. The openings will be strictly utilitarian. They will serve a purpose. She will see and will eat. She will live."

My parents nodded, hoping for more. There was more.

"And," the doctor paused, allowing the magnitude of his generosity to slowly sink into the provincial minds of the local doctors, "and, without cost... to you, that is..." he nodded at my parents in their unfashionable clothes and ugly shoes, "when she is grown, nineteen, perhaps twenty... I shall make a face for her. I will make her beautiful."

The local doctors applauded loudly. My mother, teeth clenched, nodded and held my father's hand while he sobbed. Rubbing his hands palm over backs, the great reconstructive genius bowed twice in acknowledgement.

The necessary holes were made that afternoon. Two days later I was put to the breast for the first time. Because my father could not look at me without weeping, my mother bought a rubber mask from the Burn Ward, trimmed it to fit me, sewed pink lace on the edges to soften the effect. As I grew, the masks kept pace with my clothes, a new one every few months. When summer came, dark glasses were sewn on to protect my eyes from the sun because without eyelids I could not close my eyes ever, not even in sleep.

I'm told that I was a happy child, an open air, active child. I don't remember. Happiness, unhappiness were the same. The things I loved were seen through the Mask, the food I tasted was tasted through the Mask. The world seemed a kaleidoscope of forms, smells, sounds, but a kaleidoscope in reverse, for it spun around outside. I was encased firmly in the isolating tube of the Mask.

I loved the gentle pressure of my mother's hand on my hair, and the sound of my father's voice. I enjoyed colours. They appeared like jewels to magnify the world. I longed to be beautiful like the world so that people might look at me with pleasure and meet my eyes when speaking to me. Though no one spoke to me. They responded only when I spoke to them. It was as if I wasn't really there. The Mask was a barrier between me and the world, a rigid, flat, unyielding wall that caused everyone to look at my ears when they talked to me, or to fix their stare at some point three inches above my head.

I hated the Mask. The rubber stung and pinched my skin. In the sunlight it gave off an odour of chemical putrescence. It seemed like a Death Mask, a wall between life and me. My father would not come home unless I wore it. He insisted. I resisted, but my mother begged for him.

"Please, Jamila, please! Think of others. Don't make your father cry. See how you hurt him when you push the mask up like that? You must learn to control yourself. We all have to learn control. It is not nice to offend. Not nice, not at all nice."

I grew fast as if to outrace them, but the procession of masks seemed endless. And, as I outgrew them, my mother saved them, keeping them in her drawer with my baby shoes and her wedding dress.

My classes at the Destina School for Children became progressively worse. Kindergarten had been easy in spite of the teacher who retched daily as she wiped my lunch from my face. But the older I grew the more difficult life became. I was the focus of the children's games. They played tag with me, screaming and pointing when they caught me and the bravest ones tore off the Mask. Our teacher, determined to give us a classical education, narrated stories of gods, heroes, dragons and monsters. In every quest the hero met and vanquished the monster. The children applied their classical education immediately.

"Let's play Theseus and the Minotaur! Jamila must be the Minotaur in the labyrinth." They would pull, push me into position. And I would crouch under a bush or a table or sit for hours in the back of a dark cupboard. Jamila the Medusa, Jamila the Hydra. Jamila Gorgon, Jamila Djinn, Jamila Cyclops. Eventually the course was changed from mythology to fairy tales, but the children were as relentless and inventive as Grimm. There is no end to the faces of the monster.

My school days were cut short, finally, by The Incident. One morning a small, thin girl, with curly hair and eyes like blue sapphires, blocked my way and took my lunch bag, saying, "You don't need to eat because you're Nobody. Only Nobody has no face. Nobody! Nobody!"

I smacked her hard. I scratched her star sapphire eyes until they turned to rubies. I bit her perfect little nose and am told that my teeth marks remain. Other children took her side, of course. They protected her from the Monster. Hurling themselves on top of me, they held me down. But for a moment they were at a loss: what could they do to me that had not already been done? What more could they do?

As if the same thought swept through all their minds at once, they pulled out pens, pencils, crayons, and wrote words on the Mask;

filthy words misspelled in their ignorance. They drew pictures of men copulating with animals, pictures of cocks and balls like inverted *fleur-de-lis*, all the swear words they ever heard, and then, finally, tearing off the Mask, they wrote and drew on my face, "fuckshitpisscuntkillwarblood."

I was removed from the school, for the sake of the other children's peace of mind.

"You must admit she is a disturbance. Perhaps it would be better."

It was admitted by my mother's lowered eyes.

"A private tutor, perhaps?" My mother nodded.

And so I stayed home. The tutor, our neighbour's son in his first year of trade school, taught me arithmetic, biology, grammar and Art. He spoke gently and I think he liked me because he was kind to me, yet while he taught he kept his eyes trained, like a hound, on my mother's best china at the back of the cabinet behind me.

The face-graffiti combined with the Art lessons germinated a seed in my mother's mind, and for several weeks she worked around the house with a secretive and sly look. I would notice her staring at me thoughtfully, rocking on her heels, her hands gripping her thick waist, her mouth open, her eyes half-closed. She waited for the mailman every morning.

Then one night at the supper table – my brothers on one side, my sisters on the other, my parents presiding at each end (I sat with my brothers because behind a mask gender doesn't matter) – my mother spoke.

"I've come up with a plan for Jamila."

"Another plan?" Father's eyes filled with tears at the sound of my name.

"Yes. Another plan. A good plan." My mother's plans were famous throughout the neighbourhood. Father always said she would never leave well enough alone.

"Can't you leave well enough alone?" he asked.

My mother ignored the remark as she speared another boiled potato. "I've asked the most famous painter in the world to paint a face for Jamila, pass the gravy please."

"And just who is the most famous painter in the world now? Would you be so good as to tell me, please?" Father enquired sarcastically through his tears.

Silently and triumphantly my mother handed him the art magazine she had been sitting on. The cover was crumpled but still recognisable.

Father stared and almost laughed through his tears.

"He? Never. Never. Why should he? He's the god of Art."

My mother smiled, nostrils flaring as she chewed her vegetables slowly and firmly. I counted forty-one chews before she swallowed. She reached for her glass, took a long drink of water swilling it carefully around her teeth, and dabbed her lips with the sleeve of her housedress. My brothers and sisters sat open-mouthed. Father leaned forward. I feigned indifference by staring at the light-bulb.

"He has already agreed and said yes – pass the meat and the gravy take your elbow out of the margarine – in the Louvre the Prado the Tate the Modern..." My mother had read the art books carefully.

"Everything he does is gold. Pure gold. His paintings sell for millions. When Jamila is finished with it, we can sell it. We will be rich. We will be famous. People will envy us."

Other people's envy was very important to my mother. She could not enjoy her house, her clothes, her children, unless there was someone to envy her her good fortune. I, of course, had been a severe blow in the face of such need.

Father turned to look at me. Inspired by the moment, I stared back. And unbuckling the Mask, held it on my lap. Father stared at me, hope and greed mingled, giving him strength. It was the first time he had ever looked at me without crying.

I jumped up from my chair and throwing the Mask to the floor, stamped on it.

"I hate it. I hate it." Saliva ran out of my lipless mouth as I squeezed my eyeholes in a vain attempt to force a tear.

My sisters and brothers stared at me in horror. None of them had ever seen my real face. Mother had been afraid it might stunt their growth. My eldest brother left his seat and picking up the Mask, handed it to me.

"There's ice-cream for dessert," he said.

"That settles it," said Father, dry-eyed, "when?"

There were sounds of lust, if not love, from the small back bedroom that night. Fame and the prospect of cash drove my father to unsuspected heavens of erotica. He had somehow acquired technique during the long absence from the small back bedroom.

The Most Famous Painter in the world came to see me. He arrived with five limousines, waving his beret and smiling his famous smile at the crowds. His women (girlfriends, ex-wives, new wife, secretary, assistants, publicist and chauffeurs) laughed, and bickering happily among themselves, offered their familiar profiles. With a hopeful smile the ex-wife with the famous buttocks turned her back to us.

He sat me on his knee, his hard dark eyes shiny with anticipation. Painting had long since ceased to be a challenge. He was above criticism. His most minor works drew rave reviews. He could do no wrong. His publicist remarked that, when framed, even the food stains on his teeshirts hung in museums.

He turned me on his knee and pulled my head back against his broad peasant chest. His striped cotton pullover smelled pleasantly of musk, sweat, garlic and lemons. He poked and prodded my head as if I were a clay bust of a girl, not a real girl. He looked into my eyeholes and pushed his finger through the ragged hole of my mouth. He counted my teeth. He handled me roughly, held me too tightly. But I liked it, I admit. He looked at me without disgust or shock or veiled aversion. He was as impersonal as God scooping the clay of Adam from the earth. He looked at me, saw only what I might be.

I felt my excitement rising. I was a person. I was not to be a Nobody any more.

He stood me on a chair a little way off from himself, and sitting on our kitchen stool, stared at me. He bit his knuckle and measured his thumb. The crowd was silent, hushed, anticipatory. It was known that he would not tolerate noise as he worked.

He sucked on a pencil and spat out the eraser; made a small sketch on a match cover. He chewed his thumbnail, descended from the red kitchen stool, hitched his fishermen's pants high up over his waist. He scratched his arse and pulled his ear.

"I will do."

The crowd roared its approval. Photographers who had been restraining themselves snapped pictures; flashbulbs cracked the air. Journalists fought to use our old black telephone. The girlfriends, ex-wives, secretaries and publicist lined up for the bathroom, renewing their make-up for the journey back. My mother clenched her teeth so hard that she broke a molar. And Father almost smiled.

The Most Famous Painter went away with his little sketch and three days later returned. He smiled, waved the ubiquitous beret. He shook his knotted fist for silence. Taking the Mask carefully from the seat of the sixth limousine he held Her to his chest. He raised Her in front of his face so that we could get the full import and magnificence of his gesture. He shook Her triumphantly.

"The face all men will love," he shouted. "The face all fathers will be proud of. The face that mothers will clasp their hands with reverence before." (I saw that when you are famous grammar doesn't matter).

My mother immediately dropped to her knees in prayer at his famous feet.

"We cannot ever..." she said humbly and with well-rehearsed dignity.

The Painter must have made a small motion with his head, for several people rushed forward simultaneously, tripping over Mother and tearing her borrowed dress in their haste to be the first to place Her on my head.

She was heavy, but I knew that I would gladly get used to Her. I liked the cool clean scent of Her freshly sanded wood, the pungent smells of Her blue impastos. The Most Famous Painter held a mirror. I looked into it and saw that I was beautiful. Gentle, laughing, acquiescent, delicately suggestive. My indigo shadows invited, my violet curves compelled. My lips were full and orchidaceous and he had parted them so that I could speak. She made me beautiful, and as I turned to the crowd, I felt their love and admiration flow towards me as the fingers of the ocean reach for the abandoned shell at returning tide.

The Most Famous Painter had brought with him his own Poet to commemorate the occasion. At a nod from the Master, he began to write an Ode to Her Beauty, and then as if seeking inspiration asked to see the Master's signature incised just under Her chin. The Poet's fingers were cool on my neck, but his breath was hot.

Our lives changed. Our phone now rang constantly. I was in demand. Somehow my parents found the money for insurance, for my face was worth a fortune. We put bars on the windows. A brisk argument and fistfight between museum curators ensued on our front lawn early one Monday morning. Who would acquire the

Mask? And when? My mother took deposits and rights-of-first-refusal from each. I was not consulted. Decisions were made. We argued.

"You can't sell my face. It's my face, not yours. You just can't give my face away when you feel like it."

My mother sighed, turning her face stubbornly to the kitchen wall; her mind was set. I decided never to let the Mask out of my sight, even at night. I hung Her on the wall at the foot of my bed. Hers was the last face I saw at night and the first I would see upon awaking. I was haunted by Her beauty. I dreamed of Her. We were angels, She and I. We were goddesses. We had power and influence. Wild animals knelt humbly at Our feet, We rode the backs of great white bulls, We embraced swans.

And yet She lived a life apart from mine. She received an offer for a film, even though We were the star. She agreed to promote a brand of cosmetics and Our picture appeared on magazines. Young women everywhere emulated Our blues and lavenders and painted their own profiles on their cheeks. And all that was required of me was that I be myself. That I be the body that carried Her. The One Who Wore The Mask.

I loved Her too, I admit. Who could not?

And yet when She smiled wistfully on the wall at the foot of my bed, Her eyes seemed sad, for without my sight She could not see. I was touched by Her vulnerability, Her blindness. Her need made me strong. I felt responsible for the darkness She was forced to live in without me. I began to wear the Mask to bed at night. I knew She needed me. I learned to sleep on my back, careful not to crush or harm Her face. And slept without moving, arranging my arms and legs to complement Her calm blue gaze. I became quieter, a neutral bezel for the great jewel of Her face.

We received a book of poetry dedicated to Her. Flowers followed. The Poet had not forgotten Us.

"I have always loved you," he said. "From the first time I saw you. Your nubile fragility was inspiration. Ode to the Mask of Lolita was born that day because of you. You are my Muse."

On the morning of my sixteenth birthday, the Poet and I became lovers, and I learned to make love without moving so that he could look long and lovingly down at Us. He looked deeply into Her face, touched Her gently, careful not to wear away any of the brush strokes of the master. He fingered the famous signature and kissed it reverently, humbly. But the Poet was less reticent with me.

He kissed and bit my neck. He bruised my breasts. He sank his teeth into my flat young belly. I played the part of mummy ravished to perfection. Not a muscle moved, though inside, my heart danced a fandango. I was loved. I was beautiful. Soon I was in demand, and the three of us became travellers sharing Her enigmatic silence with the world.

We were in France, having just completed a short film evocative of death, when the Master requested that we come for Her yearly touch-up. He insisted, as he had from the first, that I wear the Mask as he worked on Her. He demanded that We be posed nude. The Poet objected, of course, and was only calmed with the promise of a small sketch. I could hear him pacing outside the studio window on the tiled courtyard below.

The Master worked slowly, smiling. When We came down, my Poet's face was as white as the jasmine around us. He stared rudely at Her, without love.

"You've changed Her!" he shouted at the Master.

The Master shrugged and flipped his beret into the corner where the little brown goat stood waiting to be milked.

"Faces change. She's a woman now," he glared back. "Thanks to you."

My lover spoke firmly. "But this is my woman. This is the face I love." They enjoyed each other's strength. They were both strong men, and knew it.

"And She is my work of art." The black eyes glittered like pebbles under water. The famous finger stubbed roughly against Her chin.

"See. My name. She is mine." He would not change Her. "Next year, perhaps. We see."

We went home. My lover brooded. Odes, sonnets, haiku, all were fugitive. There was the threat of impotence, but time triumphed and when the problem reduced itself to one of premature ejaculation we both heaved a sigh of relief. We were still able to enhance his manhood.

A month later his full sexual prowess returned when another poet, seeking recognition, wrote an Ode to The Pensive Mask, inciting my lover to write feverishly in the epic mode day and night, producing at last The Mask of Odysseus. The Poet felt that he had matured, the touches of contemplation brushed in by the Master now became a reflection of his own growth as an artist. He finally understood the wisdom of the changes and saw Her sadness as his own sagacity. "The Master intuited what I was to become," he said with a tinge of almost real emotion. "Life is too, too full. My genius is just at its beginning."

We both ignored the fact that my twentieth birthday was less than a year away and the great surgeon would be returning. I was nervous, and my lover complained that I was biting my nails.

"If you must do it, don't jiggle Her face. It makes Her look ridiculous! Try to think of others, please Jamila."

I stopped biting my nails and took up macramé, and yet, I did have a secret. It was very silly, really, a girl's whim. One Monday when my lover was in town with his accountant, I had a sudden attack of bravery. Fingers aching from the stress and pull of the yarn, and tired of looking at Our reflection in the mirrored walls, I took the Mask off.

It felt strange to be naked, to be ugly again, even if I was alone with no one there to see. I was careful not to look in the mirrors, and pretended that I was as beautiful as She. Taking the pen that my lover saved only for cinquains and haiku, the one that had belonged to the Master himself, I wrote a few short sentences on the inside of the Mask. I saw that they would rest against my cheekbones. Working quickly I drew a small picture on the smooth wood between her eyes and boldly, in the inside of Her mouth, I wrote... I hesitate to reveal the content. In fact, it must remain my secret. I can tell you only that the words were a needed balance to Her enigmatic blindness. I hoped my explicit drawing might give Her a depth of perception that She lacked.

As my lover leaned back on his arms that night staring down at Us, I felt a perverse pleasure in knowing that I was facing something hidden from him. That I, too, had been able to give Her something. Love was very good that night for me, but my lover complained that I was not still enough and that Her face slipped at a crucial moment.

But time was running out. I was almost twenty and the surgeon was anxious to schedule the operations. He prepared carefully for this, hiring a press agent and lending his name to a brand of sanitary napkins. His career now hinged on the creation of the

Face. I was afraid, of course; who wouldn't be? I was facing pain and solitude. My lover talked me into waiting another six months.

He treated me like a queen during this time. We shopped for clothes to enhance Her smile. We posed for great photographers, We christened ships and babies, We named streets, We set the trends. We graced the dinner tables of the cognoscenti and We withered the uncultured with a look. Life was good, but unlike my Poet, I was anxious for the operations to begin and be over. I wanted to feel the morning breeze on my cheeks. I wanted lips that could return a kiss and a mouth that could discover. Most of all I wanted to close my eyes.

I asked that it resemble Her face. The surgeon examined the contours of my face-to-be. He shook his head. "Not possible. Life must not imitate Art."

I attempted to squeeze a tear from my lidless eyes. I could not.

"I will give you planes, angles, a whole topography." He showed me the false faces of the famous and the rich in a red leather book.

"See, they all come to me."

Months of pain. Darkness. Fear of the becoming face. Guilt at the coming abandonment of Her. She suspected, I know. She hung on the wall coldly, Her mouth blurred, one eyebrow slightly erased. She missed the sweaty adoration of Our Poet.

He would not come, could not come to see Us, he said.

"The blood, the pain... the unknown..." he murmured over the phone. "But I will create a poem... Orpheus and The Mask."

More months of bandages, of scalpels, of sutures, of tubes, of the dull echoing ache of anaesthesia. And a pain in my chest as if my lover had cut out my heart and swallowed it whole.

Everyone said that the new face was a beauty.

"Ah, the nose..."

"Oh, the mouth..."

"And those cheeks..."

"The lips..."

Lips, brows, lids, cheeks, nostrilsbridgecleftdimplecurveschin...the face was a success! A brief flurry of notice in the papers, a cover on a magazine showing Us face to Face. Encouraged, I went to see my lover. It was good to walk down his street once more, smell the sycamore, the damp smell of the moss in the wall. We had not seen each other for over a year. It had been agreed. No stitches, or bandages or hints of surgery. He was a man whose mother had raised him softly, without argument, without disruption, without confrontation. She had hoped for a priest.

He opened the door and stared blankly.

"Who?" he asked politely, blowing the smoke from his cigarette back into the hallway.

We stared at each other until finally I had to tell him who I was. He seemed uncomfortable. He looked at his feet, then at the window; like all artists his glance constantly veered to the left.

"Am I beautiful?"

Quickly, too quickly, he said, "Why, of course, no question about it." And laughed a short laugh. Then, sucked on his cigarette.

My new lips ached for his kiss. But the kiss brushed my cheek, scarcely. And he could not make love, he said. Too strange. It would seem like infidelity.

I stood on the pavement beneath his apartment window, counting the trees on the street and waiting to breathe normally again. A sound above. He called down to me. I fumed, my heart racing. "Yes?"

"What have you done with Her?"

"Mother wants the Met. Father the Louvre. The Master wants Her back. As for me? I don't know."

Later that day his manservant brought a letter. An admission to make. A guilty secret; an illness. Perhaps to be fatal, who knew? He could no longer make love, or in fact be close to any woman. No wrongdoing on his part. He begged me to believe. He loved me. Would always see that I was cared for; a large sum of money enclosed. And last, for old time's sake, might he, could he, would I allow him to keep Her? In sacred memory of me, of course. So that he would always, could always, in his solitude retain the memory, the intimacy of our love, the moments; the memory of his sighs, his pleasures, the strength in his arms, the pounding of his heart, and the memory of my still and silent whiteness bearing Her face so bravely for him.

I wrapped Her gently in purple tissue, kissing Her sad mouth and blind eyes. She would soon need a touch-up. But who would do it now? My lover would not be able to risk the Master either altering or stealing Her. But that was no longer my concern.

I sent Her back with the manservant. To Hell with Mother and the Met. To Hell with the Most Famous Painter in the world. And Father's tears had long since failed to move me.

I was happy. I was free. The wind caressing my face was all I had dreamed. With my face turned up, I ran in the rain with my mouth open to catch the drops. I knew at last the sticky joy of mango and papaya pulp lodged between my teeth. And my first lollipop. And other sticky joys. With great joy I cried. The hidden ducts were free. Now I had eyelids I could close my eyes at last, and for the first time in my life slept straight through the night and looked at the sun without dark glasses.

Now that I no longer had to protect Her famous face, I was allowed to run and jump, and learned how to swim in one afternoon. I took up fencing, ballet, archery, Tai Kwon Do. I was free.

But I must admit there were times that I missed Her. Nostalgia urged me to apply make-up that resembled Her indigo shadows; violet in the nostril, cerulean in the arch of the lid. My new face reacted violently to the colours. It swelled, became raw and itchy and burned to the touch. The surgeon advised against. In the mirror my face was expressionless and seemed without life.

"Can you change it a bit? I look too new. Too blank."

"It's up to you to change it as you use it. It will age, acquire character, become more your face. Wait. See. Live."

But it didn't. It remained raw, blank, new in the mirror; impervious to life. And behind my back (or should I say in front of my face), it betrayed me constantly by its wayward, unexpected expressions.

"Why are you sneering at me like that?" asked my closest friend after sharing a compliment paid to her voice.

The face laughed involuntarily at the recitation of my father's aches and pains, and cocked a quizzical eyebrow at Mother's tales of her pre-marital virginity. It drooped in blatant, open-mouthed incredulity at the polite white lies of the local priest, and embarrassed us all with loud guffaws at the solicitous enquiries of the town mayor campaigning for re-election. The face revealed my deepest secrets and wouldn't allow me to hide the smallest feeling.

I became unpopular. My friends left me, complaining of being deceived by my former sweet, even, temperament. "We know the real you now," they said, and they didn't like her. Too direct. Too critical. Not friendly. Not nice. I was no longer nice!

"It's not my fault. My face betrays me. My face tells what I don't know I'm thinking." They were not to be cajoled. My face showed them I didn't care even as I was speaking.

"You lie. You deceive."

I began not to care. I began to speak my mind and looked for argument. True, I was lonelier, but for a while felt braver. As the bravado waned I began to hate my face, its studied blankness mocked me in the mirror.

"Ah, you're expressionless now, but look what you do in company," I said vehemently. My face raised an eyebrow and smiled at me sarcastically. I slapped it hard. It seemed surprised. I slapped it again on the other cheek. The face tried to cry, but I forced it not to. The face struggled against my will.

"We shall see who is in charge," I said, scratching my forehead with my nails. I rubbed dust from the floorboards on my cheeks, and rubbed my eyes until they were swollen and heavy-ridded with irritation. "Who do you think you are?" I shouted.

The face glared back at me undecided.

"You're nobody. You're nothing! You couldn't exist without me. Do you know what you're made of? Flotsam and jetsam! Those eyelids that you blink so coyly are made from my thigh. The bridge of your nose is a rib. My rib. And those lips you smirk with, well, I have a shock for you, Miss Sultry Pout. They're made of labia majora... and... and..."

The face stopped smirking. We stared at each other for what seemed like a very long time. As the room darkened the sunset was our only witness. I had won. The face agreed to behave, to allow me to choose our responses and choreograph our various truths.

My life settled into a routine. I found a modest position as a window-dresser for a group of dress shops. Hoping that it might be contagious, they hired me because I had known fame. Even though I recognised that I was more comfortable with mannequins than with people, thoughts of marriage lurked in my mind. I met and discarded several men who wished to be my lovers. My fierce new passions shocked them. I could no longer lie still, white and supine, legs stretched to receive the Divine Male Sacrament. After years of enforced immobility, I craved movement – and lots of it

"Of course we want you to respond," they said reproachfully, "but respond, not take over the whole act like the only tour guide at the Sistine Chapel. Be active by all means. But in response. In response!"

I wanted to speak my love, with my newly flexible and inventive lips, shout a language of cock and cunt, ovary and testicle, sperm and egg, drop the artifice of the artificial and artful woman, break all the pedestals, erase the pure holy high, redeem vaginas from the smell of rosewater and herbs, educate them in the subtle scent of the ocean, share the violent sacredness of the cave that gives birth to the world and know at last the language of that mute mouth, engulfing and exuding without explanation or permission.

Through the grapevine I heard that the Poet was to give a reading at an embassy. A new poem. The Mask of Troy! (He was one of those artists doomed to repeat himself, forever circling his limited vision, swept up by the applause of a baffled public. If it was incomprehensible it must be good!)

I wanted him to see the new me. I planned a seduction of fire and passion that would sweep him into love's oblivion, if only for an evening. Perhaps I might inspire another epic: The Rape of Orpheus.

I laid my trap. Prepared the nest. Bought a Chinese robe and arranged my hair in the way he loved. Blue and violet maquillage on my cheeks and eyes, subtle hints of violet, purple, a reminder of the beloved colours of Her face. A topography of desire.

My face ached from smiling as the afternoon dragged on. After drinking too many cups of coffee I began to bite my nails. My plan must work. I would surprise him. He would love me. The trapped man that struggled beneath the public image was about to be set free. His disease? Perhaps it was in remission? (Exactly what was it anyway?) I had never asked. I would be his Promethea, offering flame while a slow circling of hawks rose to the sun. Our love a prayer to the sun! We were to be eagles that would fly together! My lips trembled. I was overwhelmed by the magnificence of my vision.

The reception was crowded. I was suitably late. The lobby was full, but I could hear his voice, his dark significant voice laughingtalkingtalkinglaughing in the centre of the crowd. The Most Famous Painter was holding court on the balcony at the far end of the hall, The Famous Buttocks resting on the palm of his left hand.

I wasn't recognised. People blocked my way unaware that I, too, had been one of the stars, had been a The, had set the trends they still followed.

I saw Her face before I saw his. She was facing me. Shock waves coursed through me in ripples, small electricities in my fingertips. I had not expected face to Face. She was still beautiful. In fact, She seemed younger than before, Her eyes brighter, deeper. I saw with a shock that Her mouth had been altered. It was red, and seemed wounded. Her cheekbones were higher and Her double nose more aquiline. What were these rosy tones and yellows, green? And Her hair! Not my smooth and glossy black of the past. Short, spiky, dyed eccentrically, She was punk, She was glitter! She had succumbed to other people's trends.

Angrily, I pushed my way through the crowd, until I stood next to Her. O Travesty of Travesties! She had the body of a man, just a boy, really. Slim angular breastless, he turned this way and that in shy mockery of Her womanhood. The flash of bulbs. Now this way. Now that. Hands on hips, legs braced wide, now a quick pirouette, hips thrust forward again, his genitals outlined against gold net tights. He seemed uncomfortable. Obviously an actor paid for the part, he staggered under the weight of Her face. I suspected that he was drugged.

The Poet, his hand protectively on his shoulder, steadying him seemed happier than before. He laughed, flexing his strong neck and baring white teeth. His faun in the forest pose, his innocent satyr.

She seemed distant. I can't say that She seemed happier. I stood close and watched without speaking. I didn't reveal myself. I became a stranger.

Perhaps I walked home. Or maybe ran. It was raining and I remember the water pouring into my mouth and eyes. I could feel the blue and violet streaks on my cheeks, and my hair clinging. I passed out. And slept. I woke on the floor still in the artful trap of the Chinese robe. Tears. A walk. Tea. A semblance of composure. Another walk. The evening paper.

The evening paper – Arts Section. A large photo, almost a quarter page. The three of them stood close together, locked in tableaux.

The Poet's head tossed back, showing the long neck, the gleam of saliva on the strong feral teeth; the great god Pan caught in flight (his favourite image of himself). She stood next to him. The face that all men love.

Calm, impassive, She surveyed the homage due. But Her body was a fake, twisted and contorted so that ultimately only She was real.

Next to them stood a woman. Stood, did I say? She seemed to claw the air for support. She was ugly, jaw slack, eyes half-closed in disbelief. She suffered; any fool could see that she suffered. No guile here. She was open, naked in her love and foolish hope. A needy hopeless unattractive woman caught in her moment of thwarted desire.

"Not at all nice," I could hear my mother's voice saying, "not nice, Jamila."

I knew what I must do. I gathered weapons.

I destroyed the face that, unable to lie, betrayed me with the truth. I killed the face that could not learn to cajole, coerce or manipulate. I broke the nose that forswore hypocrisy preferring honour to love. I murdered that arrogant autonomous face. I erased my enemy: myself.

The face felt no pain, and if it did it could not cry out. The face could no longer tell, it could not see without my permission. I allowed it no freedom of choice.

My lover came to the hospital to see me, braving the blood, the bandages and smells from the dying man down the hall.

"My love...," he said. "All this for me... for Us... I am so proud... your dear pain is precious. If we have not pain then what are we? It is only through pain that we mortals know existence."

I raised my arm in an attempt to save his delicate poetic sensibilities from the sight of tubes and bloody bandages. But my lover took my hands and held them tightly, looking deep into the holes where my eyes might be.

"Close your eyes, my love." I closed my eyes, and heard a rustle of paper.

The familiar smell of newly sanded wood, the sweet pungency of fresh oils, the suddenly remembered pressure of Her gold cords tightening behind my head. Her dark heaviness.

"You can open now," he said.

Her face in the mirror. Her own dear, dear indigos. Her range of tender blues. Her shy lavender smile. (A partially erased smudge of yellow and green reminded.)

We stared at each other; betrayer and betrayed.

His eyes oblique slits of pleasure, my lover kissed the mask and watched his own passion growing in the mirror. He smiled, noting how full his lips seemed, how manly the curve of his chin. Between coquettish glances, he pressed hard kisses on Her lips. But the bandages layered between us pressed harder on mine.

Under the increasing pressure my face moved and was heard to sigh. My eyes saw the mask in the mirror – all beauty; perfection realised. My slashed eyelids quivered rebelliously, and the corners of my mouth pushed outward in protest. Nose, eyebrows, curve of the cheek and even the cleft in my chin gathered themselves in structural solidarity. Small indistinct muscles rippled slowly then more rapidly, like the surface of the ocean when a storm is imminent.

My face was real. I could feel it. A face that belonged for the first time wholly to itself, defining its own aesthetic. Witness to the witness.

Yes. I saw him kiss Her in the tilted mirror, and his false shy smile.

"In dark, reflective pools I see Thine own dear face revealed..." he intoned, staring down at Her as if hearing an answer. We stared back. Rage rose in my belly like a bad fish dinner. And after a moment of brief dark reflection, it was only She who kissed him back. I wrenched my head from Her tightening cords, and left Her in his hands.

Bandaged tightly from head to toe in thin white gauze, I twisted and writhed on the narrow bed until finally I fell heavily to the floor. There among the dustballs and gumwrappers under the bed I tore at the bandages with my teeth chewing my way to freedom from the inside out. Biting through a world, spitting out my prison. By my side, dancing in circles, my lover kissed a mask in a mirror.

At last, free, naked, I ran to the open window and jumped clumsily onto the sill. My toes clenched rough grey concrete, as with knuckles whitening I tried to keep my balance. Arms outstretched, palms out, my fingertips grazed the walls. A light wind on my body dappled my skin with leaf shadows. Below me, a flower bed lay radiant, perfumed.

Turning slowly in the summer light, I unfolded damp, heavy wings, and shook them to iridescence. Then, leaping into glory, I began my flight to the sun.

GROUND NO MORE
Hwee Hwee Tan

Hwee Hwee Tan was born in 1974 in Singapore, and arrived in England via the Netherlands. She read English Literature at the Universities of East Anglia and Oxford, where she also tutored. Her stories have been broadcast by the BBC and published in PEN International, Critical Quarterly and New Writing 6. Her first novel 'Foreign Bodies' will be published this summer.

"*WAH-LEOW*," LOONG SWORE, "THE GROUND NO more man."

Gone was the white flash of concrete in the sun. Instead, a hole exposed the grey jagged underbelly of the pavement.

"*Ai-ya* I tell you if we were in Singapore this kind of thing won't happen." My father shook his head. "All these Dutch pavements, so lousy."

Spontaneously collapsing pavements were one of the many things we got used to after KLM posted my father to their head office in Den Haag. As a huge chunk of Dutch soil is reclaimed land, the earth beneath our feet used to be formless sea, and thus liable to crumble at unexpected moments.

"This cat was just walking along you know," my brother Loong said, "Then the pavement suddenly pah-boom! The cat fell in – splat! Like pancake. Good show, man."

"Cat?" I ran outside. I lifted the cat from the hole. My fingers felt the throb of its heart beneath the brown fur.

"The cat not dead," I said. "Just unconscious."

"I take care of the cat," Loong said.

"Yah, like you take care of my Snoopy – with a knife. I take the cat to the vet."

"Pa, tell her give me the cat," Loong said to my father. "I need the cat for my A-level biology experiment."

"Give cat to Loong," my father said. "It's only a stray."

I pressed the cat against my chest. Its warm breath brushed my face.

My brother grinned. Then he told my father the magic words that would persuade any Singaporean parent to let their child get away with murder – "If you give me the cat for experiment, it'll help my biology marks a lot."

Singaporeans are obsessed with grades. Take that fifteen year old, leukaemia-stricken boy who was given a full page spread in our national newspaper, the *Straits Times*. In other countries, if you're a kid dying of a terminal disease, you do interesting things e.g. try to break a world record by collecting the most get-well cards, or meet Michael Jackson.

Does the Singaporean boy take this golden opportunity to do any of the above, before he snuffs it?

No.

Instead, he studies his butt off for his O-levels. He achieves six A1s, but doesn't live to see it.

What's the use of ten O-levels once you're six feet under?

My parents don't understand, for they believed that there was a positive correlation between moral fibre and good grades.

So although my brother was a cancerous polyp on the anus of humanity, when my parents looked at him – he was mainly glasses and freckles – they saw a cross between Einstein and Francis of Assisi.

So my father pried open my arms, took the cat, and gave it to my brother.

My brother was my parents' *Loong* – their dragon. He was the strong, smart and charismatic child who would fly to the top.

They named me *Piao Piao* – 'Pretty Pretty'.

The less said about that the better.

My parents let their dragon get away with anything. When I was four, Loong's favourite game was to turn off the light when I was in the bathroom.

"Toilet monster going to eat you girl," Loong said. "His claws going to burst out of toilet bowl, grab your buttock and drag you down to hell."

I jumped off the toilet seat. My panties dangling at my feet. Loong pointed at my vagina and laughed.

Things changed when I was seven, after I attended the Methodist Girls' Primary School in Singapore. Every assembly, the chaplain would deliver a short sermon. One day he spoke about the armour of God – the shield of faith that blocked the flaming darts of the Devil, and the sword of the Spirit – the Word of God, sharper than any two-edged sword.

So the next time I went to the bathroom, I took a Bible with me. When Loong switched off the light, I sat down on the floor and pressed the Bible close to my chest.

Loong switched on the light. His dark brown rubber flip-flops slapped against the wet floor, leaving a trail of black footprints on the white tiles.

He grabbed my Bible and hit me across the face with it. It jerked my head around hard.

My face felt hot and large.

I clasped my hands, waiting for the next blow.

"Not bad, not bad. Good stuff," Loong stuck up his thumb in approval. "Love suffers long. Gooooood Christian."

He giggled. His hand swept and knocked my head to the other side. "You sit here. We going to have big fun later on." Loong left the bathroom.

My face felt thick, hot and awkward. I went to the sink and bathed my face in cold water.

The flush had gone from my left cheek but it looked a little swollen.

I sat back down on the floor. My skirt soaked up the water from the cold tiles. I shivered.

I pinched my nose to block the smell of urine. We were poor in those days, and to save money, my parents commanded us to flush the toilet only after every third use.

Loong came back with my Snoopy and a knife.

As I said, back then in Singapore, we were poor. We didn't have a proper lamp in the bathroom like we do now. All we had was an orange lightbulb that hung from a cord. The bulb swayed while the knife sliced through the air.

I brought Snoopy's shreds to my father. "I want you to kill Loong."

My father laughed. "Don't be stupid. Snoopy so old, falling apart anyway. Tomorrow I bring you to Toys 'R' Us, buy you new Snoopy, okay?"

A month before the pavement collapsed, my father announced that the Lim family was also moving from Singapore to Den Haag.

Charlie was Mr Lim's son. He wanted to join the FBI or the CIA when he grew up, thus he chose an appropriately American name for himself.

I never knew anyone who wanted to be American so badly.

Charlie was a total Walter Mitty type. When we shared a room with Charlie during our vacation at Pasir Ris, Charlie woke up at four a.m. shouting, "Battlestations! Buck Rogers reporting – Wilma, get those starboard lasers ready!"

One afternoon, when he was eleven, Charlie spent two hours tailing three cyclists.

"Wah, just like in 'Hardy Boys'," Charlie said. "You know those people who hire bicycles from East Coast Park? They not supposed to take bike out of the park you know." (We lived in an apartment that was across the park) "I saw three boys riding bicycles on our estate. Their bicycles got East Coast Park logo. So I follow them."

"So what? You make citizen's arrest?" Loong said.

"No. I saw them ride into the underpass to the park. Which mean they hire bike from the park. My suspicion correct! No need to follow them anymore."

My brother laughed.

Charlie smiled. "I was good huh? They never knew I was behind them."

Now to understand the full impact of what my brother said, you have to realize that back in the Seventies in Singapore, profanity was not widespread. Back in those days, you didn't say "shit" or "damn" until you were sixteen.

So Charlie is swelling with pride, and Loong keeps laughing. Then he says, "You know what? You're one pathetic mother-fucker."

However, Loong was the Head Prefect, and received at least four book prizes annually, so his words only made Charlie want to gain Loong's approval even more.

*

When we went to the Lim's house-warming party to welcome them to Den Haag, Charlie was constantly at Loong's side, making sure his glass was filled with Pepsi.

"Charlie, you going study at the British School or not?" Loong asked.

Loong put his hand over his glass as Charlie tried to fill it with Pepsi. "You got vodka?"

Charlie shook his head.

"In Holland men don't drink sissy thing like Pepsi. I bet you never drink vodka before."

Charlie went red. "Of course I have."

"I bet you're still a virgin."

Thus began my brother's campaign to make Charlie a *gei angmo* – a fake Caucasian.

Europe, Loong told Charlie, was a place where academic excellence and ethics had gone out of style, where it was good to be bad, and you cultivated decadence until it blossomed into sophistication.

So like Loong, Charlie got his ears pierced. Like Loong, he wore torn Levi jackets, peered through his Ray-Bans, and slouched around with a Marlboro in his mouth.

At night, they went to Loong's lab in the garden shed, where they tried to grow marijuana. They smoked pot, popped E, and got stoned on electric jelly and hash cakes. They were bad. They became European. Gone were the Singaporean, bespectacled, calculator-punching, aspiring engineer types. They were lean, mean, Continental machines.

Two days after Loong took the cat from the pavement, Charlie ran out of the garden shed, leaving a trail of vomit in his wake.

My brother laughed. "Charlie's frightened about my biology experiment in the shed."

"What happened?" I asked.

"Nothing. I just skinned the cat, took the flesh off, reconstructed the bone structure. Great experiment. I'll get an A, sure thing."

"Make sure that you burn the carcass," my father said. "If not neighbour come here and complain about the smell."

*

A week later, Loong performed another experiment in the shed, mixing Fanta orange with methylated spirits. He told Charlie that the drink was a cheap and legal way of getting high.

My father looked out of the window at the flashing lights on the police car. "I tell you if we were in Singapore this kind of thing won't happen."

Loong told the police he was sorry. He was a victim of his environment, he said. He had been nipped from the shelter of Eastern values in Singapore, and thrown into a decadent Western society, where if you got good grades, you were labelled a dork, nerd or swot. You had to prove that you were tough through drink and drugs.

The red light from the police car flashed outside my bedroom window.

Two months ago, orange hazard lights flashing outside my window kept me awake all night, for immediately after we reported the broken pavement, fixit men rumbled up with their cement truck, blocked off the hole with red-and-white striped tape, and surrounded the gap with the orange hazard lights. They fixed the hole with the quick efficiency of the experienced, like men used to patching up spontaneously disintegrating pavements. When dawn broke, the hole was filled.

After Charlie died, Loong threw himself into studying for his A-levels, and my parents never mentioned the incident again. My brother had patched up his 'accident' as quickly as the fixit men.

In the morning after the men had repaired the hole, my father walked onto the pavement, and stood there for ten minutes. I waited at the doorstep. "Everything okay," he said. He stamped his foot on the ground.

I knew better. After the ground collapsed, stepping out of the house became a great leap of faith. But after a while I pretended that the ground was a firm foundation, a solid rock. Similarly, my parents pretended that Loong was fine, that his good education gave him a concrete moral base.

Even if you can't trust the ground beneath your feet, you have to pretend that you can. You can't think of how you could suddenly be walking on air. If you did, you would never step out of the house. Staying in the house wouldn't help either, 'cos God knows, the house may collapse on you. You can't live life with that kind of fear.

Believing in Loong's explanation was like filling the broken ground with sticks, straws and stones. I told my parents about the true Rock, the cornerstone that was rejected. They wouldn't listen to me. Education was my parents' foundation. They knew no other ground to walk on.

It was the anniversary of Charlie's death last week. Loong had moved to England to read biology at Cambridge.

Everyone still believes that the boy who got all As for his chemistry, physics and biology exams, wasn't smart enough to think that orange juice and methylated spirits would get someone high.

Loong was smart enough. Smart enough to persuade Charlie to drink the lethal concoction. "Drink it," Loong must have told Charlie, "Everybody's doing it." I could imagine Loong standing over Charlie's corpse, laughing, like he did always. "So stupid," he probably said.

"Trying to get high. You're one pathetic fucker."

On my way to school, I bought five different publications.

During lunch, I walked to a coffee-shop near our school. I cut the first letter – a 'M' from *Haagsche Courant*, the second letter, a 'U' from *GQ*, the third, sixth and eighth letter 'R' from *Der Spiegel*, the fourth letter 'D' from *Rolling Stone* and the fifth and seventh letter 'E' from *OK!*. I pasted the 4x2 letters on a postcard.

I sucked my cigarette. It finished burning, and I put it out amid the shells of the pistachio.

I tore the postcard and threw the shreds into the ashtray. I sent Loong lilies instead. The card attached said, "Charlie's still dead. As always, I think of you."

Loong sent me a card with Snoopy thanking me for the flowers.

Outside, the white pavement shone like burning magnesium in the summer light. I squinted at the ground, searching for cracks, but I found none. The light bounced off the ground that burnt as white, as solid, as concrete as it did the day before it collapsed.

OFFICER
SHENSTONE'S
NIGGER
R. D. Galbraith

R. D. Galbraith was born in Glasgow in 1965 and educated at the University of St Andrews. He currently lives in Reading and has completed his first collection of short stories.

SHENSTONE MUST HAVE SEEN THAT NIGGER FROM THE bar. That was where he always stood at that time of the day on that day of the week. After the whole thing was over I had a word with Israel to see if I could squeeze anything out of him – you know, to see if Shenny was acting strange that day, if there was something out of the ordinary. Of course, the man was born useless and he couldn't tell me nothing worth listening to. Anyway, Shenny went in to do his duty by way of asking Israel (he's no Sheeny by the way, his mother just liked the sound of the word and didn't know any better), if there was anything he should know about.

"Nope," was what Israel said. "Ain't no trouble here Shenny." Israel could get a little familiar sometimes, but Shenstone knew an idiot when he saw one and never let it bother him.

Let it also be said (although I hasten to say I had a high regard for the man), that the brevity of Israel's reply never stopped our good Officer Shenstone from accepting the free beer which, if he waited long enough (and he usually did), was always offered.

I'd often watched him there. He had some style, no end of little ways about him, but always the same. There was a reliable feel to the man. I can see him as if he was standing there now, drinking his beer and drawing the first finger of his hand across his mouth to draw a little mustache of foam off. He was a quiet man, would never speak if it wasn't necessary. He'd just stand there and think his thoughts and watch himself in the mirror. His father (it was even before my time), had been a schoolteacher, and some folks seemed to think he'd come down in the world. Another thing; he'd never married, or not by that stage anyhow. That was a puzzle to some people, for Shenstone was a fine looking man.

And so on that day he must have looked to his left, creasing up his eyes at the hot brightness of the early afternoon beyond the bar-room window and seen that damn nigger just sitting on the sidewalk, up to no good.

"Israel," said Officer Shenstone. "You seen that boy before?"

"Nope," said Israel, twisting a linen cloth into the bottom of a glass. Then came one of those occasions, all entirely accidental so far as anybody has ever been able to work out, on which Israel said something meaningful: "He don't belong here."

With two inches of beer left Shenstone scowled out at the nigger, willing him to stand up and walk away. It had been weeks since his job had actually forced him to do something and this wasn't the right day to end the run of good luck. This period of peace had been earned by him sending the last nigger out of town with a lump on the back of his head the size of a Grade A goose egg. Even so, as Shenny well knew, such stories faded quickly from niggerdom's collective memory and frequent refreshers were by far the easiest way of keeping the town decent.

With nothing but a couple of slips of foam left in the bottom of his glass, Officer Shenstone stuck his thumb in his belt and walked out of the bar. He crossed the street and planted his shiny boots right under that nigger's nose, but he wouldn't move a muscle. We all thought there was going to be trouble right away. Shenny was a man with a reputation after all. All he could see of that nigger was the back of his woolly head staring down at the dirt, so dusty it was like an old man's, and his shoulders, powerful already although he was hardly more than a boy. No shoes and a pair of dungarees with more holes than threads in them. Shenny gave him a good kick on the shin and told him:

"I'm talking to you, boy."

The boy looked up, creasing his face up in the glare and seeing Shenstone's great black form, standing there like he was God Almighty himself. Alec and I had just come out of Miller's (we'd been fixing the fan there), so we stopped under the shade of the awning to watch the proceedings. Still the nigger said nothing and I thought; boy, you're going to get it carrying on like that. You're going to get it good and hard. I could see Shenny's fingers itching around the handle of his billy. I could almost feel that bump rising on the back of my own head.

Shenny knew we were watching by then. He turned a bit and glared at us like we were going to be next. His shirt was sticking to him and his face was red as a bitch baboon's ass.

"Where you from, boy?"

The nigger just put his head down again and stared at the street. I thought he was going to get it there and then, but at the last moment he had the sense to point up the street and say:

"That way."

"Well thank you, sir. That's an answer to my question that is. You'll tell me where you're from if you know what's good for you, boy."

The nigger pointed up the street again, like this was his own town:

"That way, about twenty miles. More maybe, I dunno. From Stenton." He settled his head down again between his knees.

Shenstone looked about himself: "Is there another nigger here, boy, or are you talking to me?"

"Stenton, sir," said the nigger.

"'Swat I thought you said. Now tell me boy, what's stopping you from going back there?"

Again he was asking for it. He said nothing, just put his head down and clasped his hands around the back of his neck. Alec was laughing and called out to Shenstone:

"Do your duty, Shenny!" but he just ignored him.

The nigger wouldn't say a word. A full half minute passed without a sound. It was like a photograph; the nigger crouching on the sidewalk, his bare feet on the burning street, Shenstone standing there with his hands on his belt, pouring with sweat, waiting for an answer, Alec and me leaning in the shade outside

187

Miller's waiting for the action. Then there was this noise like nothing I'd ever heard before, like halfway between some hound howling and some sort of siren. The sound began to break up into huge gasping sobs, and then we realised. He was crying. Weeping like a child, curling himself up like he was trying to disappear, his whole body jerking. We could hear Shenny starting to curse and blaspheme and look up and down the street like he wanted to be sure there was no one there. Apart from us four, it seemed that the whole world had died of the heat, and we could hear every word that was said.

"Listen boy, I'm not going to have some nigger bum salting the streets of this town d'you hear?" We could see that he was trying to be quiet, but it was no use. He wailed like an animal with its leg in a gin. All Shenny had to do was book him for vagrancy and run him out of town with a lump on his head, same as the last one. God knows what he was thinking of, but whatever it was, that was when the whole business started. I still can't understand it; it was all so unnecessary.

He said to the nigger: "Can you work, boy?"

I guess we were all about as surprised as each other. It certainly shut the boy up. It took him a good while (and he wasn't the only one), to realise that Shenstone was actually offering him something. He wiped his face with his forearms and stood up, tall enough to look Shenstone in the eye.

"Yessir," he said, loud and clear. "I can work. I'm willing, sir."

"Well," said Shenstone, "you can't go near decent folks smelling like that. Follow me." The nigger trooped after him like he was his foreman, round towards the railway depot.

That was the last I saw of him till the whole business was over. The rest I pieced together from talking to folks in the town. Shenstone took him to the back of the depot where there was an old standpipe and no ladies. He told the nigger to strip off and wash himself with the water from the standpipe. He did as he was told, meek as a lamb, while Jack and a couple of the other railway boys looked on from the staff rooms over the way. Shenstone disappeared and came back a few minutes later with a loaf and a couple of red apples he'd presumably bought in Miller's. He found his nigger standing there, naked, drying himself in the sun, told him sharpish to get his clothes on, gave him the bread and apples and left again, telling him that if he moved from that spot he'd give him ten days in the cells and a lesson he'd never forget.

In the half hour he was gone he crossed the town, went up the hill and called at the Athlone house. By that time it was already getting a bit seedy, but I remember it in its heyday. It was the widow Athlone's father who first made the money and had the house built before the first war as a retreat from the city. The place was run almost like a colony. All sorts of finery would come down from the north to spend the vacations (they were the sort of people who had vacations), with the Athlone's and for a month the place was like a Broadway show. Then some more money would have to be made and the house would be shut up for most of the rest of the year.

The present Mrs Athlone and her husband began to make more frequent use of the house and when he died she sold up in New York and came down here to settle. A strange decision in a way, and she's always been some way apart from the rest of the town. Of course that never stopped her from ruling the place; chairwoman of the Woman's Voluntary Committee, coordinator of this appeal or that, first port of call for the nearest Democrat. Never had much to do with the woman myself, all I know is that a few years back she was unwell and little of her has been seen since then. The house was let slip and the servants became a little free with what was left of the Athlone fortune.

Only the doctor was seeing her regular then, and after the dust had settled I got the story from him. It seems that Shenstone never intended to see Mrs. Athlone herself. She still kept a gardener then and he was the man he was after. He went to the outhouses to find him but before too long was accosted by one of the house staff and told that "Mrs. Athlone would see him now." I laughed when I heard that. That was the widow Athlone alright, that was her through and through. So what could he do?

He was shown into the ballroom which I guess hasn't been danced on in a generation. Apparently it was all but empty; just one small corner by the window at the side which was furnished like an old-fashioned parlour. From there Mrs. Athlone could look down the driveway and watch the comings and goings, including Shenstone's coming. It seems they got off on the wrong foot from the very start. Shenstone explained (or made up as the case may be), the idea that he had heard of some work that needed doing about the place and that he had a young man who needed a few dollars worth to pay his way back home.

"I can't imagine why you have heard that, Mr Shenstone. I gave no such instructions."

Shenstone explained that he'd heard it from the gardener.

"And did you think that I employ a gardener to make decisions for me?" Shenstone said he was sure she didn't, he must have been mistaken, excused himself and was on his way out when Mrs. Athlone decided she was interested after all. She had little enough human contact then and I reckon she wasn't about to let go of it whether she liked the sound of it or not.

"What sort of young man," she asked.

"Just a young man down on his luck," said Shenstone. "A young man who needs to make an honest dollar or two to pay his way back home."

"A young man you would prefer to get out of town, Mr Shenstone?"

"I think that's what we'd all prefer, mam. I just thought there might be another way of doing it. If there's any work to be done I thought it might be convenient. I understood you had, well, social interests."

This irritated her no end; "presumption" she called it, "height of presumption."

"A young man, you say."

"That's right, mam. A young, man." That was the only way Shenstone described him. The doctor said she seemed obsessed by this, went on and on about it like he'd lied to her. They were a sly pair, I'll say that. Then Mrs Athlone started to worry about the money.

"I am expected to facilitate this young man's departure?"

"It's normal to pay a man for his work, mam, but I wouldn't want to impose. If you can oblige with some work then I'll put something aside and you can decide later what it's worth."

She just turned round and returned to her gazing out the window, dismissing Shenstone with the opinion that if he thought it was wise he could tell his young man to come and talk to her gardener. And that's how they parted, I suppose with some sort of an understanding but exactly what wasn't easy to say.

Shenstone walked back to the centre of town, leaving a five dollar bill on the salver in the hall as he left. When he got back behind the railway depot he found his nigger there squatting in a patch of shade, apples and bread gone, sleeping like a dog. The boys in the staff room were a few hands further on, but otherwise hadn't moved from the table by the window. He gave him a vicious kick, waking him with a jolt.

"You don't smell much better, do you boy?" The nigger stood up smartly and looked Shenstone in the eye.

"I've got a chance for you if you're willing to take it."

"Yes, sir."

"Let's make sure we understand one another first. This town isn't a charity. You get a few dollars-worth of work and you use it to get out of here, to go back where you came from or wherever you like. No one here will care. Got it?"

"Yes sir," said the nigger, "I understand."

"Follow me," said Shenstone and off they trooped up to the Athlone house.

When they got there the gardener had been spoken to by Mrs. Athlone and everything seemed straightforward. One of the sheds by the side of the house had a heap of raw wood in it from trees in the grounds that had been blown down in the big storm the year before. The gardener handed over an axe you could have shaved with, told the nigger to heave that wood out, put it on the block and get choppping. I never heard any complaints from the gardener. It was a day to sweat your life out just standing still, but he never stopped. After a while he just rolled his dungarees down to his waist and kept on going till sundown. Doctor told me that Mrs. Athlone never took her eyes off him. She must have sat by that window a third of the day, her face white as death, just watching that axe rising and falling like it was part of some machine. Before the end he must have disappeared behind the pile of chopped wood with Mrs. Athlone just sitting in the gloom listening. I was up there myself some weeks later or I wouldn't have believed it. The gardener swore that no one had touched the pile since that night. There was one last thing that capped the whole business. By the time it was full night they had to tell him to stop, but they wouldn't give him his money. They told him to come back the next day to finish the job and then he'd get his bill. I don't take sides in these matters, you know that. All the same, it was a mean way to save five dollars.

By the time Shenstone next saw him there was a small crowd there already. It was the sort of news that travels fast. Like the rest I'd heard it on the rumour mill and got there a little before him; I'd been doing a bit of work on that side of the town. They'd done it from the old walnut tree. There was Officer Shenstone's nigger (as he was soon to be known), hanging there from the one big bough that stretches over the water. His head was all cricked to one side, the rough rope cutting into his neck. They'd stripped him naked, cut off his manhood. There were already flies clustering around the wound and on the surface of the river the ripples of a big catfish moving below, stirring up the dirt, smelling his blood. The Sheriff and some of his men were there, standing around. There was even a couple of Feds taking notes and photographs before getting into their fancy car and driving off to make their report.

Shenstone arrived a couple of minutes after I did. I suppose he must have known what to expect; I got the impression he'd had the chance to prepare himself. He had that stiff way of walking like he was about to bang someone on the head as soon as they stepped out of line. He planted his boots in the mud right by the edge, stuck his thumbs in his belt and stared at the nigger without saying a word. The body began to sway a little as a breeze picked up, the rope creaking on the bough. There was a fair amount of business behind him; the Sheriff and his men talking and the growing number of onlookers asking each other to explain the obvious. The Sheriff's men began to go around asking and I told them what Alec and I had seen the day before, which at that time was all I knew. They didn't seem interested, for the very good reason, I suppose, that they already knew about it. Everyone knew about it, but we all wanted to pretend otherwise and Shenstone's frozen, silent back was making it more difficult by the minute. Before long an itchy silence settled over us and people began to move away. Others who hadn't seen the show yet, looked from a distance but didn't come right down to the bank. One of the Sheriff's men crawled along the walnut bough and cut the rope, another waded in to grab the end and pull the body in, yanking it onto the mud like he was pulling a boat up a beach. He let it drop just a few feet from where Shenny was standing. He turned with nothing in his face, just nothing and walked out of there without a sound, without a look in the eye for any of us.

Now I don't know if this is true, but it don't take much to believe it. The word was that a few days later Shenny received an envelope from the Athlone house. From Mrs. Athlone, I suppose, though there was no name, no letter, just a five dollar bill.

Well, it was never the same for Shenstone after that. Within a few weeks most us weren't ever to see him again. I caught sight of him once, years later, in the city. He was still in uniform, still looking a fine man, but he wouldn't look at me. A lot of people could never quite forgive him for what he did. It came as a terrible shock to some to realise that a man in whom they had put their trust could be so... how to put it?

So unsound.

IT'S CALLED EVIL
Susan Smith Barrie

Susan Smith Barrie was born in Massachusetts and has lived in England, France and Ireland where she graduated from Trinity College, Dublin with a BA. Her short stories have been published in New Woman and have won prizes in competition with the Writer's Bureau and Sunk Island International.

IT IS A COOL JANUARY MORNING AND MOLLY EBT IS hanging out her washing. Last week's snows have given way to an unseasonal warmth. Molly knew it would be a good day for drying outside. There was a robin sitting on her bedroom window ledge when she woke. She rolled over to tap her husband. "Look at that," she said dreamily, her fingers bouncing off Jeff's bony shoulder. "A robin. It must be good weather."

There's just enough of a breeze to make the hanging sleeves of Jeff's work shirt wave. Molly is a crazy sight – so says her neighbour, Mrs. Richard Stedman, who can't help noticing everything that goes on next door – her corkscrew curls stand out at right angles, her dressing gown hangs open. She has a short, satin night shirt on underneath, but this is baldly offset by a stout pair of rubber boots.

"And that child," Mrs Richard Stedman, née Elda Evert, exclaims to her coffee pot.

That child being young Will Ebt, all two years and twenty six inches of him. He is busy crawling around his mother's rubber-booted feet, waiting for the moment in which a clothes pin will slip from his mother's basket. Will thinks clothes pins come from Heaven – he hasn't reached the stage where he will look up and see

195

that their source is much more earthly. But for the moment he is content to accept that everything that lands before him has some higher origin. He has already been told that God is great and God is good. It is his infant's presumption that God is also a master carver of wooden clothes pins.

They make a pretty picture, Jeff Ebt thinks, as he sees his wife and child from the bathroom window. He's all lathered up and razor-ready, but he holds back on the hot tap for a moment. Just another moment to watch his family. Molly dressed like a vagrant, save for the flashes of short, expensive satin whenever the wind catches the edges of the ragged, old bathrobe. Will scrambling around the damp ground like an earnest adventurer. Each clothes pin that falls before him is treated with surprised reverence. It makes Jeff's heart swell in his chest. I helped create this scene, he thinks. I was at the origin of this moment.

Elda Stedman ducks when Molly turns her way. She knows that she has been seen, but there's something in her blood that stops her from doing something benign, like waving. It's been that way ever since the Ebts took the house next door. No neighbourliness. Just surveillance.

We really should be friends, Elda thinks. We could have coffee together in the mornings. Jeff and Richard could discuss the price of mulch or whatever it is they both spread on the lawns in the warmer months. We could take turns watching each other's houses whenever someone goes away. I could babysit. Richard could help Jeff put up one of those clothes lines that attaches directly onto the back porch. Then she wouldn't have to be out there in her smalls. And those men's boots. With her hair all over the place and her little boy rooting around in the dirt like a piglet.

As a blackness buzzes around Elda Stedman's heart, half a world away an anti-personnel missile slams into an apartment building in Grozny.

At the same moment, Jeff Ebt is drawing the razor across his stubbled chin. His fingers slip on the excess of shaving foam, and for a moment the plastic razor he filched from Molly's side of the bathtub nips malignly at the vein running over the edge of his jaw. Sheer chance saves Jeff from what he will later call "my very close shave". He has heard something, an unidentifiable noise, and has turned his face at the exact moment the razor was about to slit his vein wide open. There's a nick, though. Just a small slice into the rough skin which puckers and oozes a tiny red dribble in the white foam on his face.

"Did you say something?" Jeff is running out of the house as he shouts this. The hot water in the basin had clouded the window, and he suddenly had the back-of-the-neck tingle that something might be wrong outside.

"I think I felt it before I heard it," Molly says, her smile fading. She's fine, just fine, standing there with the washing basket in her arms. Will is fine, too. He's looking at his father with a big question mark screwing up his smooth, undefined features.

"A strange noise," Jeff says, walking over to Molly. "Like a boom."

"A boom?" Molly repeats, as if it's a word she's never heard.

"Like Batman," Jeff mumbles, putting his arms around Molly's waist and pulling her into his chest. "When he's fighting with the bad guys. You see words like 'Boom' and 'Kablamm' written on the screen."

"I never watched it," Molly replies, her voice muffled by Jeff's shoulder. She shivers despite the warmth in the air.

Jeff looks down to see Willy holding up a clothes-pin.

"As long as you're all right," Jeff says.

Molly's answer comes with sudden, and unexpected tears. "I thought it would be warm enough to hang some clothes outside."

Jeff feels her frailty. It squeezes his swelling heart, makes him suddenly wish he could completely enclose Molly, protect her from the very sun that is trying to pierce the incoming cloud.

"I don't know what's happened," Molly whispers into Jeff's ear.

But she's thinking, Something did happen. Something to send a shock wave through their suburban garden and bathroom. Something scary enough to draw Jeff out into the back yard and hold her like the world's about to end.

Elda Stedman, her head a raging hive, knows what it is. She's felt it before. Years before. When a bullet took Kennedy. When her own son lost his life in the Vietnamese jungle. When tanks rolled into Prague. It stayed in her ears like a distant, constant hum throughout the Cold War years. It turned to a thunderclap the day her father died of a heart attack before the ambulance could get to the house.

It's called evil, Elda thinks as her head rages. She would say the word out loud, but the last time she did this she had the sudden, and terrifying sensation that her tongue had turned black.

There's a momentary lull in the hornet's nest. Elda reaches for the cloth hanging behind the sink and holds it under the cold tap. This is a childhood trick, a mother's cure. Hold a cold, damp cloth to the forehead of the aggrieved and count to ten.

"One," Elda gasps. She can see mortar flying, negative images, a coil of angry, black smoke spiralling up into a winter sky.

"Two." There is a sudden silence that can only mean death and destruction.

Three is the aftershock. Four, the realisation of the damage. Five and six, the onset of pain. Seven, suffering. Eight and nine, the long, lung-searing gasp back to life. Ten, the recovery.

Elda wanders across the lawn towards the Ebt family. They are a secure unit of three, the child balanced on his mother's hip, his arms around his father's neck.

Molly sees her coming. She pulls away from Jeff, lets Will slide down to the ground. She sees something dark and troubled in Elda's eyes. Perhaps she knows what's happened.

"Did you hear something?" Molly asks, her voice faltering.

Elda stops mid-stride. A lifetime of visions and humming rush over her like a sharp breeze from the north. She intended to tell the Ebts about the evil thing that has just happened. How they should realise that there's more to this morning than hanging out washing or shaving. How their son should be warned against the folly of putting dirty clothes pins into his mouth.

A blank look crosses Elda's face. She forgets what she's come out here for. There's a man and a woman and a small, dirty child standing before her. They look concerned. They look like they think she's some sort of crazy old woman with a head full of snakes. Or...

"Hornets," Elda says, and sees Jeff flinch.

"I think it was a plane," Jeff says, and puts a protective arm around his wife's waist. "Breaking the sound barrier."

"I heard nothing," Elda says, her voice raised above the hissing noise in her ears.

Molly reaches for Will. "It was more like a sensation."

A damp cuff of one of Jeff's shirts reaches out in the breeze. It touches Elda's shoulder, beckons her back.

"It was evil," Elda shouts, and runs back to her house, her hands pressed against her ears.

Past midnight and Molly is standing over a pan of slowly-heating milk. Sleep has taken leave of her this night, avoiding her side of the bed in favour of Jeff's, laying him out cold before Molly could ask him about the morning's events. Reassurance, then, must come from a saucepan of frothing milk, just as it did years ago when Molly was Will's age.

Nor can Will give comfort. This night he, too, has succumbed to trouble-free sleep. It might just be that he has finally reached the age when he can drop off without tears. Molly has prayed for a night like this for months, but now that she has it, she wishes it was otherwise.

Give me a crying baby or an insomniac husband, Molly thinks. Give me something that makes for more noise and distraction than a pan of boiling milk.

She switches the radio on and the soothing tones of a late-night news bulletin weave around the midnight kitchen. As Molly pours the steaming milk into a mug, she picks out the words 'air strike', 'residential zone' and 'destruction'. She puts her hands around the mug to leech some of its warmth. She glances around at the familiar cabinets and marble counter and feels a tingle of relief that all is still standing.

Something terrible happened on the other side of the world. And here, something drew Mrs Stedman outside, inspired her to say those strange words. Molly leans over the kitchen sink, her eyes closed, and thinks of the exact moment. A vibration had rocked through her. Even Will looked up for a moment, dropped the clothes pin he'd been savouring. And then Jeff came out, his chin bleeding and his eyes full of worry.

It was nothing, Molly thinks. A coincidence. How could an event so far away have repercussions here? Could evil be an airborn particle, something that vibrates through airwaves or atmospheres, disturbing calmer climates, driving old women outside to shout at their neighbours?

Molly opens her eyes and feels sleep pressing on her like a

feather pillow lined with sand. She wants to drop off, to go back upstairs and measure her breaths against Jeff's warm chest. It's just the thought of what she saw. Of the moment when Elda Stedman opened her mouth to say 'evil'. Her tongue looked black.

ENGLISH AS A FOREIGN LANGUAGE
Fiona Curnow

Fiona Curnow is 31, of mixed Celtic background, currently living in Malvern – though imminently returning to Powys – with partner Andy, daughter Rhiannon and cat Marmite. Over the past four years her poetry, short stories and articles have appeared widely in both commercial and small press publications – most successfully in the emerging genre of women's erotica – and she has recently discovered the joys of judging literary competitions. In April 1995 Poetry Life published her first full-length poetry collection 'I Dreamed That Pigeons Came In Every Colour'.

"JESUS GOD!" SHE SNAPPED AS SHE FLICKED OPEN THE passenger door. "You're dripping!"

I cradled my raw thumb absently in my other hand. I'd already spent two hours trying to hitch along this washed-out Cork by-way. From her expression, I might be spending another two.

Then it softened.

"All right, get in. No – wait a moment. I'll just grab you a plastic bag to sit yourself on."

I settled in clammily. She lit another cigarette from the butt smouldering in the graveyard ashtray. As an afterthought she stabbed the pack towards me but I shook my head.

"Where you headed?" she demanded as she crunched the car into gear.

"Baltimore. You know it?"

She snorted through the smoke.

"Pig's arse of a place. Only reason to go there is to catch the ferry." After a moment she added, "So what do they call you then?"

"Pearse," I told her.

I'd become comfortable with the lie. It was the name I always felt I should have been given. It's the name I give to strangers when they've no chance of tracing the thread back and calling me a liar. It's the name I give when I'm creating me.

Her red-shot eyes narrowed as she took another drag – in disapproval or at the smoke I wasn't sure.

"Pearse," she said eventually. "Hope to God you're not one of those seventeenth-generation Yanks come home to trace his Irish roots."

"Can't you tell by the accent? I'm..." I stopped short of saying "I'm English"; it wasn't wrong but it wasn't right, either. "I'm living in Manchester just now. My folks were from Cork city."

"Ah."

She took another drag and there was silence. In her eyes – green, I realised, and they might have been quite stunning if it wasn't for the nicotine – I was probably on a par with that hypothetical American. Eventually, I tried, "Are you from round here?"

She shook her head.

"Dublin. I teach." Then she smirked. "English."

I smiled a little and she continued abrasively, "I suppose that tickles you? You're thinking, 'What's a body like her doing trying to teach the Queen's English?' "

"I wasn't thinking any such thing."

She finally stubbed out her cigarette around Timoleague. But she'd lit another by Clonakilty.

"Does this bother you?" she asked vaguely, waving the hand that was never on the steering wheel.

"A little."

"Tough. Most young people in Ireland smoke. You'd better get used to it."

I shrugged.

"If you're staying of course," she continued. "But you're not. Your type never do."

I sat there and took it. I know what you're thinking: what man would? But I was in her car. I wasn't dry and I wasn't warm but at least I wasn't getting any wetter. And the sign we'd just passed said twenty somethings to Baltimore – miles or kilometres, in Ireland you can never quite be sure.

Suddenly, after a quarter of an hour of fields and nothing moving but pissed-off cows, there was a sign for a pub. One-handed still, she swung the car roughly round to park in front of it.

"My belly thinks my throat's been cut," she explained. "We can get some bread and soup or something here."

"I'm paying," I said automatically because I had a feeling she expected me to. "It's the least I can do – for the lift."

"Okay, big fella. I'm not arguing."

The bar was empty. Cold Formica tables and a TV in one corner tuned to satellite sports with the sound turned down. As we waited for bowls of microwaved canned soup she chuckled and said, "So what did you expect – the fucking Murphy's ad?"

"Am I that transparent?"

She nodded and blew smoke down her nose.

"You never told me your name," I prompted after the soup arrived, hoping it had put her in a better mood.

"Paula," she replied.

But she'd hesitated a moment before saying it, much as I'd hesitated before saying "Pearse". She grinned then and we both knew it hadn't gone unnoticed. Such are the signs by which we liars find each other out.

"So what's for you in Baltimore?" she asked.

"Like you said – catching the ferry."

"Well it can't be the language school – must be birdies."

"Pardon?"

"Folks only go to Cape Clear Island for two reasons: the Gaelic summer school or the bird sanctuary."

"Perhaps I just wanted to make the trip."

She looked at me and said nothing. Despite the strangeness of her look, I raised something that had been troubling me.

"How far along the road can you take me?"

"Till you really piss me off."

"Listen, Paula, I'm bursting. If I nip out for a leak, what are the chances you won't have done a runner by the time I get back?"

"About even, I'd say. But I'll tell you something for nothing." She looked at her almost-empty glass. "Unlike folks in the movies,

I'd never walk away and leave a drink."

"That puts you over the limit."

"Don't be so fucking English."

"I have to sit beside you."

"You do not. And it's still a fair walk to Baltimore."

I sorted things out with the girl behind the bar on my way to the gents. She looked about thirteen. When I came back, Paula or whatever her name was smiled up at me – still there.

And when we got outside the rain had actually stopped. Later, as we edged down the last hill into Baltimore, weak sun was showing through.

I fumbled in my rucksack for my flap-eared copy of the *Rough Guide*.

"Put that away," Paula snapped as she jerked the handbrake on, "or I will not be seen with you. If you're wanting the ferry details, it leaves from down there, you've got three quarters of an hour till the next one sails and the return ticket's twelve punts – but eight if you give me the money to buy it for you and keep your gob shut."

I stared at her as she heaved a carry-all from the back seat.

"You're catching it, too?"

She nodded.

"Well, well. Birdies or college?"

"College," she sighed. "Requirement of my job I spend two weeks a year brushing up my Gaelic. I ask you, teacher in an inner city – what the fuck does Gaelic mean to me?"

"Tried to get my mum to teach me once," I admitted softly. "She wouldn't. Said all she could remember how to say was 'kiss my arse'."

Paula snorted again.

"I like the woman. I've never even met her but I like her. Now come on, give me the money. I'll meet you in the pub up there. You might want to change some more travellers cheques: they'll do it for you. Mine's another lager."

I'd already trusted her once that day. Some might have told me to quit while I was ahead – but what the hell? I was standing at the bar having just taken back my passport along with crisp portraits of famous, dead Irishmen when a small hand reached round and snatched the slim book from me.

"Peter," she said, flicking through it. "I was wondering what your real name was."

"All my family call me Pearse."

"Sure they do – after you've spent at least five years refusing to answer to anything else. Come on." She took her lager and downed it in a six second pause. "We've a ferry to catch."

It was about seven o'clock by that time. Over Roaring Water Bay the blue sky was criss-crossed with bars of pink cloud as if a finger-painting giant child had gone crazy on the walls and there'd be hell to pay when Mum and Dad got home.

"I'm going to call you Peter," she announced as the tiny ferry duck-waddled out of the harbour.

"Why?"

"Because it's your name. Because by denying it, you're hating a part of yourself. That's not healthy."

I raised one eyebrow.

"Sure I can be serious sometimes," she continued lightly. "Just promise not to tell anyone about it."

"It's easier calling myself Pearse," I said as I looked away and leaned over the rail. "It says something. I always felt it's what my parents would have called me if they'd been thinking straight at the time. I feel in-between. In England, I don't feel English. I get the 'thick Paddy' routine at least three times a week. And if I come over here I get treated like you've treated me. You just don't get it, do you? You're so bloody sure of what you are."

I turned back to her and got smoke blown in my face.

"Am I? Why are you so screwed up about it? What's wrong with being in-between?"

"Everything. If you don't know, I can't explain. When you meet someone, what's the second question they ask you after they know your name: where are you from? I never really know what to say."

"Then don't. Say, 'Hi, I'm Peter. I'm messed up and I'm from all over the fucking place but, hell, I'm cute so like me anyway'."

"Cute," I echoed with a laugh. "Is that why you stopped the car for me?"

"Sure it is. You looked just like a puppy I found on this building site once, sheltering in a steel drum from the rain. Wanted to take it home – Da wouldn't let me."

"Thanks. Thanks a million."

She gave a short, smoky chuckle.

"You're going native already."

She dropped the cigarette end into the sea and didn't light another.

"Last summer," she continued very quietly, "it was just about here I saw a dolphin. Didn't stay for more than thirty seconds but Jesus that was enough."

"Wow," I breathed. "What did it feel like?"

"What do you think? I nearly fucking wet myself. Does it bother you, by the way, a lady swearing?"

I shook my head.

"Not at all. At least it doesn't put my health at risk."

The boat had slowed down, if that was possible; we passed into a big-mouthed bay and the cliffs stared down at us. Finally, we wallowed up to a concrete quay.

"You sorted yourself somewhere to stay?" she asked as we made the leap for solid land.

"Kind of. At the hostel."

"I know it. I'll walk with you. There's only two roads out of here but you're bound to take the wrong one."

I let her get away with it. But we must have taken the long route, I guess, because ten o'clock found us still by the ruins of the old lighthouse staring out across the sea to the fully-automated winking of the new one on Fastnet Rock. She snapped open a third can of lager from her carry-all and passed it to me without asking if I wanted one.

"Fair's fair," I said eventually. "What's your real name?"

"Finuala," she told the waves.

"You're crazy – that's a lovely name. Why d'you want to ditch a name like that?"

She turned back to me smiling, half sad, half playful.

"Born in a fourth-story flat just north of the Liffey. And my parents go and name me for some swan maiden in the soppiest Irish fairy tale there is. Walk round with a name like that and people think you're away with the fairies yourself. No, Paula is... Paula sounds like she can take care of herself."

I chuckled, lay back and Paula's beer missed my mouth and trickled down my cheek. We just watched the swallows, heart-stopping in their blue-black backs and salmon bellies, clicking and whistling as they swooped for insects making the most of the long evening. I decided it wasn't worth calling her a hypocrite.

"They say they piss off to South Africa every winter," Paula commented. "That's a fuck of a long way for a little bird."

I grinned again and thought, so, they don't exactly belong anywhere either, then. They don't look too bad on it.

THE PHILOSOPHER NABEL AT THE KAFFEEHAUS ELEGANZ

Tom Saunders

Tom Saunders began writing while taking an English degree as a mature student at Kingston Polytechnic and later went on to do the Creative Writing MA at the University of East Anglia. Born and brought up on London's not-so-wild western edge, he now lives in Oxfordshire with his wife, Jean, who is an environmental activist. Tom's story, 'Blue Sea With Boats' was published in Acclaim magazine.

THE PHILOSOPHER NABEL, A PLUMP OF LIMB, DOLL OF A man with a billy goat beard the colour of cayenne pepper and a soft, flat nose, sat with his chin on his fist in a booth at the Kaffeehaus Eleganz, his green felt hat, jade-topped malacca cane and kid gloves on the table before him. His tongue, fat and pink against his palate, burnt with the sour grittiness of the oil-beaded mocha steaming in the cup at his elbow. Sucking on his moustache, he sighed a long, aching sigh. But it was over too soon. With a grunt of impatience, he shook the silk handkerchief from the breast pocket of his jacket and dabbed at his eyes; the tobacco smoke clouding the café coiled as thick as a Baltic fog and the sting of it had made his lashes moist with tears, blurring his vision.

The Eleganz was a faded establishment with large, dusty windows opposite the old leather market, its atmosphere (bourgeois patrons out in search of the picaresque were frequently overheard praising the 'authentic atmosphere' of the place) a far from subtle amalgam of abandonment and complicity. For five weeks now, Nabel had been powerless to keep away. The reason for this was no conundrum, he was invitingly acquainted with the compulsion that had drawn him there even if he was surprised at the suddenness of his surrender to it. He had, purely in passing, his mind engaged with the important but mundane problem of drafting the Ideal Letter of Complaint, tactful yet firm, regarding the recent mauling his shirts had undergone at the laundry, looked up into the face of a whore working the corner of the square – she did not proposition him, she just smiled – and the instant her softened features became part of his consciousness he knew it would be unimaginable for him to continue with his life until his knowledge of her was total. Too upset, at first, to make an approach, he was forced, sweating like warm sausage despite the bitter wind, to become a spy, his nose wetting the powdery stone of one of the rococo columns of the Opera House portico. A dumb show that continued until, close to an hour later, she stamped her feet to warm them, shrugged to herself like a card player throwing in a losing hand, and, stifling a yawn, set off down a street, her hips renouncing their sway as she went.

It was a moment of decision for Nabel. Shuffling hesitantly out into the open he had stared at the empty space she had left behind her and then strode with short, rapid strides across the square.

It was following her then that had transported Nabel forward in time – his actions circling back on themselves as if to parody, in his head at least, Nietzsche's doctrine of Eternal Recurrence – to where he now sat, leaning in a trance of expectancy on the stained table top of what, from force of habit, he had come to think of as his own personal booth at the Kaffeehaus Eleganz.

Then again, if she (Trudy, that is, he had watched as her three friends greeted her noisily, called her name) had not collapsed in a swirl of skirts and petticoats on to the bench against the wall and kicked off her shoes and stooped to massage her sore feet through her stockings on that evening of initiation, the juicy bud of his curiosity might have shrivelled and died prematurely in the unhealthy climate of that long, airless room. But that is what she did. That is what he saw; and heard; her chaste groans of pleasure as she caressed her stiff-jointed toes sending a ripple of longing through him that was as irresistible as an irrefutable argument.

Nabel had a private obsession: he revered the form, the texture and the fragrance of the feminine foot. There was no denying that, both in their real and imagined guises, breasts, buttocks and legs were inexhaustible dispensaries of carnal delight to him, but when it came down, in a manner of speaking, to feet, it was love in the truest sense of the word. They tiptoed, their pale pink perfection laced with buried lines of inky blue, into both his dreams and his daydreams; sweetly incongruous fantasies of flesh these last often were, disturbing him pleasantly when his thoughts should have been on a less corporeal plane, when lecturing at the Academy or at his desk writing his treatise for instance. Ever since puberty – maybe even before; because there were footsome feelings, or the spectres of footsome feelings, haunting the hazy fringes of his memories of early childhood, although he preferred not to think about them too closely – he had suffered with an almost overwhelming need to gaze at and pet and nuzzle and kiss the feet of women who attracted him physically. As a preoccupation it was preposterous, not to say embarrassing. Because how was it to be interpreted? It placed him, he felt, on his knees both metaphorically and actually. It was not a problem that could be discussed openly even within the mordant salon society in which he was required to move (and yet not move); amongst its ranks buggers and adulterers were commonplace and left to pursue their sensualities unremarked, but a harmless fetishist such as himself could be sure that, no matter how real his ideals were, sinning with bohemian elaboration was one thing and appearing ludicrous was another.

Trudy had remarkable feet. Nabel, a man made clairvoyant by the particularity of his lust, saw this despite the drooping heels and stretched insteps of her shabby pink cotton hose. Smoothly-arched, delicately-boned extremities they were, the toes splayed and mobile, crowned by a pair of exquisitely-sculpted, equine ankles. Others might have considered them to be a touch on the large side, but for Nabel beauty demanded scope, cried out for dimension.

If it had not been for the teasing of her three friends, Greta, Agnes and Katrine, Nabel might have sat and watched and waited and left as quietly as he had arrived.

Greta had called across the aisle to him in a soprano loud enough to bruise the already bruised pastries arrayed on top of the counter, her red lips and ripely-rouged cheekbones forcing his eyes reluctantly upward. "Hey there wee fellow, don't sit with your face pressed to the shop window when you can afford to step inside."

"If you can't afford to buy you can't afford to look." The bent peacock plume hanging down over the brim of Agnes's hat had danced a wistful dance as she planted her hands on her hips and shook her high, pointed bosom, the stones of her heavy jet necklace glinting as they clicked against one another.

Tucking the lottery ticket she had just bought from a fellow in a red velvet suit into her beaded purse and turning with a crooked grin to survey her friends, the tall, consumptively-skinny Katrine had joined in: "What say you we let him have it free, girls, put a bit of a quiver in those fat little legs of his, tire him out then keep him as a mascot?"

"Rub him for good luck."

"His, you mean."

Every rogue and slut in the place had laughed at this, or so it seemed to Nabel as he pushed his cup away and collected his things together.

"It's you he wants, Trudy."

"You can keep him on a string tucked inside your draws."

"She might sit on him."

"Poor little fucker."

"Get a smile from those red whiskers when she's least expecting it."

Trudy had caught up with Nabel a few yards down the street, the tap of her finger on his shoulder causing him to wheel around with the growl of a cornered dog.

"They are good girls," she had said after he had apologised and she had taken his arm, "doing the best they can. You shouldn't pay them any mind."

Their first time together was not a success. The hotel room was way upstairs in the attic and not much bigger than a boot cupboard and the bed-clothes had reeked of fried onions and anxiety. And at a humiliatingly inopportune moment, Nabel had thrust his left knee through the threadbare sheet and into a hole in the rotten ticking of the old, sway-backed mattress. A mishap that saw Trudy covering her mouth with her hand, her eyes wide and wild with suppressed laughter.

From then on he insisted they went to one of the more expensive hotels on the far side of the square. The room was quadruple the price and the desk clerk had to be encouraged into doing what he swore would cost him his job, but the money was well spent.

It was their third meeting before he was relaxed enough in her company to ask her shyly if he might wash her feet, a request that injured her pride even though, when he promised her extra payment and she allowed him to go ahead, they turned out to be filthy, the toenails chipped and grey-crescented.

Trudy had wide apart blue eyes and she had sat naked on the rim of the bed and stared down at him blankly as, like a mother with twin babies, he took first one foot and then the other and bathed them gently in the porcelain bowl from the night stand. When they were pink and clean he dried them by placing a towel across his lap and resting them there, tracing the yellowy hardness of their callused undersides and the softness of their high, blue veins with the tip of his finger as he did so. She only flinched momentarily when he bent forward and began to kiss her toes one by one; soapy smelling toes with a faint redolence of freshly-picked mushrooms. But then, like a farrier shoeing a skittish horse, he had to hold on tightly to her bucking heel as the tickling of his lips and beard made her wriggle and jerk away from him squealing with laughter.

Now, five weeks later, they had a fixed routine, playing out a charade designed by Nabel for his own delectation. He would sit in his booth at the Eleganz and send across coffee and a selection of flyblown pastries for the quartet of whores sitting by the door to the kitchen and wait for Trudy – posed coyly with her skirt up and her shoes off – to leave, and then, having looked on with ecstatic impatience, jump up and follow her, a damp aching in his groin and his heart leaping loose inside his badly-laundered shirt.

This evening, decided Nabel, Trudy and her three friends seemed strangely muted. With the exception of Greta, who had a blackened swelling below her right eye that her face powder could not wholly conceal, they had nodded and smiled when he sat down. And now they were eating and drinking and swapping jokes and laughing almost as freely as they usually did. But for some reason the invisible wall separating them from him (the kind of wall that could not, he had discovered, even be acknowledged let alone breached) had thickened and toughened, so much so that, unlike all the other evenings they had sat just as they were sitting now, he was unable to sense even the slightest breath of the warmth they shared with one another on his skin. There had been no teasing, no sly winks, no jokes about the mad infatuation that kept him coming back for more, paying for more. If he was alive to them tonight it was not in the same way he was alive to himself. This should have made him angry, he knew, but somehow all he felt was fear.

As the air stirred and a shadow came between the booth and the light from the street, the whores whispered conversation faltered. Turning with a frown and looking up, Nabel found himself having to acknowledge the introductory bow of a pomaded young man sporting a white carnation in the buttonhole of his too-tight, office clerks' suit. "Yes," he said, failing to hide his irritation, "what is it? What do you want?"

"Rainer Munterkeit, sir," said the boy. "One is loathe to break in so barbarously on your musings, Herr doktor, but do I have the honour of addressing the renowned, no, no, the esteemed professor Jacob Nabel, philosopher, writer and teacher?"

Even where it is at home formality tends to embrace the absurd, but in the Kaffeehaus Eleganz this was too much. Nabel covered his sudden cough of amusement with a clearing of his throat, flattered and flushed despite himself. "Well, yes, perhaps. Nabel is my name at least. As to the rest, let us say that aspirations are not always the same thing as accomplishments and leave it at that."

Pulling out a chair, Munterkeit began to sit down.

Nabel raised his hand in protest. "Young man, please," he said, "not right now. Whatever it is you want will keep a few hours, I'm sure. If it is advice you are after, why not come along and see me at the Academy?"

Impervious to what was being said to him, Munterkeit continued with what he was doing, smiling pleasantly as he arranged his body comfortably at the table. He had a wide mouth and his small, white teeth shone like wet china. The pink skin of his jaw was stretched tautly on the bone, a just-shaved smoothness to it notwithstanding the lateness of the hour.

With a blink of disbelief, Nabel pursed his lips and inflated what there was of his chest. "Excuse me, but are you deaf? I think I said not now."

Munterkeit eased back, flipped open his jacket and wedged a fat knuckle in the pocket of his waistcoat. "I trust you were satisfied with our Trudy? She's a beautiful girl don't you think? A bit thin in the ribs, but perfection is always hard to find."

Sitting up, Nabel looked the boy over, narrowing his eyes in an attempt to intimidate him. He did not, with his carefully barbered hair, high celluloid collar and black, professional mourners' tie, look like a procurer... though Nabel, who had been called upon over the years to delineate and categorise all manner of things, had no reason to think himself an authority on the style and demeanour of such an individual.

"And she's past that wonderful, tender age. Where would you put that? Sixteen? Fifteen? Earlier even. It's such a pity she doesn't have a little sister for you to sample. There's nothing, is there, quite as soft as a young girl's skin?"

Nabel wanted to put his hands over his ears. "You have no right to speak of her like that," he said, shaking his head as if to rid himself of the words.

"Oh, but I do," said Munterkeit. "And who is to prevent me?" He nodded down at the table. "It isn't often you get to see something of that quality. Unusual, too." Following his eyes, Nabel became aware of the cane beneath his hand for the first time, the smooth, mottled wood cool against the pads of his fingertips. "Did you pay a great deal for it? I'm sure that you did. The best does not come cheap and I wouldn't see a person like you counting the cost where excellence is concerned."

Angling his jaw, Nabel aimed the red tuft of his beard. "I find your comments unbelievably offensive, young man. I have no stomach for this conversation. I suggest you leave."

"Offensive?" said Munterkeit in an innocent voice, his eyebrows arched with concern. "Forgive me."

"Forgive yourself. If you can. And leave me alone. If you don't I'll have you thrown out. There are plenty of other tables, please sit somewhere else." Over Munterkeit's shoulder, Nabel met Trudy's gaze; immediately she glanced down and began toying with the rings on her fingers.

After holding Nabel in a cool, empty stare for several seconds, Munterkeit tipped back his head like an actor in a play and barked with laughter, the pure, rich brown of his eyes bright between his squeezed together lids. Then, just as abruptly – his amusement cut cleanly through – he stopped and looked across the table. "Are you trying to tell me," he said, his lips full and wet, a catch in his throat, "I'm not free to sit anywhere I want? Surely the two of us can stay or go just as we wish? And when it comes to having people thrown out I'd keep quiet if I were you, seeing as I happen to own a half share in this place. Somewhere you seem to have grown quite fond of lately."

Reacting to this in the only way open to him, Nabel reached for his hat and gloves, his eyes searching unsuccessfully for Trudy's. "If you won't move, then I will," he said.

Munterkeit shrugged. "If that's how you feel. But if you get up from this table I'm afraid that you'll have a very lonely evening ahead of you."

"If Trudy wants to leave with me you can't stop her."

"Well I think perhaps I could. Nevertheless I'm certain I won't need to."

"I see. X equals Y." Nabel threw his gloves, one, two, into his hat as if he were tossing ingredients into a pot. "She has no mind of her own and she will do whatever you tell her."

"She has a mind of her own," said Munterkeit lowering his voice and bending nearer with the sweetly dimpled smirk of a mischievous child, "but it's not her mind we are talking about now, is it?" He sat up with a wave of the hand. "Put it like this, Trudy and I are business associates and she has come through experience to respect my views on the way our joint venture should be conducted."

Nabel grunted with disgust. He was seldom able to summon up the additional mental energy – the unalloyed negativity of it demanded more of him then he was prepared to offer – necessary to loathe a fellow human being, but here he was after no more than ten minutes thoroughly despising this sad, glib creature sitting opposite him. " 'Experience'," he said, enjoying his own pomposity. "Ah yes, only a man of your sort would impoverish that word, strip it of all its richness and ambiguity."

Munterkeit, he was now convinced, his eye drawn once again

across the room to the swelling on Greta's cheek, was a savage.

"I see no need to speak directly of these things."

"You mean pain so why don't you say pain?"

Munterkeit spread his palms. "If you wish. You cannot deny that it's an efficient teacher. Thankfully, the threat of it is usually more than enough. Governments are well aware of this fact. How far would they get without their power to punish? Not very far, I can assure you. If there was any other way I'd gladly use it. Because I take my responsibilities seriously. I like to think of the girls and myself making up our own small republic. Granted, I could be seen as a despot, but not one that is ever cruel for the sake of being cruel. We have our rules, sensible rules geared strictly to the business we're in, and, as long as no-one disregards them we get along happily enough. Because I love my girls. There's nothing I wouldn't do for them, believe me. Nothing." His eyes shone as he lived out the weight of these words in his head, listening to them and gobbling them back down with injury and sincerity. "And," he went on, passing a hand quickly across his face, "as our little enterprise thrives and prospers I hope they will continue to be of loyal service to me, and if they are they will be correspondingly rewarded. That's the law of the marketplace, isn't it? The fact of the matter."

Sighing, Nabel pulled out the chair next to his and put his hat and gloves down on it. The boy is quite mad, he told himself, and as with all madmen I must do my utmost not to humour him. "What is it that you want?" he said. "Explain yourself... if such a thing is possible. I cannot imagine what your ridiculous rationalizations have to do with me. You have chosen absolutely the wrong person if you are hoping to excuse your inexcusable behaviour, I can promise you that."

"I want nothing," said Munterkeit, frowning as though Nabel has somehow misunderstood a point that had been carefully explained to him. "Just to talk, that's all. You see, I greatly admire what you have achieved in your life, the respect with which you are held. As a child I hoped for something of the same sort for myself, and, maybe, but for fate, I might have attained it."

Nabel, wiping his eyes once more with his handkerchief, snorted dismissively even before Munterkeit had stopped speaking. "Ah yes, fate, that convenient concept, always there to take the blame.

The culprit that can never be captured, that has always left the scene of the crime."

"Quite so," nodded Munterkeit, his bottom lip thrust out like a carp's to show the seriousness of his deliberations, "I understand your reservations, of course. I have often had cause to think that way myself. However, the truth is that if my poor, dead father had not bankrupted himself through his own greed and incompetence, not to mention his cock-happy conduct with every sly girl who gave him a friendly wag of her arse, I would have at least had the benefit of a decent education. As it was, as soon as the bills weren't met they kicked me out of my private school and I had to go on with my studies as best I could with a bunch of jug-eared peasant boys for classmates." Munterkeit laughed and smoothed back his clipped hair nervously, the cheap, eye-watering perfume of the pomade liberated by his fingers. "You should have seen them with their heads shaved and painted blue because of the lice. Most of them dressed up like clowns in cut-down clothes and great big boots. Boots that slopped about like coal barges on their feet even though their mothers had wadded them with strips of waste paper to waterproof them and make them smaller." Conscious of Nabel's contemptuous glare, Munterkeit added with a shrug: "Of course, apart from their routine stupidity and their sentimental attachment to violence and each other, there was no harm in these people. I've no doubt that most of them have matured into hard-working, good-for-the-want-of-a-chance-to-be-bad young men, fathers in truth or prospect to more of their kind. But I was made for better, I can tell you. It was all I could do..."

"I went to a charity school," interposed Nabel quietly, telling himself that he was being obliged to speak out in order to qualify the argument. "And my boots were never of the snuggest fit."

Munterkeit, moon-eyed and confused, his train of thought broken into, assimilated this silently. Snapping to suddenly with a blink and a shaking of his head, he said: "Really? You? I find that very hard to believe. If it is the truth, then my admiration for you is multiplied. What an elevation. Yours must be uncommon flair. My intelligence, like the vast majority of our sort, is closer to the middle-ground. Which, as a child, gave me less resilience. A plant with moderate powers of growth can only flourish if it is properly nurtured. It will wither away when left to fight its way above the weeds."

Nabel was unimpressed. "You seem to me to be in a remarkably fine health for such a shamefully neglected flower."

As he said this he became aware with a fluttering of his heart that Trudy was staring at him, the glint of her eyes bright at the periphery of his vision. But when he turned his face to hers she still refused to meet his gaze, starting guiltily and lowering her lashes with an insect quick movement.

Munterkeit smiled his youthful smile and caressed his paunch as though it were a favourite cat. "An unfortunate metaphor, I agree, given my appetite for the world and all its pleasures. And a well-worn one. But you take my point, I trust?"

"As a generalisation, possibly. But then again, generalisations are almost always evil."

"I see. What you are saying," said Munterkeit with a frown, "is that you agree with me but it hurts you to admit it."

Feigning horror in a deliberately tired manner, Nabel drew back in his chair. "Agree with you? In my case agreement is not so easy to come by, my friend. I specialise in disagreement. When it comes to the difficult questions, the questions we all attempt to avoid, it has been my experience that we agree far too much and think far too little. We bicker about details and mouth vague inanities when it comes to anything larger than the small lives we elect to lead. Well, some problems are much too important to be simplified out of existence. Complexity is a benefaction, the measure of who we are, we must not stand back from it in fear." The gradual thickening of passion in his voice was an embarrassment to him. A nerve began to fibrillate in his eyelid. To camouflage this he put his hand up to the side of his face and his elbow on the table and leant forwards as if ready to parry a response.

But a stillness had settled on Munterkeit. His expression had a sleepy self-absorption to it, his eyes misted over. The background noises of the Eleganz, the talk and laughter, the clank of plates, the hiss of boiling water, the scraping of chair legs, rose louder and louder. In their corner, Trudy, Greta, Agnes and Katrine were smoking and debating quietly and intensely, their faces circled in on one another.

"Well..." began Nabel, shifting in his seat and making ready to leave.

Munterkeit sat up with a twist of his neck to settle the collar of his shirt and tugged at his waistcoat. "You're not a big man," he said, "don't you ever worry about wandering around this part of the city by yourself?" There was a new remoteness in his tone, his manner companionable but business-like.

"As of this evening, yes," said Nabel, deciding that there was something he should be very careful of here. The strained rigidity of Munterkeit's spine now that he had moved in closer to the table echoed that of every petty official that had ever sat in judgement behind a desk.

"You don't worry then?"

"Of course I do," said Nabel, getting to his feet, "but I would be an even smaller man if I let my fear rule my life."

Munterkeit shook his head impatiently. "You might be tempted to write that in a book, but you don't really believe it. Everybody's life is ruled by their fear."

Nabel retrieved his hat and gloves from the chair. "Or set free by their courage."

Munterkeit rested his hands gently on the table and smiled down at them. "The shorter the general the taller the words," he said to himself, and then added without raising his eyes: "Give me your cane."

After a momentary hesitation, Nabel, whose fingers were already stretching across the table to claim the malacca, carried on as if nothing had been said, but when he went to pick it up Munterkeit's palm slammed down on the shaft and prevented him. "Didn't you hear me?" he said. "The cane is mine."

"This is ridiculous," said Nabel, his voice shaking as he tried to prise the stick free, "childish."

"How would it be if I told all your fine colleagues over at the Academy what you've been doing with your evenings of late?"

"They would be surprised, then amused. I could tell you spicier tales about them, I'm afraid. Even if they disapproved it would be kept quiet... the faculty does its best work when prevailed upon to keep inconvenient facts quiet."

"Really?" Munterkeit stared hard at Nabel in an attempt to read the truth in his face.

"Really."

"As an intelligent man you must see that I have no need to play this game. Let go."

"No."

"You don't care if Trudy gets hurt?" said Munterkeit softly.

Nabel pretended to frown. "What is that, some kind of threat?"

"At last we're in agreement. Now let go."

"She has nothing to do with this."

"You think so?"

Nabel knew he was beaten, had always been beaten. He was in the grip of circumstances and the grip had tightened to the point where he had nowhere to go. If he went to the police what could they do? Laugh at him behind his back, most probably, an educated fool who had got out of his depth. Asking for it. Using these words against himself in his thoughts had a choking effect, his chest and throat aching with rage and stifled tears.

Munterkeit tilted his head. "Perhaps she is worth less than the cane?"

Nabel released his grip and stood back. "Take the stupid thing, then," he said, his breath ragged. Now that he was able to look around he saw that everybody in the Eleganz – especially Trudy and her friends – had stopped what they were doing to watch them.

Munterkeit bowed and twirled the stick in his hand. "Thank you. A wise and generous action."

"Anything for you to leave us alone."

"And now," said Munterkeit, "I'll do something for you."

Nabel's hands shook as he removed his gloves from his hat and put them on. "There is nothing you can do for me. Nothing."

Munterkeit smiled as he pushed back his chair and got up. "No?" The second he left the booth the room came alive again, the rising buzz of voices broken by quick, edgy waves of heartless yet heartfelt laughter.

Trudy's face was composed and impassive as Munterkeit squatted down on the floor in front of her. Leaning into her lap, he pinched her narrow chin between his thumb and forefinger and began to speak, pausing whenever a reaction was appropriate and working his arm up and down so that she was forced to nod her head. She did this without the slightest resistance or protest, her widely-spaced blue eyes, their lashes blinking slowly and solemnly, watching him intently as if understanding what he was saying was the most important thing in the world.

Not knowing what was expected of him, Nabel stood numbly in the aisle and waited. To avoid making matters worse, that was his main task. To avoid making matters worse.

Midway through the morning of the next day, Nabel, his thoughts in a spin, tried vainly to recover his place in his notes while tiers of amorphous student faces peered down unforgivingly at him. There was an inquisitorial aspect to the rising ranks of seats and desks in the lecture theatre that had never struck him quite so potently before. And what was on trial? His skill as a teacher? His morals? His lack of physical prepossession? The clarity and rigour of his thoughts? His good humour in the face of their slowness? The grace of his arguments, of his rhetorical embroidery? He was being observed and reported on. Enquired into. He was being observed and reported on and he did not care. He was beyond all harm after last night, which had been spent in one of the big hotels by the river. He was safe. Trudy had been wonderful, alive to his touch in a way he would not have imagined possible. Sensitive to him. Seeing him. Asking him to speak about himself for the first time. Laughing and smiling without constraint, letting him see her close up as he had only seen her before from afar. Listening to him when he fumed and cursed over what Munterkeit had said and agreeing, her eyes coyly downcast, with surprising readiness when he offered to find her an apartment. They would be together and he would look after her, he had promised, cradling her thin shoulders in the warm bed and kissing her forehead, she would be free of the Kaffeehaus Eleganz and the life she had been driven to lead, free of the streets and the square and the young man with the too-tight clerks' suit and jade-topped malacca cane.

The pages of Nabel's notes were more confused than ever now. He was perspiring despite the breath-fogging cold of the theatre, and the students were beginning to fidget and fret amongst themselves. Without looking up, he felt for his handkerchief in the breast pocket of his jacket and began to mop his brow.

It was a giggle from the one female undergraduate in his group, sitting on her own at the end of the first row, that initiated the laughter; a wet, snorting little explosion into the quickly-raised palm of her hand, the sound of it halfway between that of a sneeze and a fart. In seconds the whole room was roaring, the high walls alive with cattle-like shufflings, with nudging elbows. When, with a sigh, Nabel gave in and lifted his head he was mystified as to what was going on. Then, following their eyes, he glanced down and saw he was clasping in his fist not a clean, silk handkerchief but a pink cotton stocking, grey and worn around the heel and toes and smelling, teasingly, of love.

HOLES, EMPTY SPACES
Kirsty Seymour-Ure

Kirsty Seymour-Ure was born in 1965 and was brought up in Kent. She read English at Durham University and since then has lived in London, working as a freelance editor in illustrated publishing. She is just about to transform her life by moving to a tumbledown farmhouse in Italy. Kirsty has had a number of poems and short stories published, and it is her constant hope that one day she will be able to make writing more than a hobby.

IT WAS NOT THAT EMMIE HADN'T KNOWN PEOPLE WITH bits of them missing. Her grandfather had lost an arm in the war, had to have his food cut up for him, couldn't tie knots. One of her brother's friends, a mountaineer, lost a couple of toes from frostbite, had to learn all over again how to walk, how to keep balance. She felt sorry for them, sorry for what they had lost.

And now she felt sorry for herself, about to lose something. The lump in her breast had proved malign. An exploratory operation had been performed, and it was likely that a mastectomy would be advised. This meant the removal of her breast: Emmie knew that.

The doctors and nurses were kind. They explained all the technicalities, didn't try to blind her with science, spelt out the jargon, gave her strong coffee without sugar when she asked for it. But the fact remained, these people wanted to cut her breast off. No amount of kindness could hide that.

"We'll give it a month," they told her. They were waiting for more test results. In the meantime they put her on chemotherapy. Gave her the name of the hospital's counsellor. Wrote down a helpline number to call if she felt really bad.

She did feel bad, in every way. She had never felt so bad. At the beginning, she thought she was waiting to die. When the shock passed – if it ever really did – and she realized the treatment meant she was not going to die, not right away anyway, she waited for her hair, her beautiful, long, shiny hair, to begin to turn brittle, to fall out in tufts, to stop growing. This was something they had warned her about. She couldn't bear the thought of it. She was more worried about that than the disease, than losing her breast, even than dying. So she had it all cut off, in its prime, two and a half feet long, she had it cut close, close to her skull, and she tied a bright silk scarf like a turban around her head. The hairdresser – practically weeping herself – did up the hair in a parcel for Emmie to take home. She had been going to burn it but in the end she kept it to look at sometimes, to stroke, like a pet animal, for comfort.

Emmie also drove her lover away. Feeling fallible, vulnerable, raw, all that came out was aggression. Raging, she forced him to leave. Took the clothes he kept at her place and shoved them in carrier-bags and threw them in his car. Took the keys to her flat off his key-ring, dropped them down a grating in the street. Returned to him the keys to his flat, though he posted them back to her the next day. He didn't want to leave her. She didn't know how to be helped.

It was late spring and to Emmie the world had never seemed so alive. Even in the city there were shoots pushing through, the trees in blossom, flowers everywhere, everywhere the sap rising and bursting. For a couple of weeks Emmie went wild. She drank. First she drank at home. The telephone stacked up the messages for her. Then she took to going out to a late bar and drinking there. She found she became less depressed, less self-pitying in company than alone, even if the company was a not very reputable crowd of late-night drinkers.

In her turban she was striking, beautiful, exotic; her solitude was splendid. It was inevitable that men would try and pick her up – what else would she be there for? – but after the third night, the barman decided to take her under his wing. Emmie imagined he thought she was a bit crazy. Crazy, but harmless. One night he said to her, "That's nice, that turban thing you wear. Unusual." Then he laughed. "What is it," he said, "you bald underneath?"

It was not unkind laughter. He could not possibly have known the truth. She burst into tears. People turned to look at her as she snuffled. The barman was alarmed. "God, I'm sorry love," he said, "didn't mean to upset you. Here, have this on the house." He gave her another glass of vodka. He eyed the bottle as he poured the shot. "Dangerous stuff, this," he said. Emmie looked at the hand that held the bottle; there was something strange about it. He followed her gaze with his eyes and grinned. "Accident with my brother's chainsaw," he said.

His hand had only three fingers: thumb, forefinger, middle finger. Missing, the little finger and the one next to it. She hadn't noticed before. He gripped the bottle tightly with his thumb and two remaining fingers, like a claw. When he picked up a glass and began to wipe it, the action with the damaged hand was surprisingly delicate.

That night she waited for the bar to start closing up before she left. The barman was stacking chairs on tables. Emmie came out of the Ladies, the last customer. He looked surprised to see her, then his eyes became comprehending.

"Would you see me home?" she said.

"Well, all right. Are you sure?" A fractional pause; a shrug. He glanced at his watch. "Give me another fifteen minutes or so, I'll be with you. Here." He took down a chair and motioned for her to sit. His face was mild, curious. She sat meekly, feeling her heart working hectically in her chest. She had never done this before, asked a man home with her, a man she didn't know. A man, now she came to think of it, whose name she didn't even know. She thought of his missing fingers. What would it feel like, that hand, with its area of conspicuous absence, travelling over her skin?

She had expected awkwardness once they were home but there was none. He was polite, cheerful, interested. He seemed disarmingly simple. She liked him, although in the bar he had been nothing to her. In bed he unwound her turban, the brightly coloured silk trailing away over the quilt. She closed her eyes. He ran his hand – his whole hand, the hand that was whole – over her head, the short, bristly hair. "Soft," he said, smiling like a child. He traced her body with both hands, gently, head to toe, back again. It seemed to take hours. He said nothing, breathing softly.

Emmie wondered if he could feel the disease inside her. She felt his missing fingers upon her like ghosts. When the blunt stumps brushed her flesh it was a shock.

"You don't mind?" he asked.

"Don't be silly."

"Only, some women find it puts them off."

"No," Emmie said. "Not me." She liked the way he'd said some women.

Afterwards she said, "Did it hurt, your accident?"

"Of course it fucking hurt," he said, holding up his hand. "It was a chainsaw for chrissake."

She felt herself blush. "I thought that really great pain made feeling sort of blank out. I thought you went numb."

He regarded her. "You're a strange one," he said. "Pain is pain. There's nothing can blank that out."

"Can you feel your fingers still?" she asked. She'd heard about that, people still feeling sensation in the amputated parts, the limbs that weren't there any more.

The barman held up his hand, seemed to examine it, thoughtfully. "No," he said. "I feel nothing. It's like they were never there."

He looked at Emmie closely and shook his head. She thought his eyes were full of depth, knowledge, sadness. She tried to imagine the pain. She said, "They're going to cut my breast off." She took his injured hand and put it over her breast, made him feel the lump. He pulled away violently.

"God almighty," he said. "Jesus Christ almighty." His hand fell slack onto her stomach.

She had to persist. "But you don't feel – any different, then – with a part of you missing?"

"No, I bloody don't." He shifted uneasily beside her. "But, God, it was just a couple of fingers. Not –"

She felt hard and cold.

Then he put out his hand again, his two fingers, thumb, and ran them slowly, gently, over her breast. He stroked it, lovingly. She felt it respond to his touch, straining towards the source of the pleasure, desiring more. How could this cease to belong to her?

After that experience Emmie didn't go out for some days. She didn't go back to the bar. She was trying to think things out. She was trying to work out what was happening. How much did you have to lose before you were a different person? When did you stop being you? She thought about her lover, whom she'd driven away: missing him, she felt his loss physically; the lack of him slowly becoming a part of her, like a sediment settling just under her skin. She couldn't tell if she was the same person she had been a month ago. She wondered if she would be less or more truly herself once the disease had been cut out of her; sometimes she thought she didn't want it to be gone.

When she was a teenager she had dated a boy whose front tooth had been knocked out. The first time she kissed him there was an extraordinary sense of shock, her tongue probing along the hard wall of teeth and suddenly coming across – nothing. A hole. It was an indescribable sensation. Not unpleasant, but unexpectedly shocking, even though she'd known it would be there. And her tongue had returned to that soft place again and again. Each time the thrill of it, as if she was touching something forbidden, or breaking a taboo.

Recalling this, Emmie wondered idly what it would be like to make love to a man with no arms, or no legs. She began to think about it all the time. One morning she went out to buy some food, and coming back on the bus there was a man whose leg was missing from the knee downward. He was young, looked fit, competent, normal. He was carrying a bag of groceries, easily. She watched him. He joked with the bus conductor. As he got off the bus she saw him greet a girl, and they walked along the street together. He used a crutch to help him walk. His empty trouser leg was pinned up behind him to the back of his trousers. Emmie imagined making love to him. She imagined his stump, naked, pressing against her. She visualised herself caressing it, feeling its smoothness under her fingertips. She could see all of this clearly in her mind.

But when she tried to imagine the two of them actually performing the sexual act, him on top of her, inside her, she couldn't: she couldn't see it. She couldn't imagine the lack of weight, the empty space where his leg should have been. She just couldn't. Her hand strayed to touch her breast, soon to be absence, just so much emptiness.

She had an appointment at the clinic. She forced herself to go. When she stepped into the consulting room the friendly doctor and nurses were waiting for her. They gave her a cup of coffee, invited her to take her coat off. It seemed almost to be a social occasion.

"Good news!" said the doctor after she'd sat down. Emmie looked at him without expression.

"Results on those last tests we did came through just yesterday," he continued after a pause. "And they're good! Very good! We think we won't have to remove the breast after all. An operation, to be sure, to remove the lumps; continue with the chemo for a while. But a full mastectomy: no!"

He was beaming, bouncing with joy, as if the reprieve were his. Emmie stared. She couldn't take it in. What was he saying, everything was going to be all right? Exhaustion washed over her in great, terrible waves. She wanted to go home, lie down in darkness, sleep for weeks.

Before they let her go they did some more tests, gave her some more medication, admired her turban.

She put her hand to her head, touching the silk. "Thank you," she said. They were the first words she'd spoken since she'd arrived.

She saw a glance pass between the doctor and the two nurses. "Have you been to see the counsellor?" asked one of them.

She shook her head. Another glance.

"The thing is," she said suddenly, "the thing is, my grandfather lost his arm." She remembered, when she was a child, tugging at the empty sleeve that hung down from his shoulder. It was a game. That was her only memory of her grandfather. He had not been old when he died. His arm was somewhere in the North African desert. The rest of his body was buried in a pretty church graveyard in Hampshire.

In the silence Emmie became aware of them looking at her encouragingly. She said, "My brother's friend had two of his toes amputated. After frostbite. He was on the mountain for three days before he was rescued. They thought they'd have to take off his whole foot." She was shaking. "But it turned out to be just two toes. His big toe. The one next to it."

"Ye-es...?" The doctor's voice was very tentative.

She didn't know what to say. "To start with, he fell over a lot," she said. Then she said, "He took me dancing."

In the end they wrote down a date. Day, month, year. It was the date for the operation.

Some days after this the barman came to her flat. It was the middle of the afternoon. Summer was starting to come and the air was light and sunshiny, the street filled with bright glints from cars and windows.

"Haven't seen you for a while," the barman said, standing on the doorstep. "Wanted to make sure you were all right." His face was friendly, anxious.

"I'm fine," Emmie said, pressing her cheek against the cold edge of the door.

He held out something to her. Flowers. Emmie looked at them. Irises, purple, yellow. The barman shrugged, his hand dropped to his side, the tall irises pointing downward, nearly brushing the ground. She looked to where they were pointing, the concrete of her front step. Then her gaze followed the slender green leaves back, to where the barman's hand clutched the cellophane-wrapped stalks. His three-fingered hand, his delicate claw.

She gathered herself, held the door open. "Come in," she said.

Inside, they put the irises in water. "I had these fantasies," Emmie told the barman. She felt he would not misunderstand her. "All I could think about was having sex with men with missing limbs."

He laughed. His laughter was fresh, real, unthreatening. "Is that what I done to you then?" he said.

She shook her head. They were mixing drinks in the kitchen, afternoon sun streaming in. The barman had brought a half-bottle of whisky and was making cocktails. He shook the ice in a metal jug with his hand over the top, then poured whisky over the ice and shook some more.

"It's like this," he said. "It's not what's missing that counts. It's what's still there."

Emmie realized he was consoling her. He tipped liquid into a glass, held out the drink to her and she took it.

"It's what's still there that counts," he repeated.

She thought she should tell him about her reprieve. The words were difficult to find. She said, "They've decided to give me another chance. With the drugs."

The barman's face broadened into a smile of delight. "Bloody brilliant!" he exclaimed. "Bloody brilliant!" He chuckled and held up his glass to her in a toast. Then he put the glass down again. "What's up?" he said.

She was feeling confused. She was feeling almost on the brink of something. She held herself very still. The barman pushed the ice around in his glass with his two fingers. Emmie looked at his open, perplexed face. The truth was, she no longer knew what it meant to be whole.

BARCELONA
Jonathan Carr

Jonathan Carr started out as a solicitor, following a degree in Law; that bored him, so he gave it up to write. Over the last two years, he has completed three novels, several short stories, and is currently working on a musical project.

IT'S NOW SIX MINUTES SINCE THE PILOT INFORMED US – with, in the circumstances, what seems to be unjustifiable calm, that both of the engines have failed and we are sinking towards the earth at an alarming rate. In fragments, he tells us the present score, which is that flaps have been flexed to stall our descent, flammable kerosene has been dumped, the airport knows there is something up and radio contact is being maintained. There's nothing to worry about. I'm listening to the announcement and I'm not sure what I think or feel.

He came on the cabin speaker system and told us and the immediate passenger response was disbelief. He said that about a half hour ago one of the two turbines had spluttered and died, but that the other had been fine. We could fly normally with one engine. During this half hour, while cabin staff sold duty free and collected empty plastic glasses, he had tried to restore the engine to its previous form, but it was having none of it, and sat limply on the wing, nothing but an unwanted extra in the drag coefficient to which we are all now unpleasantly awake. When the other engine followed suit, he decided to share the news. Thanks, Mr Pilot.

It would have been nice to have longer to panic, was my first thought. Perhaps just for once the standard paternalism from officialdom could have been dropped and we could have decided, as adults, how to handle our disaster. But I wonder – does it really make any difference?

In the first minute following the announcement, the passengers sat in a bewildered lull. There is surprisingly little to do when you've been told of your imminent death. Conversations and tears followed, flowed, in the second minute, and the cabin crew swept along the aisles comforting people. In the third minute, some of the cabin crew broke down too, and the economy class cabin was seized then of the scale of its misfortune. People stood up and paced about. A queue for the toilet developed. Sick bags were used.

By the fourth minute, a delirium had settled among a group near the exit, that gazed out hopelessly at the static turbine, at the shuddering wing. Beneath us is one of the most beautiful views I've ever beheld from a plane, London at night, but today, I can't really focus on it. I'm beside my father on the window seat of a Boeing 737 from Barcelona to Heathrow, and he's in the aisle and looking around and I have no idea what he's thinking. My father and I look alike, and in old pictures he is the image of me at twenty-three, which is what I am now, and has retained some of his looks. At the check-in the woman at the desk grinned at us as she passed the boarding cards through a machine.

"How nice!" she cooed. "A father and son on holiday together."

My father grunted and I tautened my lips into a sort of smile to cover the fact that the whole trip has been a mistake and we currently loathe each other more than ever.

Dad is not a very wealthy man, but he cut a couple of deals late on in life that netted him nearly a million and so travel is one of his main pursuits. After I'd packed in my job and had some free time he invited me out to Spain to hang out and maybe catch up on some things we've missed and no doubt tell me what a mess I'm making of my life.

If I think about it I am back there listening to him. His voice quivers as he grandly issues the invitation. I know that the subtext is that I can barely afford cabs, let alone plane fare, and that he's doing me a favour. When he asks me, I'm kind of not with it and I'm not sure.

"Um, I don't know, dad," I tell him, my hostility building. Why the fuck should I do this for him? He's humiliated me enough. I have never been to Barcelona, and I think of the city becoming inextricably linked in my mind with my dad and somewhere I then, because of him, don't want to go back to, like Tokyo, where he ridiculed me in a restaurant, age thirteen, for asking him to send my food back because it was cold (it was sushi), or like Dallas, where I supposedly ruined his chances of a deal with some fat oil people by meeting up with them late for dinner, and in jeans, and talking too loosely about my dad's business at home in London.

"I'll, em, call you back, dad," I say on this occasion, and as he replaces the handset I can hear my mother saying, in a loud whisper the new phone captures fully, "He doesn't want to go, Michael." And then there's a click and I feel ridiculously predictable and despise both my parents for knowing how I'm feeling.

So then I flick through Spartacus and Barcelona looks pretty good and I call back, with forced jolliness, and tell him I'd love to go.

In the fifth minute, the cabin crew are offering people drinks and handing out doubles of things until there is nothing left and in the nonsmoking section people are breaking open packs of duty free cigarettes and chain-smoking them. The pilot comes on to say we might not make the runway but there are other places to land, maybe Gatwick, which is closer, and he's checking out his options, but it may be that we'll have to risk a landing in a field somewhere near the M25 and I'm not really listening and I'm thinking about my drugs in the hold and wishing I could take something but then I realize that nothing I have would probably kick in before we crash so it would be a futile exercise. Then I'm wondering whether they do a post mortem on the bodies they find in a plane crash and thinking about my mother's embarrassment when she is told by someone that her son's blood was rich in amphetamines and marijuana, but in the end this thought is quite funny and reminds me of when she used to tell me about putting on underwear you wouldn't be embarrassed to be found wearing in a car accident.

Then I'm thinking about us travelling economy and my family's frequent accusation that my dad would never pay for first class seats because it's a rip off, and I'm wondering if the irony is amusing to the people up front in Club Europe, because although they paid three times as much as we did, death will sweep through their section of the plane first.

I smile to myself about this for a moment and I remember that Richard Branson once said that if the seats in an aeroplane were arranged to face the rear of the craft the statistical chance of survival in a crash is masses higher, and then I'm sad to think that even though all of the airlines know this, none of them have tried it because they're worried that nobody will then fly with them. And I have a vague recollection of a product my father once sold that was basically unsafe and I remember him justifying this to himself and saying that safety doesn't sell anything and as I look at him now I want to ask him about this and find out if he thinks it's kind of ironic.

Even though dad will not fly first class, the family all have these Executive Club lounge cards so we can have free drinks and newspapers pre-flight, and I can see that my dad thinks it's pretty cool to stride past the peasants in the common areas up to the lounges, although these lounges are consistently full of drunks and plebs too. We were in the lounge today and I had three large gin and tonics, quickly, and my dad watched me and sipped orange juice because since he became richer he's stopped doing unhealthy things and clearly intends to live longer. "Afraid of flying, are you now?" he asks me, his copy of the *Financial Times* being folded and replaced on the rack beside him.

I glare at him and light a cigarette, and his mouth tightens further. "Not... afraid... of flying," I reply calmly. "I just need a drink."

My dad checks his watch and though it is past noon in Spain, London is an hour behind and my dad obviously thinks this is a bit early for a drink. "It's a bit early," he comments, evenly.

236

"It must be opening time somewhere," I tell him, looking up at the departure screen which lists a whole lot of flights I'd rather get on, in particular one to Rio de Janeiro which will be hot and full of horny boys and most importantly is six thousand miles away from my father.

"In fact," I add tersely, "it's opening time in bloody London."

My dad shakes his head slightly, as though I am impossibly wayward and he cannot believe it was from his loins I sprang in 1972. But then his face softens and he smiles a little, which is a bad sign as it generally precedes some little recherché snippet of wisdom.

"I suppose when I was your age I was smoking and drinking all the time," he tells me. "But it was different then, smoking hadn't been linked to cancer. You could drink and drive... people never talked about cirrhosis." He tails off, and I laugh out loud at the idea that a responsible person needs a law to explain to them the dangers of drinking and driving, at the idea that knowing about the risks of smoking drives people from it, rather than intensifying its appeal. My dad probably wants to ask me what's funny but doesn't, maybe afraid of what I'll say, and now picks up *The Economist* and studies that. But then he mutters, "You'll be sorry when your body packs up when you're forty-five. Your forties are much closer than you think."

And I'm thinking about the drugs I take and if they quicken the ageing process and I realize with a shock that in my suitcase is some grass and some whizz someone in a gay bar in Barcelona gave me, and which I hid in the pocket of the case because I knew my dad wouldn't look there and I have almost forgotten about it. I can picture the scene at Heathrow clearly, with the normally calm and obedient patrol dogs dragging the guys along on taut leads, foaming at the mouth, dashing round, and the guilt on the faces in the customs queue draining away, replaced with disdain as the dogs land on my case, flattening it, barking madly. Also, I know from my friend who was searched that customs people have lots of extra powers to detain you that aren't available to the police, and I think about this and it frightens me a little.

"I think... I want to stay in Barcelona a bit longer," I say to my dad, as I think of ways to get my case off the flight.

"Eh?" He puts down the magazine and frowns at me. "What do you mean?"

"I want to have a couple more days," I say.

"But I've not got that type of ticket," he says. "You'd have to pay for another ticket." My dad thinks I am being ridiculous and that this is to do with spending the flight with him. I stare at him and my fantasy of the dogs at Heathrow expands to accommodate the shocked and unbelieving face of my father and I can't be bothered to argue and in some ways think it might be worth it just to see his face.

But as we sit together now, six minutes after the announcement, I'm wishing like hell that I'd got off the fucking plane and stood my ground because now I'll never get to see my dad's face at the imaginary drug bust and the whole plan is ruined. My dad is turning the safety card he's plucked from the seat pocket and is looking it over thoughtfully, but it now seems absurd, a story about a perfect crash landing, as smooth as an ordinary one, with women's high heels off and everyone bent forwards, then everyone sliding down inflatables in an orderly, dignified line to the hard, real tarmac.

"We're going to be okay," my dad for some reason decides to tell me and I stare at him and after a long time I say, "Why are you... telling me this?" He doesn't reply, just keeps on staring at the safety card, holding onto it, and the stewardess leans in to us and querulously asks us if we want something to drink.

I am looking at the stewardess and she looks artificial and exhausted, and young, maybe not more than twenty, and she tries to smile at me but she is too upset to reassure anyone, and I realize that she is the person who went through the safety announcement just after take off. I wonder what she has been taught about how to behave in a crash situation but I find I have no idea what the training might be.

"I'll have a Jack Daniels," my dad tells her and she passes him two little airline bottles and looks at me, waiting for my order.

"Um... gin and tonic, please," I say, and I get the bottles and she forgets to give me tonic and as she walks off to another row of seats I'm looking at her and wondering why she's forgotten and I shout her over and my dad spins round and looks at me and says, "Christ." Then he falls silent, slowly snaps open one of the bottles and drinks all of it in one go. Moments later the stewardess is streaming along the aisle saying the bar service has been "suspended".

I get my tonic and mix the drink and watch it slowly go flat, not touching it, and outside the ground looks closer but then I'm not sure and there are so many lights I wonder how the fuck we can land in between them and I wonder for a while whether the pilot is allowed to put the plane down where he wants to, even if it's in a residential area and people will be killed when we hit the ground. I develop an urge to go up front and watch the crash from the cockpit and sit behind the pilot as the nose of the aeroplane dips towards a field and finally splinters and the glass in the windows shatters, but then I decide that it wouldn't be like that, that what's more likely is that the cockpit is just instantly crushed and there is no time even for glass to respond by breaking, and I turn this thought over and eventually it makes me smile.

"I was once in a plane crash, you know," my dad tells me. "Well... not a crash, as such, but a fucked-up landing."

I listen to my dad say "fucked" and I realize I have never heard him say it before and he seems a bit more human for a second, but then the content of what he's said takes shape in my head and it's just incredibly irritating, because my dad has always done everything before and you can never have an experience he hasn't had. I remembered the restaurant choices I advanced in Barcelona when he consulted me about where we would eat and how each time he'd been there or knew somewhere better until in the end I just lost it with him and said, "What the fuck did you ask me for, then?"

So now I think about ignoring him but he clearly wants to talk, so, still staring at my gin and tonic I tiredly say, "Oh yeah? When was this?"

"When you were about four, in Rio de Janeiro."

"You've never mentioned it before," I remark, suspicious, wondering if he's making it up. Not that this would surprise me, since he must find his way to be equal to or better than any situation, even if it is his own death.

My dad shrugs. "Never thought about it. I was going to

239

Argentina, and we had a stop in Rio, and everything was fine until we landed, when the plane suddenly veered off to the left and I was sitting in the upstairs cabin in the jumbo and it was obvious that the brakes had failed or something, and we were heading for the terminal building." He pauses, and I am looking at him in a new light – a crash survivor, and I think that actually, this is not a bad story, although I am annoyed by the casualness with which he's absorbed the experience, and long for him to admit he was – even momentarily – not absolutely confident that he'd get through it.

"And then the plane eventually stopped and by this time all these red lights had come on, and the emergency exits were opening and there was this announcement in French, because it was an Air France flight, and everyone had to get up out of the crash position and get down the chutes and run, so we did that and ran from the plane. When I looked back, one of the engines was on fire and the plane had buckled so that its, like, back was broken, but there were no injuries and it was all okay."

I take all of this in and stare at him, and the stewardess comes back and sweeps away the drinks, looking nervous as hell, and around us people are agitated as they feel the plane judder and lurch towards the ground, with a steepness I haven't experienced before though I have flown a hundred times.

I try to think about dying and what that means, but my mind is turning over and going back to the first night we had in Barcelona at a restaurant my father had chosen and I am miserable at the table because near us is a group of four gay men and my dad has been watching them looking at me and admiring me and we both know we have no words for this and that we'll ignore it, and as I light my fifth cigarette since we sat down and look again at the menu, which makes no sense to me, one of the guys says something to another and they all look over at us and laugh. It's like, the most embarrassing thing.

"You're smoking an awful lot," my dad observes. I stamp the cigarette, just lit, out into the ashtray and fold my arms and try to steal an unsuspicious look at the only one of the gay guys who is attractive but I can't quite pull it off and so I just lift my beer to my mouth and almost drain the bottle. My dad smiles blandly at me and hoists up his menu.

"So, what would you like?" I stare at him and back at the menu.

"It's all in Spanish," I halfheartedly complain. "I don't know what stuff is."

Now that I have cued him in, given him a role, my dad flexes his Spanish, which he is depressingly good at, like he's good at everything, and he begins to translate the menu.

I decide to get drunk and once we finish the meal my dad suggests we go to a bar, and so we trawl the streets and somehow wind up in an area that's gay and I'm hoping that my dad doesn't realize but suddenly, excruciatingly, he says, "This looks like your kind of neck of the woods," and I nearly die and just keep walking.

Eventually we get back to the hotel, and the bar is full of locals and my dad decides we're going to have sangria and we sit on bar stools by two women in their mid-thirties who are alone, and tourists. My dad leans towards me.

"What do you think?" he says, teasing me but not funny.

"About what?" I ask.

"About..." he looks over at the two women, and one of them, who is taller and quite attractive, smiles back. I can't believe that, seeing as I have come out to him recently, he would say this to me, even as a joke.

"Dad," I say, and my face is a humourless mask, and I realize that I cannot talk to my father, that I can't bear his company.

"So, ladies," my dad asks one of the women, "what are you drinking?"

I shudder and turn away, and although I know that my dad is just fooling, I imagine him on other business trips, away from home, and wonder if he's had affairs, if he's been unfaithful.

"Oh," one of the women is saying, pleased, "white wine."

"White wine," my dad nods, and he motions to the barman to refresh their drinks. He turns to me and I sense that I am about to be introduced and I try to assemble some sort of smile as my dad says, "I'm Mike and this is my son, Mark." My dad gestures to me apologetically and adds, "He's, um, a bit shy."

One of the women nods and smiles and says, "I'm Alma, and this is my friend Michelle."

"Hi," says Michelle, displaying crooked teeth, and I notice that her face looks stretched over her cheekbones and I think for a second that I can see little scars, maybe from a facelift, but as I'm revising my estimate of her age upwards she turns away and it's too dark, really, to see.

My dad is smiling at the women and we watch as they are served with wine.

"We're from Birmingham," says Alma, playfully, and I place the accent and groan quietly and my dad nudges me as though I am some troublesome child. The three of them are staring at me and then Alma turns to Michelle and smiles. "A father and a son on holiday together," she says. "Isn't that nice?"

"Yeah," Michelle agrees, looking us over, "that's very nice."

I have had enough and I lose my smile and announce that I'm tired and I want to go to bed. My dad glares at me and I glare back and stand up, and it seems that in this look he gives me now is summed up all the disappointment I have caused him, and I realize that no matter who I become or what I do I can never please him, and it will never be enough. He turns to the women and says, apologetically, "Well, have a good night. It's been nice..."

"You stay, dad," I say, almost aggressively, but my dad doesn't seem like he wants to.

"What's up with him, Mike?" Alma asks and I'm already turning away and leaving the bar but I am close enough to hear my dad chuckle softly and say, "Oh, problems at work and... stuff. He's, em, going through a few changes."

I am walking quickly towards the lifts and my dad is two steps behind me and I just want to get away from him and sleep.

We are all waiting for the pilot to come back on and tell us what is happening, but he doesn't, not yet, and I'm starting to panic and wish I'd drunk the gin and tonic and I stare at my dad with about a million things to say, saying none of them. And now I'm thinking of the last conversation I had with my mother, which was a not untypical one.

I am sitting in the living room of our house and I'm watching MTV and there are all these great new videos on and I'm, like, engrossed, and my mother comes in and starts asking me what I want to eat for dinner.

"Well... I'm not bothered," I tell her, still staring at the screen, but she just stands there and she's tediously going through the options and it seems like we've had this conversation a million times and it seems like it's the only conversation we've ever had.

"Mum... just... whatever, okay?" I say, but still she persists and will it be steak or maybe a takeaway and eventually she gets so irritating I have to huffily put a tape in the video and record what I'm missing on MTV and turn to her and listen.

"Mum, steak is fine. Whatever you want is fine," I tell her, and she gives me the saddest look and looks at the TV set and then retreats from the room. And it doesn't seem like a very good last conversation to have had with your mum, to me.

The pilot comes on and tells us we are to make an emergency landing at Gatwick and this will happen in about three minutes, although from the window I estimate that had we been flying normally the height we have left to lose would take twenty minutes of flying time, and I can feel the plane dip and head down with shocking purpose. And the stewardess comes on and in a voice with at least a shred of confidence, says, "Seats upright. Place your forehead on the back of the seat in front of you. There will be several bumps. Leave all your hand baggage and move as quickly as you can to the exits and slide down the escape-chutes. When you are on the ground – run."

So I'm starting to really worry and I hunker down as she's instructed and from this new vantage point I can see that my father is, like, trying not to cry and then I can feel the pressure of tears and I try to ignore them and then I say, "Dad," but not loud and he turns to me and smiles, and then grins.

"We'll get through it, son. Don't worry."

And I want him to give me a hug, like he hasn't in years, and I say, "Dad," and I'm choking and the plane seems to be sliding somehow to the left.

"I love you," my dad tells me and I frown and say, "I love you too."

He says, "I'm sorry we couldn't... get it together this weekend. I'm sorry for... things. But you're my son and I love you."

I listen to this and I think red lights have come on in the cabin and there's this terrible silence as we wait for the impact and the plane makes hardly any noise, which is just, like, so fucking eerie, and I wonder where the ground is and if we'll make the runway.

"Dad," I say again, and I'm not sure what else I can say but I feel kind of close to him and it feels, actually, okay.

The 737 smacks the ground and I can feel the fuselage shudder and rock and my ears press and my head feels like it must be through the seat in front and I'm barely aware of it but my teeth are locked together and my eyes are closed and I'm waiting for something, like a searing heat or sudden pain but instead there's just this tug of Gs at my body and while my head is shooting forward my legs think they're being pulled through the floor and I can see my sunglasses jump from the rack and shoot forward beneath the seats in front of me.

The plane is shooting down the runway for what seems like forever and there seems like there's this hesitant application of brakes and then more and I'm shunted into the wall and then the plane begins to vibrate spitefully and then actually jump and even leave the ground and now I'm thinking, oh fuck, it's not going to stop and I think of the story Jimmy, my boyfriend, told me, of how his convertible left the road and went into this spin but that in the end it stopped and he was, like, fine, and I hope that we'll be lucky too.

Now there's this crunching sound and the plane feels like it's turning and the tail is developing all this weight and suddenly, there's a jolt that I think almost breaks my neck and the plane stops.

For long seconds nobody can believe that the plane has come to a halt but the air stewards are rushing down the aisles and as I sit up there is this noise which I realize is seatbelts clicking and the exits are open and I notice that the oxygen masks have come down and all the overhead lockers have flown open and there are jackets and bags in the aisles. A queue forms along the aisle and people are quiet but press nervously towards the exit as we wait for the stewardess to tell us the chutes have inflated, and women are pulling off their shoes. People are saying, "Please, please," and the stewardess is telling people to sit and jump and the plane clears at surprising speed, although it's full. My dad catches my eye and kind of smiles and when it's our turn we slide down the chute and run from the plane which I now see has scooted off the runway and is about fifty yards from the terminal building. People are crying, but there is exultation and the grass is strewn with people lying down and the stewardesses are trying to comfort people, and the plane looks fine from where I'm looking, not buckled or broken, not in flames, and in my ear I can hear my father talking to me, looking ragged but fine.

"Well, I told you we'd be all right," he says. "This was all right."

I smile at him, and right there on the grass, in total shock, I step towards him, and give him a hug, which he returns powerfully, and it's all over.

SWEET WILLIAM IS THE SCENT

(for Henry Hale)
Jeannette AlLée

Jeannette AlLée grew up in Idaho, Colorado and Montana. After finishing school on an Indian reservation, she worked herself round the world for over twelve years as a nanny, a schnappseller, an English teacher, a deckhand on a German freighter, etc. She now lives outside of Seattle and is working on her first novel.

A HOUSE WITH A TURRET AND AN OLD, BLACK CAR with a snoot, that's what I'd dream about, all those listless nights, lying in the sunken-down bed of my childhood town. Nothing to that old town; milkweed, stinkbugs, chiggers in the lawn. Sometimes I'd lie still so long mooning, the back of my head would pool cool blood.

When school finished, the daydreaming just seemed to lead me. So I packed up my old hat box and long-stemmed umbrella, walked down that dusty road leading to the highway for the last time, and rode the bus into Reno.

For the first few days I was nervous, wearing a rhinestone choker, short-skirted and teetering around on high heels serving cocktails in a casino. But the glamour of it all evaporated quickly as I came to know the other girls: plastic-nailed, pinched faces, always squinting out the next big tipper from across the room.

I took tips reluctantly, I never learned to master the professional pause with the just-emptied tray, so that gamblers, hands grubby from digging through coins all day, might drop a few in my little tip tub. I know I walked away while coins were chosen choicely for me. They'd call out a "Hey missy!" and with a reddening face I'd walk further away. How could a person just stand there nonchalantly? I never could. The other girls sensed this weakness and approached me accordingly.

"Your cheeks is shiny," one said accusingly.

"Oh, I just took a bath before I came in," I answered.

She blinked at me impatiently, and grabbed a bar cherry from the garnish dish. "Ain't you got no make-up?" she said, looking me over. Her gold-crowned teeth glinted in the dark, green decor of the club as she gnawed on the plastic-red cherry.

"Well, I only wear lipstick," I found myself saying almost apologetically.

She reached over and wiped the stickiness off her hand and onto one of the napkins on my tray. "Yeah but I'm telling ya, your cheeks is still shiny!" she snapped and stomped off in clunky heels.

So they left me, and what they considered my mysterious stupidity, to work in the quieter slots, with the cheaper tippers. I didn't mind. The other girls could lose their hearing, working in the dollar slots where the metal pans were made to rattle and echo, greedy and loud. Or they could reap their cut-throat rewards by working under the high-rolling pressure and hair-trigger tension of the pit.

I gladly stayed in the back, with all the first-timers, last-chancers, and gaggles of elderly, white-haired ladies who sat at the nickel slots and readily took me into their confidence, and under their wing for the evening. I meandered happily through the crowds, delivering drinks and bringing luck with the throw of my fingers to certain machines for special customers. I served shots of whiskey to shouting, burly boys, and silent outlaws, intent at their show-downs with one-armed bandits. Brides in white gowns saddled stools and called me over to confer "Should I order a Virgin Mary or one a them Pantydropper drinks, what do you think?" Even careful Irish grannies who had travelled as far as Portland just to play our lucky leprechaun machines would live it up with us, ordering frosty, mint grasshoppers over their usual plain sodas. With white-gloved hands, they'd pat me lovingly on the back, spill nickels across my tray, and say I really ought to meet their grandsons.

Of course I never did meet any grandsons. Girls back home, heavy with child, started dropping like flies out of school early on. They were groomed for desperate lives, raising babies on stump farms that the banks owned in the end. It made me curious and cautious about the draw of men. As for these city girls, all they talked about was how they wouldn't go out with a man who didn't make a certain amount of salary, or wasn't a particular height. I didn't understand what loving could ever have to do with that. I just held on to a hope, a trust, as simple and direct as any good child's, that love would one day come. I thought maybe this belief could be seen, be recognized, by the right man.

"You must be new," a croupier said, taking a seat across from me in the break room. His eyes were eager and awake.

"How did you know?" I asked.

"You're still smiling," he said with a smirk, and offered his hand out for me to shake. "I'm John. Pleased to meet you," he said with a firm, reassuring grip.

Croupiers were given a break every hour, and John found his place across the table from me whenever I took dinner. One night he looked over at me slyly and said "You know, there's something very special about you, something unique. I wish I could put my finger on it."

I think I actually blushed to that compliment, but said cheekily, "Thank you, but you better keep your hands to yourself." We both laughed, and when I looked up, John was holding me tenderly with his eyes. Before dinner was over, he asked if he could offer me a ride home. There had been warnings all day of rain and possibly flash floods.

I met him down at the time clock. Out of his bow-tie and white, pressed, tuxedo shirt, John looked like an entirely different person. He was wearing knee-split jeans, and an embarrassing T-shirt from the musical Cats. In the parking lot he put his arm around me to lead me to the car. It was one of those low, toy types I always think men buy to get a flash of a girl passenger's underwear. When getting in, I caught my stocking. The dark silk split and laddered ominously up my leg as we drove home, and I could feel the run exposing bare flesh under my skirt.

When we pulled up in front of my apartment, John turned to me, and reached over to brush back a lock of hair that had fallen across my cheek.

"I know a gorgeous hot springs up in the mountains," he said. We could go there this weekend, get some fresh air. It's a way off the trail, so we don't have to wear a thing. I'll bet the dimples on your butt are real cute."

I stumbled all over the place getting out, and never sat with him again.

Usually, when I'd return home from work in the evening, I'd take a long, scented bath. Afterwards, I'd carefully powder my body and comb out my hair. When my hair had dried, I'd tie it up in a hanky the way my granny had shown me, so that in the morning I'd untie it to find soft, full curls. Usually I'd pass the evening by reading library books to the slow tock of the tail of my Kit Kat Klock, or listen to the most far-off radio show I could find.

Lacking companionship, I was sometimes drawn to the mirror, wanting to see another face looking back at me, but instead found my own puzzling image. In photographs, I was always surprised to find my beauty mark on the opposite side of my face. Once a family of dark foreigners had stopped me on my rounds at work, and pointed at it in awe, then nodding vigorously in agreement, they all gave me a thumbs up sign, and stood back as if in honour. They had acted as if I had magical powers, and on evenings when I considered my image in the mirror, my long neck not the current fashion, I'd try to place the era where I belonged. But I didn't know. I'd look hard and long imagining, but all I saw was my young, too-trusting face. If I'd been crying, my eyes were small, and I looked more like a kindly old elephant, sad and gentle, waiting for just one peanut, or a pat on the trunk.

Often I'd fall asleep to the sound of trains passing in the distance, and think of what it would have been like in the days when they carried young men off to war, leaving behind indelible loves. One night I had this beautiful dream...

In the dream I am standing in the middle of a street. There are orderly houses down both sides of this street, but no cars, and no-one else is in sight, only me, standing in the middle of the road. On the horizon, headed straight my way down that straight street, is a tremendous, whirling funnel of a tornado. I have my head thrown sensuously back, with my eyes closed, and I'm smiling in ecstatic anticipation. My smile is so wide and earthy it is almost shocking, and my arms are thrown open as if to welcome a lover. I am standing there, waiting, to be caught in the eye of the tornado, and carried off.

I felt giddy from this dream for days on end. It gave me that strange warm feeling inside, just like when that suave New York band leader would slip my name into a song as I was passing by the casino's cabaret.

"Your eyes are blue and your kiss is too,
Oh Colette, I can't believe it, I'm in love with you!"

I held on to these lyrics, that odd dream, and then one day, Henry appeared.

In truth I'd already seen him walking around town, from one end, all the way to the other, a few times now. He was a dapper little fellow, always strolling trim about the town, adorned in a hat of some sort, boater or fedora, and naturally vintage-suited. One hot, end-of-summer day, he came jauntily around a corner wearing a pith helmet, and I was so endeared by the sight that I nearly dashed down the street after him. But what would I say?

Now here he was, standing at the back of the cabaret while the band was starting into "Around the world, I searched for you." The music billowed and swayed, and pushed me right up to him.

"Good evening, sir," I said.

"A fine, fine evening it is," Henry answered.

We stood side by side for a moment, watching the band together.

Then I couldn't help myself, I said "I think you're an incredible gentleman."

He tilted his head to the side, surprised, and suppressing a flattered smile, he said, "Well bless your sweet, sweet heart." Then he pretended to adjust his spectacles, adding, "And I must say you're an awfully beautiful gal. You know what they say don't you? Birds of a feather flock together."

We stood there awkwardly for a few seconds, then introduced ourselves. But as soon as we'd finished, Henry tipped his hat, said goodnight, and took his leave. I called out a singsong, second goodbye, and he walked so lightly away, I thought him to be twenty years younger than his eighty-two.

That evening I went for a cooling walk along the river that wound through town. The breeze rustled through the leaves, high in the trees, that particular sound of valley birches. I stopped along the bridge and looked down. The river was fast-moving but shallow, and famous for being the place where people came to throw their wedding rings away when their quick Nevada marriages went bad. The similarities in the people and the river seemed funny and sad. People (shallow people?) rushing into forever like a flood that will only end up stranding someone sooner or later. I pulled my sweater on, searched for the moon, and walked home.

At the back of my mind all that week were thoughts of Henry. What had brought him into the club in the first place? He didn't look like a gambler or drinker. I wondered where he lived and how he spent his days. Early on Friday afternoon, when he sauntered in, and I thought I might ask him.

"Why Good Afternoon to you," he said, as if that introduction was already an understood jest between us.

"Hello Henry, I was wondering if I'd see you again."

"You're looking lovely as ever, my dear. You know health is wealth."

"The only kind I believe in... what are you up to today?"

"Well, I'm just passing through, wishing you all the best for the rest of your day," he said, and strolled on out into the sunny street. He'd snuck so quickly away, and our next few meetings were exactly the same. We'd just get started talking, then suddenly he'd disappear. Finally I caught him.

"Henry, can I take you out for coffee sometime?" I asked, as soon as he'd said hello.

"Oh, no, dear, I'm afraid not. I'm too busy." He said it with such kind but simple finality, I was puzzled.

"Do you mind if I ask what you're busy doing?" I said, thinking that he did not have a job or family to report to.

"Why my career," he said. "Everyday I practise my singing and my dancing, Vaudeville, you know, I've been in it for over sixty years." He leaned in closely as he spoke, as if he were revealing a secret he didn't want others to know about just yet.

"Now you see, I practise singing to records at home, and then of course my tapping I can't simply do just on the floor. Neighbours downstairs, dontcha know. So I sit on a chair to soft-shoe lightly. I might get my big break yet."

Henry cleared his throat, as if he had suddenly become tired from talking. In a weaker voice he told me that he was mindful of his health, didn't partake in any liquor or tobacco, and that currently he was studying something called Reflexology.

Wistfully I watched him walk away that night.

On my day off, I dusted and swept my room, aired my pillows in the sunshine, did my laundry, and dropped off a copy of one of my favourite stories to a young cashier at the Horseshoe Club. I'd met him once when he was handing out peanut butter and jelly sandwiches to the toothless bums down by the railroad tracks. I was struck by his clumsy altruism, it reminded me of 'A Tree, A Rock, A Cloud'. I dropped the story off without my name or address, and later I took a bus out to MGM to see an old film. I walked directly to the front of the theatre, sat in the third row back and centre, and watched other lives unfold, while I waited for my own.

After another full month of his hummingbird-like visits, Henry being his bright, agile, and fleeting self, he actually agreed to lunch with me. I was delighted. We were to meet downtown. It was raining heavily out and I was concerned, afraid that he might not show up after all. But there, standing stylish in front of the restaurant, was Henry.

"Well, bless your sweet, sweet heart for coming," Henry said.

"Were you all right in the rain? Hey, that's a handsome trench-coat you've got on."

"Why, thank you," Henry said, smoothing down the sides of his coat, "I wear it belted to accentuate my slim waistline."

We walked arm-in-arm together up to the dining room for lunch. I had the vegetable soup and Henry ordered a roast beef sandwich that was so large, with mashed potatoes crowding it off its thick plate, that when the waiter set it down before him, Henry googled out his eyes behind his already thick lenses, blinked his thin eyelids, and said with a gulp, "I do believe I need a cannibal to help me eat all this." We giggled over that for the longest time.

After that, Henry was always popping in at work to say hello on his way down to Circus, Circus where his friend Bill played the organ. Then on my days off, we met for milk (Henry convinced me it was better than coffee) or for a stroll, with our arms entwined, down the avenues and through the parks. Henry spoke at length about his career, and the benefits of Reflexology, and sometimes in his mystical mood, he would turn to me tenderly and claim I'd been sent to him.

"You're an angel come to abide from above," he said. "According to the laws of incarnation and reincarnation, life was meant to be this way for us."

I never shushed him. We fell into step so easily together, with such a natural understanding of each other, that we could just tell the rest of the world to go away. But we didn't. This closeness only seemed to lay the world out more perfectly for us, offer it up invitingly at every turn. We came across rare books together, found old films and lost music, and even a pair of black gloves for me that buttoned right up past the elbows. Henry said my noble arms had been deserving that kind of attention.

When I was granted the grand honour of visiting Henry at his apartment, his birds, recently renamed after us, suddenly stopped chirping as we entered.

"My two little birdies have been singing sweet songs all morning," Henry said. "I'll bet instinctively they know things we don't. They're natural creatures for sure."

Henry tried coaxing them into song, and I came up close to the cage and whispered a soft hello, but two little birdie profiles just peeked quietly back at us.

"Now isn't that something," Henry said, shaking his head. "Why come to think of it, it's been about five years since we've had a visitor here," he chuckled. "My birdies are just a bit shy to meet you."

Henry's apartment was small. The paint on the walls had grown creamy with age, and rose-covered draperies sagged on their hooks at the window. The cozy rooms smelled of vitamins and Marmite, and in one corner stood a high bed with a chenille bedspread. In the other corner were two card tables covered with a cloth and littered with faded photographs. Henry sat us comfortably down and brought out boxes of memorabilia; studio shots (Henry in hat and tails with his cane properly poised), photographs from road shows, USO tours, marquees with his name in lights (billed as 'The Perfect Gentleman'), and even a picture of a girl in a bathing suit frolicking on the beach who Henry said had been Johnny Weismuller's girlfriend too.

"Too?" I asked. Henry got up silently to chose some music to put on the record player. Something about the back of his head, the way his ears had slowly moved, told me he was smiling on the front side.

I stood up to stretch my legs and take a polite snoop around. On the wall, next to a large, faded map of the world, I saw hand-written signs that read:

SELF-EXPRESSION THRU ART
IS THE ONLY THING WORTHWHILE

and

TONGUE EXERCISES
HEAD EXERCISES   PRAYERS
HUMMING   DANCING   SINGING
IMAGINATIONS

The word 'imaginations' was written in wavy, roller-coaster script.

I was drawn to the gentle scent of a small bouquet of sweet william that sat upon a miniature shelf, when above it I saw another sign, printed in block capitals with only the slightest show of a tremble. I swallowed hard as I read:

YOU *MUST* TALK TO YOURSELF

Suddenly I understood why Henry had declined my invitations all those times, yet still kept coming round to say hello. He had been on his own, alone for so long, he needed a warm-up, rehearsals, for our big show.

He danced for me that day. I sat on the loveseat and he opened the door to the kitchen like a stage and tapped on the bare linoleum. And he sang for me. He sang 'Buffalo Gals Wontcha Come Out Tonight', and 'I Don't Want To Walk Without You, Baby' and 'That Old Gang Of Mine'. He was running around getting different props and quickly changing selection after selection on the record player, singing and dancing just for me. He was singing of love and loss and love again. He was singing with his arms out and open to me. I was trying hard not to cry, asking Henry to please sit down and rest awhile, rest awhile please. Many songs later he collapsed down beside me and squeezed a weak hug. I looked to him in absolute amazement. His lips were chilly as he gave me a thin kiss.

I brought my hatbox and Kit Kat Klock over at the end of the month. Henry and I are currently studying Reflexology, and we often go over to MGM to see old movies, or down to Circus, Circus to visit our friend Bill who plays the organ.

Sometimes when Henry and I are out for our nightly stroll, I catch looks from boys my age. I don't know exactly where my young life is leading, but Henry believes I'm his angel and I know I will lead him gently to that good gate. Everyone should have a chance at coming into their own time on earth, and love only makes sense.